TROUBLE IN SUMMER VALLEY

Trouble Cat Mysteries #4

SUSAN Y. TANNER

KaliOka Press

Cover design by Cissy Hartley
Formatted by Priya Bhakta

For Will, my firstborn grandchild. He holds a piece of my heart, now and always.

CHAPTER ONE

*A*ugust is - by far - not the most congenial of months in central Alabama. Invariably, a thunderstorm, brewed by climbing afternoon temperatures and typically quite fierce, will mar the washed out blue of the summer sky. And, as a matter of interest, I do believe that is thunder I hear rumbling in the distance. A soaking is not my preferred method of hygiene by any means, but the late afternoon breeze carries the faint but unmistakable scent of a fast-approaching storm. What I wouldn't give for a dark and brooding English day.

Nevertheless, here I am at the base of the courthouse steps, sweltering in the heat rising from the sidewalk, and here I'll remain until I enter the next phase of my assignment.

I've had company for quite some time, though the broad shouldered man has not shifted his position since he stepped from the silver embellished, dark pickup truck, sliding equally dark sunglasses into place all in one smooth move. The only interest I've seen him exhibit was toward the motorcycle rider who sat rather conspicuously upon his bike across the street for some time. And even that interest waned when the gentleman — and little though I like to judge by appearances, I use the term gentleman sparingly — donned his helmet and went on his way.

There is something about his demeanor that refutes idleness and I've given him more than a fair share of side looks in the hour or so since his arrival. I do so again, in time to see him push away from his seemingly somnolent position against the hood of the truck. Forewarned, I turn and am rewarded for my patience at last. There, decidedly less fresh than when I watched her arrive at nine on the dot this morning, is my target. At some point, those rich tresses escaped their smooth upsweep and now tumble into dark curls. Earlier, I'd judged her hair to be ebony but the strands hold the late afternoon sun just enough to prove them dark brown instead.

She looks more like her photographs now than when I first laid eyes upon her. That could be due to the diminished strain upon her face, a lessening which mayhap signals a favorable change in her circumstances. I certainly hope so. The differences are subtle and likely difficult for human eyes to discern, though quite evident to a feline as observant as myself. There is a distinct decline of trepidation in those wide, expressive eyes, a slight easing of the tension along her jawline. And, I must say, it is a remarkably firm jawline for, if my research is as impeccable as ever, a woman of forty-nine years maturity.

I see no evidence, now, of this morning's dread and anger when she was confronted on these very steps by her 'significant other' as I believe the ridiculous phrase to be in current vernacular. They had a somewhat heated exchange as he insisted she would lose the battle ahead and suggested vehemently that she 'cut her losses' and sign the papers he waved in her face. If I'm any judge of circumstances and people – and I believe myself to be quite astute – he was wrong.

It was apparent to me that the man was already near desperation. If I surmise her victory correctly, he will be even more desperate and very likely dangerous as well. My role could turn – as it so often does – to protector as much as investigator.

So now I must find my way to this 'working' horse ranch she is purported to own and manage with a certain flair for the unusual. I must say that such an outdoor and very physical lifestyle could contribute to the supple lines hinted at by the slim fitting skirt she wears with a tucked-in blouse. Her lightly tanned arms, as well as the calves of her legs, are nicely shaped so that would fit as well. Yet, there is also a certain elegance about her light movements on black stiletto heels as she descends toward me, an elegance that could well suit a boardroom career. I should know, as I've breached that world in the line of my profession as well. A definite contradiction, so we shall see. She may, perhaps, be merely the owner with an entourage at her beck and call in the stables and paddocks and a well-fitted home gym where she spends her days in air conditioned comfort while others labor on her behalf. But I think not.

And, there now, she is close enough for me to bring into play my Sherlockian skills in order to catch her attention. If I have misjudged her, the proverbial goose – mine! – may well be cooked.

AVERY STARTED in surprise as a solid black feline leapt lightly onto the step just below her feet. Her inclination to give a moment of attention to the striking creature was outweighed by the knowledge that Craig would soon be emerging from the courthouse behind her. A Craig wrapped in the fury of his defeat.

With that knowledge pressing in on her, Avery sidestepped rather than stopping as she normally would have to let her fingers glide through the gleaming onyx fur. The cat surprised her, yet again, with a move that placed him firmly in her path. The movement was so precise it seemed almost intentional. Despite her haste and the remnants of dread that gripped her still, Avery allowed herself to smile and stooped to stroke the animal. "What a beauty you are," she murmured, as the cat arched in appreciation against her caress. The expensive leather collar and sleek condition of the cat's coat told her plainly that this was someone's beloved pet. If that had not been the case, she would gladly have taken him home with her.

Green eyes regarded her calmly but the sound of voices – angry male voices – had Avery quickly straightening her back. The thud of heavy footsteps warned her it was too late to turn her back and exit gracefully. She would look cowardly if she did so now and Avery was not a coward. Knowing how fiercely Craig hated cats, she ignored all precautions about handling unknown animals, particularly a breed known for its disdain and intolerance of clumsy humans. Without a second thought, she scooped the cat up in her arms. She had a quick vision of Craig booting the innocent creature out of his path, if for no other reason than having seen Avery pet the animal.

Avery shifted to one side of the broad steps, giving plenty of room and silently willing Craig to take his venom elsewhere. Her ex came down the stairs, his attorney following close at his heels. Andrew Morgan appeared as irritated as Craig looked irate.

Craig came to an abrupt halt just inches away and Avery resigned herself to enduring one last ugly scene. Ugly was the best word she could give to anything to do with Craig these days. She marveled at the change the last five years had wrought in the man she'd once believed in and trusted completely. The handsome, energetic man at the height of a successful career had been replaced by this gaunt caricature of a person with poorly cut hair and ill-fitting clothes. She recognized the expensive gray suit. She'd selected it for him, as she once had all of his clothing and, at the time, it had fit his muscular shoulders to a tee.

"You won't win," he snarled at her.

Avery said nothing, knowing nothing she said would make

any difference. Reminding him of the fact that she *had* won would do no good and serve only to fuel his resentment.

Andrew Morgan, once his closest friend and advisor and still his attorney, laid a hand on Craig's shoulder. "Don't do this, Craig. Let's get that coffee now."

Craig ignored him, thrusting his face closer to Avery. She stood her ground, despite a tremor of alarm at the lack of control in his expression. She couldn't let him see that it affected her. Her silence seemed to infuriate him even further. His pale face darkened with red blotches.

"Don't think this ends here."

"It has ended," she said finally, quietly. "It's done, Craig."

His harsh laugh had the cat tensing in her arms and she instinctively snuggled him more closely to her chest.

"You stupid bitch! You would've been a hell of a lot smarter to take what I offered and gotten the hell out of Alabama. That ranch is mine, every acre, every horse."

She could see the hatred in his eyes where once she'd imagined she'd seen love. And she supposed Craig could see with equal clarity the emptiness she felt when she looked at him.

"Over my dead body." She kept her voice steady by sheer strength of will. Her exhaustion was bone-deep. "The judge gave you twenty-four hours to remove the rest of your belongings from the ranch. Carlee is welcome to continue on with me."

"Carlee is my daughter, just like that ranch is my property! Over your dead body?" he mimicked her words. His lips curled. "I hope you mean that ... because that's just what I'm going to step over to take back what you've stolen from me."

"Craig, what the hell ..." Andrew Morgan scrubbed a hand over his face in disgust.

Shock and fury hit Avery in a tidal wave of heat. "I can and will defend what's mine." Her voice was hard with the reminder of all she'd been through, all he'd put her through. "You should listen to your attorney, Craig. He might just keep you out of jail."

"Don't threaten me, you emasculating bitch."

Even more shocking than his threats, Craig grabbed her shoulders, his fingers digging in so hard she sucked in her breath. As bad, as nasty, as things had gotten between them, Craig had never laid hands on her – until now.

In one, blurred moment, she felt rather than saw the cat swipe unsheathed claws at the hand on her shoulder.

Craig howled and jerked away with a string of curses more vulgar than she'd ever heard from him. He flung drops of blood from his hand, staring at the gash in disbelief before lunging forward. Avery could not tell if she or the cat were his target.

Andrew tried to restrain Craig but his ineffectual attempt proved unnecessary. Before Avery had time for real fear, she watched in amazement as a complete stranger stepped past her, effortlessly pulling Craig's arm behind his back so hard that Craig's features contorted with pain rather than anger.

The man leaned in close and spoke with quiet effect. Avery wished she could hear the words that drained all resistance from Craig's taut body. Craig glared in disbelief then jerked backward as the other man loosened his grip.

The stranger turned his back on Craig in dismissal. A cool, assessing gaze skimmed Avery and the cat. "Mrs. Danson."

Avery was vaguely aware of Craig stumbling past them, his attorney trailing behind.

"Ms. Wilson," she corrected automatically. She'd taken her own name back as soon as she'd filed for divorce more than two years earlier. For a moment, she stared at him. His eyes were hidden by dark, aviator style glasses but she could almost

He could feel her scrutiny but when he looked up her expression was a careful blank. If she was irritated by his high-handedness in ordering for her, it was well-hidden.

As the waitress walked away with their order, Dirks removed a small fold of leather from his back pocket and withdrew two cards. Silently he handed her his credentials. One was his military ID. The other was styled as a business card with his position and responsibilities. The latter had only been created and printed a week earlier.

He watched her face as she studied them. Only when those truly incredible eyes lifted to gaze into his, did he speak. "You applied for the wounded veteran program. Equine therapy."

Those eyes widened with what he hoped was excitement and not dread. He banished that thought as swiftly as it came. He had a job to do and this unexpected allure had no place in it.

"I'd given up," she admitted. "I knew the government moved slowly but ..." She gave a little lift of her shoulders.

Dirks schooled his expression, not entirely sure where this was headed but entirely prepared to follow whatever lead came his way. "Your application crossed my desk about eighteen months ago," he prompted.

"I didn't mean to insult you or imply you were the hold-up." She shrugged again. "I just expected someone sooner."

Which gave away exactly nothing, he thought. He found it interesting that she toyed with the elegant black napkin which had been artfully folded around the place setting. He also noted with even more interest that there was no pale circle around her slender finger. She had not waited until the divorce was final to remove her wedding ring. From what he'd read of her husband, he couldn't say he blamed her.

"We do eventually get to every applicant."

He lost the opportunity to judge her response to his words as their waitress arrived with their salads. When they were alone again, he noted with interest that she'd resumed her watchful pose once more. He shrugged mentally, perfectly willing to retrieve the gauntlet he'd tossed and she'd ignored.

"When would be a good time for me to tour your facilities? Do you need a day or two to regroup?"

She blinked. "Regroup?"

"I assume this morning's court appearance was successful given your husband's - ex-husband's - reaction but it must still have been difficult."

The corners of her eyes crinkled into a smile and she went instantly from attractive to astonishing. Whoa, he reined in his reaction.

"Difficult describes the last few years. This morning?" she shrugged. "I'll take a few hours drama in exchange for peace."

"What will you do with that peace?" The question, he was honest with himself, had less to do with his purpose in being there than with the woman.

She didn't answer right away, and, for a while, he thought she wouldn't at all.

"Be me."

She didn't elaborate and he realized she didn't need to add anything, not for her or for him. Those two simple words were profoundly revealing. He wondered if she realized just how revealing. What kind of a lie had her marriage imposed on her existence? And would that lie figure into his investigation?

Realizing she had said all she would, he leaned back in his chair. He had to focus on the business at hand.

"Tell me about the horses you use in your veteran assistance program." His word choice was deliberate. Use. Not plan to use. They both knew that no veterans had been referred yet. Would she correct his word choice? Would it mean anything if she didn't?

"My horses?" she asked. "I could talk about them forever. They all love what they do. They know their job and they love doing it."

She didn't remind him that she was still waiting for the first veteran to be sent to her facility, didn't explain or apologize for funds sent but not earned. Dirks put away his disappointment, reminding himself it wasn't really self-incrimination, and listened to the rich Southern cadence of her voice. He'd lived in so many places over the course of his career, in and out of the states, that he himself had a diction that could have placed him anywhere and nowhere, depending upon the language he chose to employ.

Her eyes brightened as she described the animals, one by one, rarely noting bloodlines - some of which he already knew were impressive - focusing instead on their personality and backstory. How they came to her and how she felt about them were clearly more important than their sires and dams.

"I know what rescue animals are, of course, but is a *kill* pen as ugly as the name implies?"

Sorrow, and something he suspected was anger, touched her features. "Unfortunately, yes. And sometimes I hear about horses with great potential too late. I have contacts at several facilities who do what they can for the animals. I wish I could take them all but there are other people besides me who help save as many as possible."

"How do they end up there? I saw a news report once that implied most of them were vicious killers."

Her eyes flashed with pure anger now. "That's just not true. Yes, some are mistreated to the point they strike back, but most?" She shook her head. "Animals are an investment of time, income, and energy. So many people realize that, too late, and throw them away like so much trash. Then, there are horses injured in competitive sports that need healing time and others simply too old to continue. Their owners don't want to be bothered feeding and caring for them as they heal or age. They just move on to the next new toy. These are the ones I can usually take and train and make into a really useful instructor horse. Some, who've been abused, I find I can't help at all."

"What then? I'm certain you don't send them back where they came from."

"No. Never." She sighed. "There are a few rescue farms in the area that take them when they can, but I also have a pasture full of horses that are nothing but an expense."

"Of the ones who have worked out for you, do you have a favorite?"

"Jack," she said without hesitation. "He was a hunter-jumper and one of my first finds for Summer Valley Ranch. He's got papers a mile long but he was injured early in his career and his owners no longer had any use for him. He was a stallion, which is pretty rare in a successful working competitor, but so gentle. If he had made it to some big stakes wins, I never would have gotten him. He would've been put to stud. It took him a year to heal and another year to learn what I needed from him. I can't wait for you to watch him in action. The amazing thing with Jack is that he is a producer and his offspring are equally talented, equally gentle. I've been offered a small fortune for any one of them but they aren't for sale and won't be unless I think they're needed someplace more and will be well-treated. And even then there will be stipulations to the sale."

"Stipulations?"

"If they're no longer needed where they are, they'll come back to me at the same price I was given originally."

He raised his brows at that. "Could get expensive for you."

Her quick grin was a sucker punch to the gut, one he wasn't expecting. "Hasn't come to that. I haven't found a potential purchaser who meets my standards."

He kept her talking with a well-placed question or two, listening as intently to her words as much as to the warm honey of the phrases that interspersed anecdotes about the animals she loved. He found himself hoping she was everything she seemed. She was either very clever or had absolutely nothing to hide.

Conversation flowed easily throughout their entrée and he found himself disappointed when she placed her fork aside. She'd finished only half her meal but he suspected it may have been more than she was accustomed to eating. She laid her napkin on the tablecloth.

"Thank you for the meal. Truly. I have to get back to take care of things but you're welcome to come out anytime. I cancelled classes today so my instructors won't be there. Tomorrow would probably be more helpful to you."

"You have guest quarters?" He asked it as a question although he already knew the answer.

He found her momentary hesitation another disappointment. He didn't want her to have anything to hide.

"We do," she admitted, "but they aren't prepared for guests. Most of our students use the bunk houses. The guest quarters – except for the one my ex-husband's been using – haven't been used or deep-cleaned in several months although we do keep the cooling and heating on so they're aired."

Her voice trailed away as if to give him an opportunity to offer to stay in town.

When he remained silent, she sighed. "I guess I could bring some towels and linens out but you'd be *much* more comfortable in one of the hotels in town. There are several that are truly nice."

He leaned back in his chair, every instinct heightened. The woman most definitely did not want him staying on her property.

"I don't need much to be comfortable," he said blandly, "and it will be easier for me to see what I need to see if I'm there during various times of the day."

She frowned. "You plan a lengthy stay?"

"It will take some time to evaluate everything I need to review."

As her frown deepened, Dirks wished he hadn't felt such a swift and unexpected attraction to her. It was almost certainly an appeal that could go nowhere.

CHAPTER TWO

*D*irks Hanna paid the tab and they walked through the dusk back to the courthouse parking lot. The energy she'd felt as she talked about her horses had faded and exhaustion seeped back into her until it was the familiar dead weight she'd known since things had gone so badly wrong with her marriage. It had been so long since she'd truly been able to rest. Not since this fight had started, not since she realized there *was* a fight. She'd won but she didn't fool herself. Despite her words to Craig, she knew it wasn't over. He wasn't just going to go away. Maybe someday, but not yet.

As they walked, a slow sense of dread blended with the exhaustion. Along with threatening her over the course of their long, drawn-out court fight, he'd threatened the horses as well. They meant nothing to him except as a means to an end and that end was money. Always money. For newer cars, nicer clothes. For gambling. She'd realized too late the siren call that dice and cards held for him. Not to mention the women, always younger than her. When had *she* stopped being enough for him?

The carefully preserved oaks, so pretty by day, seemed to crowd the sidewalk with shadows. She experienced a sudden sense of urgency, a feeling she should have gone straight home.

Avery heard Dirks' growl of anger before she saw her SUV. She wasn't surprised to see the shattered glass of her windshield. She wasn't even surprised to see the elegant black cat pacing the sidewalk beside the slashed tires. She had, she realized, almost been expecting ... something.

WELL, I hope these two enjoyed their dinner for the games have certainly begun and I've eaten nothing since lunch, which was quite fine, I'll admit, but has long since burned away with my efforts.

Unfortunately, my pretty lady is going to assume that her nasty ex-husband is the only culprit. He, I suspect, she could handle rather well, at least with my assistance. Somehow I've got to ensure that Mr. Military realizes a knife may have slashed those tires but there is a bullet somewhere behind that ruined glass, a bullet discharged by a very skillful hand with a gun. A gun with a silencer no less for it drew absolutely no attention from the busy street. Methinks such machinations are beyond the abilities of the slovenly ex.

It is only a slight hindrance that these two have not yet deduced my heightened feline abilities. Ah, well, one does what one must, even resorting to the 'trite' but true. Hmmm, a clever line, that. I do believe I must commit it to my excellent memory for my yet-to-be written memoirs. Meanwhile, there is much to do in the moment at hand.

"I'LL CALL THE POLICE." Dirks, as he'd told her to call him, pulled his phone from his pocket.

"I can't wait for them. I've got to get home," Avery said, staring at her ruined SUV. "Now! You've got to take me."

She blessed the fact that he didn't argue. He just took one glance at her face and gestured toward a dark-grey, almost black truck parked close to hers. Before they took more than a step or two, however, the cat snagged a paw in Dirks' trousers.

Dirks uttered a mild oath as the cat sat down and stared up at him intently. When Dirks stepped forward again, his pants were snagged again. When he stopped, the cat sat. "Okay." Dirks hesitated. His expression said clearly that he felt more than a little stupid for talking to a cat. "What?"

The cat stood and stalked back to Avery's SUV. Dirks looked at Avery. "Your cat wants to show us something."

"You're crazy. He's not my cat. And I have to get home!" Avery knew her voice had risen slightly with each short statement.

"Two minutes," Dirks answered and he followed the cat back to her SUV.

Avery trailed after him, fighting a sense of panic and tears. Crying wouldn't help, it never had, never would, and she'd given it up long ago. Panic didn't change things either, she knew, but the tears were easier to quell than this horrific sense that something terrible was going to happen to things that truly mattered. If it hadn't already.

Dirks made a closer study of the windshield, studying the broken glass. He whistled softly. "Does your ex own a gun?"

"Craig? Absolutely not. He hates guns, though I own several. Are you saying ...?"

She stepped closer, trying to see what Dirks was studying.

"I'm saying you have a problem." He opened the door to the vehicle, quickly finding the entry and exit for the bullet that went through her front seat. Avery waited numbly while he continued his search in the back seat and pocketed two bullets. "I'll get these to the police later. Let's go."

He turned with an odd expression to the cat who had observed him from the hood of the car without moving.

"I know you didn't make this trouble, but you sure found it, didn't you, guy?"

Dirks didn't seem any more surprised than she when the black cat leapt lightly into his truck with them and settled on the console. "Let's go, then, Trouble."

Dirks started the engine and Avery put her head against the headrest, anxious to be home but dreading what she might find when she got there.

She listened as Dirks made a series of phone calls. With each one he was careful to tell the person on the other end that they were on his truck speakerphone. First the sheriff's office, giving brief pertinent facts of what they'd found, of Avery's concern for the safety of her property. He affirmed they were on their way to the ranch and gave the address without glancing at her. Even the oddity that he apparently had it memorized couldn't edge past her growing anxiety sufficiently to make her question the fact. The next call seemed to be to a travel agency canceling a flight for later in the week. And then one so cryptic she couldn't tell if it was to friend or family or someone he barely knew. Nothing seemed to be in whole sentences and the sentence fragments could have meant anything.

Although the distance to her property wasn't great, the change from town to country was abrupt and complete. Stately homes fell away within minutes to long, rolling hills. His headlights swept field after white-fenced field. All familiar to her and dearly-loved.

He drove smoothly, expertly, and very, very fast for which she was grateful, particularly if it was in deference to her anxiety to be home. She supposed a military man might be expected to be obedient to speed limits. She was glad he wasn't, at least for this trip.

She didn't miss that he didn't need to ask directions and turned without hesitation into her drive. On some level that bothered her, on another she almost expected it.

She would've liked for Dirks to first see the place in the light of morning. She'd worked hard, poured her very heart and soul into it, and she knew it was impressive at first sight, but he'd see little of its beauty in the dark. She wanted him to be impressed, to approve her application to provide equine therapy to wounded veterans, but nothing mattered in this moment as much as knowing her horses were there and unharmed.

As the truck skimmed along the lengthy drive, she realized every light blazed from all three stable areas. Her heart stuttered in her chest.

She was almost nauseous by the time he had the engine off and was barely aware of him coming around the hood to open her door as she stumbled out without waiting. Kicking off her heels, she took off toward the barn at a run, leaving Dirks to follow – Dirks and the cat he'd named Trouble.

THE SOUND of weeping was clear in the evening air. Avery felt the blood freeze in her veins well before she reached the huge sliding barn door, standing wide in a manner that was not the norm for this time of day. She believed that horses, like humans, thrived on a set routine for meals and rest. Blessedly the days of having to give riding lessons at odd hours to adjust to her clients' work and school schedules were well in the past for her.

The sight of Carlee sitting against a stall door, head in

hands, nearly stopped her heart and her steps slowed. She touched her step-daughter's hair lightly and Carlee looked up with tear-drenched eyes and shook her head. Seeing no sign of injury or trauma, Avery forced herself to move past Carlee to the first stall, and drew her first breath of true relief as her beloved Jack thrust his head over the stall door and nickered at her. She caressed his broad forehead and moved on, one stall at a time, one barn at a time, relief growing as she was greeted by each beloved animal in turn. She touched each in turn, quickly, lightly, reassuring herself they were unharmed, and that all was well. With them at least. The same was not true of her step-daughter.

Turning, she hurried back to the weeping Carlee, already knowing that Craig had come and gone. Dirks was crouched in front of Craig's daughter but she had turned her face from him. Carlee was a private person and she would not appreciate having a stranger see her in an emotional state of any kind. Avery dropped to her knees beside Carlee, aware and grateful that Dirks discreetly withdrew.

"Carlee?" She kept her voice calm, though she was anything but calm inside. Despite knowing her horses were safe, her nerves jangled from the events of the day – the scene with Craig and the damage to her vehicle – and now dread at the realization that something had gone terribly wrong here as well.

Carlee turned to her, eyes as blue as Craig's and long, dark lashes that never needed mascara, drenched with tears, as others streamed down her face. "Oh, Avery, I'm so sorry. I tried to stop him. He was wild, absolutely wild with fury."

Avery's stomach clenched. "Are you hurt?"

Carlee shook her head vehemently. "No, of course not.

He'd never hurt me. He's my father." But her voice did not carry any conviction.

"What happened here? What did he do?" She could not bring herself to so much as say Craig's name.

Head down in shame, Carlee waved a hand toward the tack room where the bridles were always maintained in meticulous order and cleanliness.

As Avery stepped through the doorway, she could not stop her gasp. Dozens of valuable bridles fully tacked out with bits and reins were heaped in the middle of the floor, costly leather headstalls slashed in half.

"I tried to stop him. I truly did," Carlee's voice carried softly from the hall of the barn. "He was screaming and just pushed me away like I wasn't even speaking to him." Carlee's voice was openly troubled. "I don't think he even knew it was me talking to him, begging him to stop. He just kept saying you had to pay, over and over." Carlee stopped abruptly, clearly stricken by what she was admitting about her own father.

Avery expelled a sigh as she turned resolutely away from the carnage. The bridles could be replaced. Her horses were safe and Carlee was unharmed, though shaken by the scene with Craig.

Avery returned to stand in front of her and held out her hand. Slowly, Carlee took it and rose gracefully to her feet. She was taller than Avery, but only slightly, and their eyes met. "I'm really, really sorry, Avery."

"This isn't your fault, Carlee. I don't hold you accountable in the least."

"Would it be better," her voice broke slightly, but she took a breath and finished, "better for you ... easier ... if I just left?" Carlee appeared uncharacteristically young and vulnerable, far from her usual shoulders-back confidence.

"Is that what you want?" Avery kept her words calm even as an added stress slammed through her. Carlee was her right-hand. She couldn't imagine how she'd ever replace her, how she could possibly find someone as reliable and as committed to helping Summer Valley Ranch succeed. And on a personal level, she would miss Carlee terribly. But Avery knew she had to do the right thing for the girl. Craig's daughter was caught clearly in the middle. "Would it be easier on you? I know these last years have been as difficult for you as they have for me. I'd make sure you were okay financially if you feel that's best for you."

"No." Carlee's expression was one of pure shock at the suggestion. "I never want to leave here. This is my home. We've built everything from nothing." Her lips quivered. "Me and you. Together."

Avery heaved a sigh of relief, acknowledging a familiar wave of affection. She and Carlee were a good team. "Well, that's that then." She smiled though she didn't yet feel like smiling. "We'll get through this like we have the rest. Your father will get a grip eventually and move on. He loves you, Carlee, whatever he said about or to you, it will be okay."

Carlee shook her head and her mid-length layers of hair swirled slightly with the movement. "You didn't see him, Avery. I'm not sure he can pull himself together. His hands were shaking – not just trembling – but shaking and he was talking wild. Kept saying 'they' would be angry and he wasn't going to take the blame for what you'd done to him."

"They?" Avery was completely confused. "They, who?"

"I don't know. I asked. He wouldn't answer me."

"Don't worry about it for now," Avery said firmly, shifting into mother mode. "You're exhausted and so am I. We'll get some rest and clean up this mess first thing in the morning. I'll finish and lock up here. You go on inside."

Carlee didn't seem at all sure about leaving Avery and turned her attention to Dirks for the first time. Her eyes narrowed in warning. "Who are you?"

Dirks gave his name and held out his hand, waiting patiently for Carlee to shake it. Avery could see her hesitance and offered as much explanation as she could.

"Mr. Hanna will be staying in the guest quarters while he checks out what we can offer wounded veterans." She was relieved to see Carlee's shoulders lose some of their tension.

"Welcome to Summer Valley Ranch," Carlee said, with more welcome but still no smile.

Avery suspected she didn't have much 'smile' left in her after the episode with Craig. "Get some rest, Carlee," she said gently. "I'll get Mr. Hanna settled and see you in the morning. Everything will seem better with the sun."

Carlee gave her an 'I'm not so sure look' but she complied, giving Avery a light, quick hug before turning to leave. At the door of the barn, she cast a final backward, slightly anxious glance.

"She's worried about you," Dirks offered.

Avery sighed. "Well, that's two of us." She brushed tangled hair from her face. "I'll show you to the guest quarters and let you take your bags in while I get some fresh linen."

"What remains to be done out here?"

The question surprised her. "With the horses? Nothing." She glanced toward the tack room with the tangle of ruined headstalls. "Nothing at all."

Well, how interesting was that? Ms. Gorgeous hardly appears old enough to be playing mother to a young woman of Carlee's age yet the relationship seems to work for the two of them. And, of course, in terms of pure age, it is entirely plausible.

Beyond a doubt, there is much to be done in short order. My beautiful Irish Rose, Tammy Lynn, must be reassured of my safety, so computer access is essential. Fortunately, there is no need for a conversational exchange. Tammy Lynn will realize at once that my presence in Summer Valley is directly tied to the string of worrisome e-mails she has received from Ms. Gorgeous. Though they don't see each other often, they remain good friends. I'd thought to find and settle a simple case of harassment from a soon-to-be-ex-husband but the current situation is certainly more than that. What worries my Tammy Lynn worries me and must, therefore, be resolved. And that is where my sleuthing skills shall be directed.

Once Tammy Lynn is aware of my location, my next task will also require my excellent online skills as I have yet to confirm that Mr. Military is as legitimate as he seems. So there is that to be accomplished along with sorting through the divorce drama to determine the identity of the puppet master pulling the strings of the ex-husband. Reaching a suitable conclusion is likely to be draining so my first order of business must be nourishment to sustain me as this looks to be a rather lengthy investigation.

CHAPTER THREE

*A*very was an early riser by nature on top of which she'd not rested well. Even after her body had demanded she crawl between her soft-as-silk sheets, her mind had skittered among worry over her horses, hope that she was handling things well with Carlee, and trepidation over Dirks Hanna's arrival in the midst of this mess. Long before first light, she was at her computer, coffee mug in hand. She'd intended to do some research on him, the same as she did on any students or potential students who came her way, particularly those whose needs originated in trauma of some sort. It was essential that she always know what she was up against in her efforts to help her clients, sometimes merely to reach them, connect with them. Added to that, she was exceedingly particular in accepting clients she actually thought would benefit from what she had to offer and never those whose past indicated they would be a menace to her animals or her family.

She also had to read through more of the financial documents that Carlee sent her faithfully. Avery had given Carlee complete authority to execute purchase orders and pay bills, but Carlee adamantly refused to do anything that Avery had not first reviewed and blessed. The younger woman was always careful to send her a summary, telling her what documents were included and what response was needed. Avery never let her know that she sometimes did no more than skim the summary and forward her e-mail approval for the contents. Carlee was an absolute genius when it came to all things financial. Far be it from Avery to second-guess the rock-solid choices Carlee made in how and when to spend their resources above and beyond the necessities of feed and supplements, vaccinations and de-wormer, routine dental, and – always – the farrier.

Checking her e-mail before she did anything else was now more habit than necessity. There was a time, when she was first starting Summer Valley Ranch, that checking daily – often multiple times a day – for potential new clients was a must. She couldn't afford to miss any inquiry in the early days. Now, she was flooded with clients. All came to her by word of mouth. Summer Valley Ranch did not, and did not need to, advertise.

Seeing an e-mail from her friend Tammy Lynn brought a smile to her face. She hadn't thought she'd have anything to smile about today but the book seller had been such a good friend to her since she'd moved to the area and opened the ranch. Avery didn't have much leisure time but what she did have she spent reading. Tammy Lynn's "Book Basket" was her favorite place to find reading material.

Her first read of the e-mail, however, left her confused. Her smile faded as she re-read the words her friend had written.

"I'm glad Trouble is with you. I have no doubt he wouldn't be unless he was certain he was needed. I know you'll take good care of him, you're that kind of person, and I know he'll take good care of you, he's that kind of cat." She'd ended with one last comment. "I enjoyed the Skype."

Avery leaned back in her chair and took another drink of her coffee while her mind tried to assimilate the message. Skype? Of a cat named Trouble? Tammy Lynn's Trouble? Sure, she knew Tammy Lynn had what she swore was a smarter-than-average black cat but ...

Feeling eyes on her, she turned slowly, knowing those eyes were going to be a brilliant green. "Mister, I don't know if or how you did that, but you are one scary-smart cat if you actually did."

Trouble matched her stare for stare before leaping lightly to the desktop. He placed a deliberate paw upon the mouse, then withdrew it to curl up neatly on top of the mousepad. When he closed those guileless green eyes, Avery knew she'd been dismissed.

"I think I need another cup of coffee," she murmured. Snooping into Mr. Hanna's existence could wait as could the several dozen other e-mails.

COFFEE AND FRESH AIR. She stepped out of the well-appointed kitchen, rarely used these days, to the wrap-around porch. Cup in hand, she sank into a cushioned wicker chair, letting the early morning coolness wash over her.

Before she had time to relax completely, her cell phone rang and she wasn't surprised to see the sheriff's name displayed. His daughter had been one of her first students. Long before she owned Summer Valley Ranch, she had been a riding instructor at a fairly large, local riding school. She'd learned enough to know she could make it in the business. She and the Farleys had remained friends.

"What the hell, Avery?"

Little as she felt like laughing, she couldn't help herself. "Good morning, Ben. What the hell, indeed. I take it you've seen my vehicle."

"Seen it, combed through it, and had it towed. You'll get it back when it's fixed, but we're not done with it yet. Do I need to bust Craig's ass?"

"I wish." She sighed. "But you can't, Ben, and we both know it. Craig may have slashed the tires but you'll never prove it. And he doesn't own a gun."

"That you know of."

"Oh, Ben, come on. You know he doesn't carry."

"What I know is he's not the man he once was or the man I thought he was. We can't be sure what he would and wouldn't do at this point. You watch yourself, Avery. Watch yourself and I'll watch him."

Avery's throat tightened. So many good people here, so many who cared about her. And a hell of a way to have to find out how many, a tiny voice chimed in. She ignored her own cynicism.

For a brief moment, she considered telling him about the destruction Craig had wreaked upon some extremely expensive tack. The thought of Carlee being questioned about her exchange that night with her father, of Carlee's comments being a factor if Ben decided to arrest Craig, deterred her. She would not pit daughter against father. She thanked the sheriff and he rang off, reiterating that he'd have her vehicle towed to a repair shop and returned to her as soon as their investigation allowed them to.

Avery didn't put much faith in that investigation but she didn't say so. Not that Ben Farley wasn't as smart as any big city sheriff, but it'd be a long shot if he managed to pin it on Craig, even as convinced as he was that Craig was guilty.

She wasn't convinced. Craig might be just brave enough and just cowardly enough to slash a woman's tires, but bullets, no, not so much. No, if anyone could figure out what had happened she'd put more faith in Dirks Hanna than the local law enforcement. But she hoped he wasn't around long enough to solve any mysteries for her or anyone else. She wanted him to see what he needed to see and go back to whoever needed to hear it and declare Summer Valley Ranch more than adequate for the veteran equine therapy program. She had her heart set on it and would have been more frustrated by the delay than she was if the drawn out fight with Craig hadn't taken so much of her time and energy.

Her gaze was drawn to the row of small guest bungalows. She'd put Dirks in the one farthest from the main house and wasn't surprised to see a light already on. His air of confidence and authority was appealing. She could acknowledge the fact while also accepting she wouldn't allow herself to be drawn to him for that or any other reason. Like strong hands and broad shoulders. She'd once found Craig's strong hands and broad shoulders just as appealing. See where that had gotten her. She shook off the thought, determined not to go there. It was time to move forward and forward was showing Mr. Hanna that she had a perfectly viable program, medically approved to help veterans regain some sense of normalcy and control of their own destiny. The medically approved part he should already know even if he'd no more than skimmed the surface of her application. But the viable part – that much she could *and would* demonstrate to his satisfaction.

By the time her first client had arrived - she refused to call or even think of them as patients - Avery had downed another cup of coffee with two slices of whole wheat toast, showered and pulled her hair back and up with a clip. She would have preferred to forgo makeup completely, but her mirror said otherwise. She refused to go about appearing wan and dreary, like some heroine in a tragedy. The judge's ruling had averted the tragedy she'd feared and there could be no heroine without a hero, and Craig was no hero. The last thought brought a glimmer of a smile as she brushed just the slightest bit of color onto her cheeks.

She waited for their eight o'clock client at the first paddock. Rob had been just weeks from his high school graduation when a car crash had taken his closest friend and left him with debilitating injuries. He'd been referred to her by a neurosurgeon who believed Rob's own mind was deliberately holding him back from fullest recovery. Rob had been driving when the accident occurred. The parents of the deceased friend had forgiven their son's friend, but Rob couldn't or wouldn't forgive himself.

Rob greeted her with a shy smile. That smile had taken weeks to surface but Avery didn't credit herself. It was Rob's bond with Mr. BoJangles – or Jangle as he'd come to be called – that had wrought the slow change in a young man who had everything in life ahead of him but wanted nothing but the one thing that life could not offer. A second chance for his friend.

The youngest of her instructors, Leanne, brought Jangle to the paddock and stood waiting patiently in the center for Rob to come to her.

Avery remained at the paddock opening as Rob walked slowly but with increasing steadiness across the soft smooth dirt of the paddock.

"Why didn't she bring the horse to him?" Dirks' voice came from behind her.

Avery turned slowly. "You're very quiet on your feet." It wasn't *quite* an accusation.

"Habit. Training. Sorry, it wasn't intentional."

But she wondered if that were true. He was here, after all, to scrutinize everything about her. The thought should have bothered her, she supposed, but she was glad the government cared enough about the men and women who had served and been injured for their service to see that they received good care. She had reason to know that wasn't always the case and not just because of the bombardment of bad press about veteran aid. She was still angry at how long it had taken for her brother to get the help he needed and, even then, it had been too little, too late.

Pulling her thoughts back to Dirks' question, she said, "Rob came to us six months ago in a wheelchair. He had to *want* to walk before he could *learn* to walk. Jangle has a way about him that makes people want to come to him. Leanne was smart enough to use that fact to full advantage."

She turned to look at Dirks and found he was watching the young man and the horse. Jangle never took his wide, dark eyes off Rob despite the slow process, never shook his head in impatience. Avery knew the moment Dirks realized that Leanne had stepped away and saw only solid training held the animal quietly in position. Avery knew it was more than training. Jack's offspring – and Jangle was the oldest of them – seemed to understand intuitively the need of the humans who came into their care. When Rob reached Jangle's side, Jangle lowered his head to the young man's chest. Arms, not as strong as they surely once were, but stronger every day, circled the horse's neck. Leanne came forward with a two-step stool and stood by, ready to assist, but not offering help that wasn't needed, as Rob slowly stepped up and into the saddle. He gave

Leanne another brief smile then gathered the reins and began to guide Jangle slowly around the paddock.

Avery beckoned Leanne forward and introduced her to Dirks. "Leanne is in charge of Barn One."

She'd thought that Dirks would question Leanne but all he did was give his name and say that he was there on behalf of the wounded veterans program. When Leanne returned to the center of the ring to keep careful watch over Rob's and Jangle's progress, Dirks asked, "What does in charge of mean? Does she have a title?"

Avery nodded. "She's Barn Manager. That's what is on the books. Reality is so much more. She is in charge of the horses in her barn – there are six in each – and the clients matched to those horses. Those horses are hers to manage as far as exercise, feed, training, leisure time – whatever they need she ensures they have. When they are with a client, her focus is on that client and that horse the entire time. She must know the medical history of each client, understand their primary doctor's instructions for their therapy. Each barn has an indoor and an outdoor paddock. She's tasked with knowing when the ground needs to be worked, altered in some way, etc. Of recognizing when maintenance is needed and making it happen."

She wasn't surprised by Dirks' raised brow. "One person? All that?"

"One person. All that and more. She doesn't *do* it all mind you, but she knows the why and manages the how and the when. The 'and more' is that each barn has a part-time barn helper who cleans the stalls, makes sure water is cool and tubs are clean and horses are all fed according to Leanne's specific direction for each. She is also responsible for their performance and development as employees."

"Has she been here long?"

"Almost five years. Leanne came to me straight from graduation -- physical therapy. She didn't want to work in a hospital or clinic. She loves horses and she loves people."

"Does she live here? Do any of your barn managers? You have three barns so three managers, right?"

"That's right and she did live here for a while. The guest quarters are sometimes used for temporary residences, sometimes for clients who need a place to 'be' but again temporary. Leanne married a couple of years ago and she and her husband bought a small property not far from here. One of my requirements is that my barn managers must be within a thirty minute commute at the most."

"This isn't just a job for them, is it?"

Avery gave him a quick glance, realizing that he truly got it. "No, I guess it's a career plus a lifestyle. Like the military is for some."

She started to walk toward Barn Two. The first appointment for that barn was another thirty minutes out. Dirks followed as she expected he would.

"Why three barns? Why not one big one?"

Her answer wasn't quick or flippant because it was actually a good question. "Initially, it was because I started small and had only the first six horses to work with and not a great deal of savings or income. The first barn was built just big enough to house those six because it was as much as I could afford at the time. After I put in the outdoor paddock at one end and the covered paddock at the other, the set up worked so well that I did the same with Barn Two rather than adding on to what was there.

The horses in Barn One provide therapy for clients who have been injured, like Rob. Leanne is good with the grief and the anger and the frustration that comes with all of that - the loss of what they had, the fight to get it back."

"What about Barn Two?" Dirks asked quietly. "Who is that for?"

"Children born with disabilities, whose parents or care-givers of some sort are smart enough, care enough, and brave enough to want them to have more, to have and be everything they can and they choose horses, choose *us*, to give it to them."

DIRKS HEARD the passion in her voice, heard the caring. But caring didn't always equate to ethics, he knew. He almost hated to push on through the questioning. Not that he had a choice. The questioning and the digging were why he'd been sent.

"And Barn Three?"

"That barn I just filled over the last few months, selected the horses more carefully than I've ever selected in my life." He could hear the sadness in her voice. "I chose them for the veterans."

"Your brother came home from Afghanistan wounded."

Her feet stopped moving and he saw the slight jerk of her head, as if he'd sent the slenderest of arrows through her. She didn't question his knowledge, of course. She would've expected him to do his homework before coming to see her facilities.

The look she turned on him was filled as much with anger as with anguish. "He was passed from one hospital to another, assigned to one reviewer after another. He couldn't get the quality of help he needed from them and he wouldn't take it from me." She started walking again, seeming not to care if he followed or not.

Dirks didn't bother to apologize. There were no words

adequate. What was happening in military units everywhere was inexcusable. But there were those working hard to make improvements and he was part of that effort. No matter how pretty - how beautiful - he found Avery Wilson, he'd verify she was part of the improvement process, as well, or turn her over to the authorities in a heartbeat if he found she was not. Maybe not without a pang, but he'd do it.

The last trace the military had of her brother was that he was one of the walking wounded, lost and homeless, but – hopefully – still alive someplace, still with the possibility of recovery. There was another whole investigative branch now dedicated to finding and helping, this time truly helping, those who would let them. And still not each of them would.

Carlee intercepted them before they reached Barn Two. Dirks noted that she was dressed much like Avery in jeans and tucked shirt with her light colored hair pulled up into some kind of knot. Also like Avery she wore a minimum of makeup. These were women with a focus on their work not on their appearance.

She acknowledged Dirks with a glance and something that could have passed for a nod but she focused her gaze on Avery. "I've ordered all new headstalls for Barn One. We're using what we need from Barn Three until they arrive."

"That works," Avery agreed. "You ordered from Barton's?"

"Of course." Carlee almost smiled. "I know your preference for local and the quality is there as well as value for the price. Sam was thrilled to get the order." The smile, that never quite was, disappeared quickly. "There was an odd message on the business line. A Mr. Markham. He said his flight would arrive just after one o'clock this afternoon and he'd be around to assess the colt."

"What? What colt? Why?"

Dirks noted that every bit of the tension was back in Avery's voice.

"I don't know, Avery. That's all he said other than he mentioned an e-mail he'd sent last evening. He sounded like a Yankee or a Brit," Carlee added. "I couldn't place the accent."

"I don't care if he sounded like European Royalty. He's wasting his time. And mine. We've nothing for sale, lease, or borrow."

"I know," Carlee soothed. "I'll deal with him if you like."

"No, it's mine to do, but thank you. I've got this. There is something you can do for me."

"Anything, of course."

"I need a rental for a few weeks and I need the insurance adjustor to go by the sheriff's office and request to see my SUV so that a claim can get started."

"What are you talking about? Avery, were you in a wreck? Are you hurt?" Carlee started to sound frantic.

Avery put both hands on Carlee's shoulders. "No and no. No wreck and I'm not hurt. Someone just had a little fun with my car, that's all. Nothing a new windshield and four new tires won't fix."

Dirks realized she didn't mention bullet holes and a front seat that would need replacing. But since Carlee showed clear signs of panic, that was probably a wise decision on her part.

"Oh, my God, what did he do? He's crazy. I swear it. Avery, I'm sorry."

"Stop, Carlee. Just stop. I don't know who did it and neither do you. The sheriff may figure it out so let's just wait and see."

"Why are you protecting him?"

"I'm not, Carlee, I'm really not but until I know more, I can't accuse Craig of anything."

"Well, I can." With the panic fading, Carlee's blue eyes held pure anger. "I can and will."

"I really wish you wouldn't."

Carlee touched Avery's face lightly. "You're a saint, you know that don't you?" But she didn't, Dirks noted, give in to Avery's wishes.

Avery stood watching as Carlee walked away but Dirks' attention was split between the two women. Avery's brows were drawn together in worry as she watched her step-daughter's long strides. Carlee glanced at the black cat as he sauntered by but she didn't slow. Clearly, Carlee on a mission could be a formidable person.

"Well, okay, then." The words were quietly spoken.

Dirks focused on Avery and raised one brow.

"There's no stopping Carlee when she sets her mind on something. She's wrong though. I'm not a saint. If I could give Craig as much misery as he's given me, I probably would. Fortunately for me, he's saved me the effort." She turned at the sound of a diesel engine. A sharp, blue truck was pulling to a stop in front of the second of the three barns. "There's our nine o'clock. You can watch Tucker. He's manager for Barn Two. The youngsters adore him."

FROM THE LOOK Mr. Military is giving Ms. Gorgeous he's feeling a bit of adoration himself. A hint of romance gives such an interesting side bar to a nice mystery. Tender feelings aside, however, I'm a bit antsy as the locals might say. Nothing I can touch a paw to but my incredibly sensitive nature advises something is too quiet about the morning. I'd best keep in close contact in case my feline detecting abilities are once again called into play. Whoever fired those bullets last evening hasn't obtained the prize. I must ensure that remains the case.

For all of the conflict, the ranch provides a lovely respite. The nice fence rails all around and fat corner posts make a comfortable place to sit and watch. Not quite large enough to curl up for a nap, but my work isn't done and a nap is out of the question for the moment.

Now there's a handsome lad stepping down from the truck with unusually calm movements for one so young. Odd. He appears quite healthy but there's a distinct sadness in his father's eyes — at least I suppose the man is his father as they bear a close resemblance — as he stands back and watches. The boy walks toward a petite grey horse led by a small, wiry man with rather outrageously red hair and kind green eyes. I'm partial to green eyes. I'm not, however, overly fond of children much of the time. Regardless, I tolerate them reasonably well, particularly the polite ones. I'm not keen on horses either although I will admit they can be truly magnificent creatures. This one is a bit undersized to be called magnificent but I suppose, to a child, it could seem quite large.

I see no fear, however. The boy seems much at ease as he approaches the horse and the person called Tucker. Tucker smiles but the child does not, at least not until he settles quietly into the saddle. The smile he gives his father as he does so is breathtaking and the sadness leaves his father's eyes.

Mr. Military stands near Ms. Gorgeous as she watches the boy lift the reins. She explains that the pony is a Connemara pony and Mr. Military leans even closer, as if to hear her better, and I suppose that is a handy excuse for him. Autistic, she says about the boy, with signs of improvement. Oh my. Autism is such a hard thing for a parent to work through with a child. I know that many don't even try or give up when the progress is too little. But a child is there, locked deep inside his own prison. It is heartening to know there are ways to reach through the barriers for some.

Mr. Military seems impressed as well. Hopefully he will realize that Ms. Gorgeous is more than just a pretty face.

Even more important, however, is the fact that I heard the word lunch *pass between them. With any luck, there will be some real attempt at true cuisine and not the warmed slices of bread that passed for a human breakfast this morning. I did, however, appreciate the offering of two eggs scrambled with real cream. A bit of grilled salmon would not come amiss for a tasty midday break. We shall see.*

CHAPTER FOUR

*T*ension built slowly through Avery as she sliced fresh, heirloom tomatoes and cucumbers still warm from her small side garden. How *had* she come to be in this domestic little scene with Dirks Hanna? She didn't want to be here. She didn't want *him* to be here. She wanted him to figure out what he needed to know and go away, back to wherever he came from and give her application a thumbs-up when he got there. She wanted to spend the next hour or so pacing the floor while she worried about this unknown Mr. Markham who thought it okay to just show up for a look at one of *her* beloved horses as if he were answering a sales ad. He planned to arrive with no more than a brief voice message and an e-mail she still hadn't had a chance to read much less answer. She wanted to be peaceful, damn it. That didn't seem too much to ask.

She shot a frustrated glance through the glass door where Dirks was turning fish on the grill. Tammy Lynn's black cat wove through his legs as if they were best friends. Unexpectedly, the humor of the situation, of her own thoughts struck her and some of the tension ebbed. So, okay, she wasn't ready to feel attraction for any man, wasn't ready for the attraction she felt for *this* particular man. She didn't need to act on it. And Dirks certainly seemed unaware of her interest, of the fact that she found the intelligence in his gaze sexy and his lips tempting when they curved in a smile. He had a nice smile, nothing wrong with admitting that. No reason for the admission to kick her pulse up to anxiety level. She was behaving beyond ridiculous.

Taking a deep breath, she finished what she was doing and stepped into her office to find Mr. Markham's e-mail. She read through it twice but was none the wiser. He wrote as if she should be expecting him, expecting his e-mail, his phone call, his arrival. It was a polite note, but read as if the purchase were a *fait accompli*. His imminent arrival was beyond her control. The e-mail had been sent, he mentioned, from his iPad as he stood at the boarding gate. Well, he was destined for disappointment. Her horses were not for sale.

The sound of the door opening drew her back into the kitchen. Dirks handed her the platter of grilled-to-perfection red snapper and Trouble immediately shifted his affectionate twining from Dirks' legs to hers.

Dirks gave him a stern glare. "Traitor."

"Fickle, is he?"

"His affections appear to follow the food."

Dirks smiled and her pulse gave that tiny leap again. She felt like calling her own body a traitor but that would be far too much of a confession, even if it were a silent one.

"I thought we'd eat here, rather than the dining room." She indicated the wide, quartz topped bar where she'd already laid out flatware on napkins and glasses filled with ice and water. She didn't want him to think she was going to any trouble to impress him. Summer Valley Ranch should be impressive enough, *was* impressive enough on its own.

While Dirks stepped into the downstairs powder room to wash up, she placed the fish and fresh garden vegetables on the bar along with the salt and pepper grinders. And took another deep breath.

I'M QUITE IMPRESSED with the culinary expertise of Mr. Military. Although I suspect Ms. Gorgeous would rather he pack his briefcase and all those precisely pressed garments – yes, I'll confess to a bit of snooping in his quarters – and depart, I fear my diet would suffer in terms of variety. I'd like to say that I have no reason to question that there is more to his appearance here than ensuring the adequacy of Summer Valley Ranch for wounded veteran rehabilitation but – alas – once again things are not as they seem. My elevated olfactory sense enabled me to detect a significant amount of firepower secreted around his lodging in various locations, which I find interesting accoutrement for a desk jockey. While these two dawdle over lunch, I shall make further use of the computer in the office next door. Judging by the intensity between these two, I doubt I shall be missed anytime soon.

"WHERE IS CARLEE'S MOTHER?"

Dirks had asked a few probing questions about Craig's role at the ranch, seeming satisfied when Avery explained that he'd really had little to do with the physical management of the place. Craig had been involved with only a bit of the bookwork and he'd been an ear to listen when she needed to balance some decision. The question about Craig's first wife caught Avery by surprise and she sighed, the heavy weight of sorrow pressing on her even after all these years. "She's deceased. It's a sad story. Craig's had a lot of loss and I try to be compassionate because I don't know how much of his current breakdown has to do with that."

"Breakdown? You think he's suffering from some kind of emotional incapacity?" Dirks raised his brows and she could almost feel his skepticism.

"Honestly, I don't know all that is going on with him," she admitted, "but, in the end, I had to accept that I couldn't allow him to destroy what my team and I have worked so hard to build and he refused any suggestion of professional help. I believe that some diseases are a 'disease of choice'. The victim doesn't choose to have the disease but they do choose – or reject – the opportunity for healing. Carlee's been a Godsend to me and she's certainly suffered as much, if not more, than Craig in all this."

She hesitated, feeling a bit of a traitor to expose her stepdaughter's personal heartache. "Carlee's twin died horribly when the girls were just eleven. They were both students at the facility where I gave lessons but in different programs. Carlee was in an elevated hunter-jumper class, probably headed for the Olympics. Caren was placed with me in a therapeutic program."

Dirks had stayed silent while she talked, swirling his water glass and watching the motion of liquid and ice thoughtfully, almost as if to give her space. But at her words, he shifted that piercing gaze to hers. "Therapeutic? Had she been in some kind of accident?"

"No, Caren was born with cerebral palsy. The child was absolutely brilliant academically but walking was difficult for her. She *could* walk but was much more mobile, more self-sufficient from her wheelchair. The girls were more than close, as I guess most twins are. But Carlee ... Carlee was devoted to her sister, always came to watch her ride, cheering her on for the slightest victory. She was devastated by Caren's death. They all were. *We* all were." The entire academy had shut down on the day of Caren's funeral. She was that well-loved. Remembering, Avery focused her attention on her plate, knowing her eyes glittered with tears. She didn't want Dirks to see and construe them as some kind of weakness that might make her unfit as a business woman strong enough for the responsibilities associated with the wounded veteran program.

"Had she been progressively ill? I know a little about cerebral palsy, not much, but I know it can impact a number of organs."

Avery shook her head. "No, her death was a horrible, horrible accident. Her wheelchair somehow rolled into the pool. Carlee found her when she came in from after school softball practice. Carlee was into every sport imaginable. Margaret, their mother, had fallen asleep on the sun porch while Caren sketched. That was one of Caren's favorite pastimes, second only to riding. She was very artistic though she only had full use of her right arm. The muscles were stiff and atrophied in the other." Avery still had nightmares, waking to images of Caren slowly sinking into the pool, struggling to release the seatbelt intended to keep her safe when her chair was in use, helpless to free herself as the water closed over her head. She could only imagine the horrors that Craig and Carlee endured thinking about Caren's death.

"She wasn't just a student to you. You loved her," Dirks said softly.

"Everyone loved Caren. She was an incredible child. Loving, courageous, sunny ... in spite of her disability. It was a complete tragedy. Her mother took her own life a year later and Craig was left to pick up the pieces. Carlee told me once it hurt to the core that she didn't just lose her sister and best friend but that she wasn't reason enough for her mother to want to live."

Dirks reached over as if to touch her hand but at the last minute didn't, placing it on the table instead. "I think that's a common and certainly natural feeling among family members of suicides, especially young children."

"I won't pretend to know what I'd do in similar circumstances but I can't imagine knowingly, intentionally leaving my child to face my death and grow up without me."

"You said Carlee was 'probably' headed for the Olympics." There was a faint question in his voice.

"She lost heart after Caren died – just quit riding. Some months after her mother's suicide, Craig came back to the academy. He was desperate to distract Carlee from her grief and thought horses might help. By then, I'd made the barest beginnings with Summer Valley Ranch and he chose to bring her here, thinking it would be an easier environment."

She fell silent for a moment, thinking back to that long ago summer. Dirks' steady gaze reminded her of the reason she was sharing all of these personal, sometimes happy, sometimes painful experiences.

"Carlee didn't want lessons, not in any of the venues, she wanted only to be around horses and ride on her own. So that's what we did. Mostly long trail rides, just the two of us." It was through those months that she and Craig had drifted into a relationship. She pushed aside those memories, now tarnished by the ugliness of more recent history.

Avery watched as Dirks processed what she'd told him, and she wasn't in the least surprised when he circled back to his initial question and asked, "Do you really think – this many years later – that Craig suddenly finds it impossible to deal with the losses of his daughter and his wife?"

"No," she admitted. "No, I don't. What I really think is that I missed a weakness in Craig, missed it at the start and failed to watch it grow. I was too caught up in creating my dreams for Summer Valley Ranch, too caught up with the hard work and my love for the horses to see what was happening to my husband. And to my marriage."

"His addiction isn't your fault or your problem."

The intensity in his voice surprised her until she realized he'd mistaken her meaning. "I agree, it isn't, but I should at least have recognized sooner that it existed. I might have made different decisions." She sighed, realizing she might as well acknowledge an aspect she'd neatly skimmed over in earlier conversation. "Carlee manages accounts payables. For a while Craig managed accounts receivables. I've taken that part of the business on for the time being. I suspect, now, that he was putting a good bit in his pocket right from the first, but a few years ago, the revenue from the ranch started shrinking noticeably. I brought in an independent financial guru to help me maximize my profit. She's the one who found that Craig was pocketing nearly as much as he was depositing. I confronted him, he denied it, and I filed for divorce."

None of it had been as easy as that admission must sound to an outsider, but that pain, that drama was over and done and not anything she wanted or needed to relive by talking about it now.

Her cell phone broke the complete silence that followed her stark words. She glanced at the caller I.D., noting the time, and sighed. She looked at Dirks before she hit answer. "I guess it's show time." Careful to lighten her tone, she spoke into the phone. "Hey, Tucker."

"There's a Mr. Markham to see you. He's pulling an empty horse trailer." Tucker sounded worried and she realized immediately that she should've given her team a heads-up.

"And he'll be pulling an empty one on his way out," she said reassuringly, keeping her voice calm. "Where did he park?"

"In the main drive."

"Tell him I'm on my way. You can go back to your barn. You have a student, don't you?"

"They just pulled in but I really think I should be here with you."

She heard the edge in Tucker's voice and knew at once he didn't like the appearance of their *guest*. "I've got this, Tucker, I promise. Go take care of your student." Her years-long fight with Craig had affected more than just her. Her team had become protective of her. Too protective.

As she put the phone down, she realized Dirks had already gotten to his feet. "Not you, too." She fought the urge to roll her eyes. "I've *got* this," she said, repeating the words she'd spoken to Tucker in exasperation.

"Let's go," was all Dirks said.

Irritation washed through her and she flashed Trouble a scowl as he sauntered out of the office and through the door with them. Another alpha male. She was surrounded by them.

WELL, *this is all getting extraordinarily interesting. My time on the computer wasn't wasted. Mr. Military hasn't been a desk jockey for any length of time – if he is at all. His credentials are real but he's seen significant military action in the not too distant past. I didn't get to his current day situation in my sleuthing but time for that later. Good thing I was keeping an ear tuned to the kitchen conversation and an eye on the clock. I wouldn't miss seeing Ms. Gorgeous handle this threat to her equines for the most tempting serving of steak tartare, which – most unfortunately – I've not had the pleasure of being served in far too long. With my love of all things British, I can still concede that the French do occasionally come up with some delectable edibles.*

I must say, however, I'm not sure why such a hurried pace has been set by the humans. I much prefer a leisurely approach to an all-out hike, especially in this atmosphere of southern sauna-like heat and humidity. Nonetheless, I manage to keep pace as I follow close on the heels of Mr. Military and Ms. Gorgeous as we head toward the barn area.

My, my! That's quite a fancy rig, very flashy and shiny with all that chrome, parked directly in the middle of the drive. I daresay either truck or trailer alone cost a bomb. Together they certainly appear appropriate to the posh main drag into the ranch. I must acknowledge that someone has done an excellent job with landscaping and lawn maintenance. The rustic board fence of weathered silver is neat without being obvious. The white board railing, evident in many of the rural equine establishments, has been the rage for years, but I much favor this pastoral ambiance.

I'll stroll around the semi and trailer for a closer look while these humans exchange pleasantries they certainly do not mean. Hmmm ... now here is something of interest. I was checking for state of registration on the license plate, but find instead **TAG APPLIED FOR** *as in 'just purchased'. Apparently, no mere hired rig would suffice for Mr. Markham.*

Uh-oh, voices are rising. I do believe I must abandon my snooping to move closer to my humans and prepare to enter the fray.

"What do you mean your horses are not for sale?" *The nob speaking isn't a particularly handsome representative of the species, but with those thin brows drawn together over a thinner nose and lips compressed with the force of his frustration he is even less so. I simply do not understand the current affinity for shaved heads among human males. Every creature looks a bit better with a healthy covering of hair, or fur, as the case may be.*

"My horses are not for sale. It's that simple." *Ms. Gorgeous is keeping her cool thus far but, somewhat incongruously, that silky tone is marvelously menacing.* "I cannot fathom that you would travel from Canada without asking first."

"I'm done talking with you. Where is your husband?"

Why, now, that comment must be extremely insulting to a self-made woman. Most certainly the result the gentleman intends, though I suppose I must use the term 'gentleman' with a certain sarcasm.

"I don't have a husband."

Oh, that's jolly. She's being deliberately obtuse with her response. I do love that in a dispute but I'm not certain it's her wisest course. I particularly dislike the manner in which the dandily dressed Mr. Markham is tapping that crop against his shiny boots.

"Impossible. Of course you do."

"Why is that?" *I can see the rising suspicion in those exquisite green eyes. Not as brilliant a green as mine – Tammy Lynn loves my eyes – but truly remarkable with the swirls of brown and flecks of gold. Remarkable and intelligent.*

"Because it was your husband who took money for the animal. Half last month and half to be paid today. Cash."

The figure he names is shockingly high if the widening of Ms. Gorgeous' eyes is any indication.

"I'm truly sorry for you, Mr. Markham. You've been cheated but not by me. I've taken money from no one because – as I said – my horses are not for sale. Not now, not ever."

What a prat! He's stepping closer, bowing his rather insignificant chest. Fortunately, Mr. Military is also moving in and he has no need for any pathetic endeavor to appear bigger or stronger than he certainly is. "I believe you're done here."

Mr. Markham clearly sees that he is outmanned, as it were. He steps back but not down. "Not until I've loaded Mr. Tarent's animal."

For some reason the name Tarent lights a match to a tinderbox. Ms. Gorgeous' hands are shaking now and not in fear.

"Tarent? Burris Tarent? That despicable man will never own one of my horses. He may be rich enough to buy from some but not from me. His mishandling has destroyed some of the finest animals in the world."

"Ridiculous! Mr. Tarent is highly respected in his field. He's obtained, and I have trained, dozens of horses to success in the show ring." *The toff is clearly offended.*

"The ones you didn't manage to cripple you mean." *Oh, the lovely fire in those eyes now. And she is the one stepping forward, ready to do battle – and physical, I suspect, as much as mental.* "Get off my property. Now. Before I call the police."

"Oh, I can promise you the law will definitely get involved. Your husband implied you might be obstinate, but Mr. Tarent's influence is wide and he's spent a fortune on this transaction. This truck and trailer were delivered from Tennessee just this week, awaiting my arrival at the airport. I assure you he didn't purchase those, as well as pay an astronomical amount for a yearling of the famous Flying Jackanapes, only to lose both the animal and the money."

"Jack and his offspring are not for sale and, if they were, it would never be to the likes of either you or Mr. Tarent. I don't care how influential you feel yourself to be. Neither of you have any power or control over me. People just like the two of you were responsible for Jack nearly being destroyed. He was put back in the ring barely healed from surgery to remove a bone spur. He tore a tendon performing his heart out for his owners, and they would have put him down for his loyalty! I rescued him just in time and his babies will never be for sale."

"Your husband took Mr. Tarant's currency. There will be consequences."

"Take it up with Craig. If he fleeced you, your problem is with him, not with me. I've taken no one's money and mine is the only name on the papers of any horse on this property and the only name that ever has been. Now get out. Go."

Oh, my, I fear the confrontation is about to get physical. Mr. Military is definitely done with the exchange and closing in for the kill. "Mr. Markham, I suggest your employer focus his attention on the person who swindled him. You have about five minutes to back this flashy rig out of here. After that you'll be held here until the law arrives and charges you with trespassing."

Mr. Markham is either a plonker or has a desire for assisted suicide. He's thrusting his chin belligerently. Uh-oh, now the dandy is eyeing Mr. Military with contempt. He'd better chose his words carefully or fisticuffs will ensue.

"Her husband said she was slutting with the hired help. I guess you'd be one of them." *Oh, I say, Mr. Markham has tipped the kettle. Even Ms. Gorgeous is clearly shocked.*

"Four minutes." *Mr. Military is a man of great restraint, but if the fists at his side are any indication, I believe he'd choose to use them instead of words.*

I would prefer this countdown not continue on its present course lest I be forced to take action in this suffocating heat. I do suspect a few feline scratches on that nice paint would distract Mr. Markham from his stupidity.

Whew. It appears the man has some sense of self-preservation as he takes one step backward and then pivots. I can see now his flanks are as narrow as the rest of him. Sharply clothed, mind you, but supremely narrow.

. . .

Dirks watched as Avery stood with clenched hands until the moron climbed back into the semi and backed it with more caution than skill down the long drive. Avery could have stepped to one side and allowed Markham to make the full circle ... the drive had been designed to offer large trailers an easy turn. He hoped Avery's pointed action was not lost on the bastard.

The tears in her eyes when she turned struck him in the gut. That they were tears of fury, rather than of sorrow, made them no less wrenching.

"I'm going to *kill* him."

She wasn't, Dirks knew, referring to either Markham or Tarent.

CHAPTER FIVE

*a*s Markham cautiously exited her property, Avery turned to find Leanne and Tucker at her heels. Both looked as furious as she felt.

"Jerk," Leanne muttered.

Tucker snorted, his glare fixed on the shiny truck and trailer. "Jackass, I'd say."

"You heard his claim?" Avery asked.

"Enough." Leanne's angry glance turned to worry. "You think he's telling the truth?"

Avery sighed. "Unfortunately, yes, which means we need to keep a close watch on things for a while. Craig's going to be frantic if he's taken that much of a man's cash for an animal he doesn't own and can't produce. Markham said 'yearling' but I've no doubt all of the horses are at risk. And for who knows how long."

"I'll put a cot by the yearling paddock tonight," Tucker said grimly.

Leanne nodded agreement. "And I'll sleep in my barn. Close to Jack. And maybe we should keep Jack and his offspring in their stalls at night for now so we can watch them. We'll just have to get them out for a few hours during the day between their appointment times."

That would be extra work for her team and Avery absolutely hated the thought of not giving all of the animals every hour of their precious paddock time. The yearlings had a long open-sided shed for shelter in their pasture, but, unless there were storms in the forecast, the others were up during the intense heat of the day and turned out at night when temperatures were cooler and the sun wasn't a blistering orb overhead. Still she couldn't disagree with Leanne's rationale.

As much as she wanted to tell her team these precautions wouldn't be necessary, she feared they might be. "It seems Craig really had expected a different ruling from the judge," she admitted as much to herself as to her team.

As Leanne and Tucker went back to their barns and their work for the afternoon, she felt Dirks' patient gaze on her and turned back to him with a sigh. None of this would look good in regard to her application. It was hard not to feel discouraged when she should have been able to enjoy the euphoria of her divorce being finalized and the ranch still safely in her name. Craig had no legal claim to land or horses but apparently he didn't plan to let that stop him.

Dirks didn't say anything for a minute then he asked, "How much of an alarm system do you have?"

She blinked, pulling her mind in this new direction. "Well, it's pretty good for foaling mares but probably not much use for preventing theft. I've got cameras set up in the box stalls. I guess we could shift those toward the main entrance to the barn and figure out how to better secure the side exits. It might take some rewiring." Avery felt completely out of her element at the thought. "I might be able to get the guy who installed them to come out and make the adjustments."

"Let me study the setup first. It may just be a matter of repositioning the cameras without moving them all that far."

Avery hesitated, looking into his eyes and trying to gauge his thoughts around what was happening at the ranch and her future plans. "You don't have to help me do this, you know. I don't want to delay what you're here to do. Getting approved by your government for the veteran equine therapy program is important to me."

Dirks raised his brow quizzically. "*My* government?"

She winced at her own word choice. "I'm not much into the political scene but sometimes I think those of us who have to work to survive have been abandoned by the politicians."

Dirks' smile was slow and devastatingly sexy. Not something she wanted to think about right now for sure.

"Let's put that conversation on hold for another time. I've read through ample files for now and I've got plenty to absorb. Sometimes keeping my hands busy while I think things through allows me to keep those thoughts productive."

"Okay." She hesitated. "Is there anything I can do to help?"

"Be on standby in case I need something from a building supply store."

"Actually, I've got some errands to run in town." It was a spur of the moment decision but he didn't need to know that. "If you find you need something, Tucker can call me."

"I've got a better idea." He pulled his phone from his pocket. "What's your number? That way I won't have to disturb Tucker if he's giving a lesson."

She hesitated only a moment before giving it to him. A moment later a soft ding sounded in the silence between them.

He looked at her. "Now you have mine as well."

The moment felt uncomfortably intimate, as if they weren't standing in the middle of her drive in the afternoon heat talking about ranch security.

"Do you need to take my truck?" It was a reminder that her vehicle was incapacitated - and why.

"No, there's a work truck. It's not pretty but it runs well. Carlee uses it more than any of us when the ranch needs something that isn't big enough to schedule a full delivery."

"You'll be back before dark?" His tone was entirely too casual and he smiled at the scowl she shot him and lifted his hands in a gesture of innocence. "Hey, in case I need you to bring back something to ensure security here is as effective as we can make it."

Although she still suspected his goal was to make sure she was safely at the ranch before nightfall, she didn't argue the point. There was peril out there. She couldn't even begin to guess the next direction Craig would take. In fact, if Carlee wasn't back when she returned, she'd check on her as well. Touching base for safety's sake was something they'd rarely felt necessary in the past but it certainly seemed warranted now.

My dilemma ... Do I remain here and secure the perimeters? Do I dog the heels of Ms. Gorgeous? Now there is an apt turn of phrase. Dog the heels. Canines are such insecure and servile creatures, continually at their masters' beck and call. Felines, thank goodness, do not serve. We do not have masters. We have humans we select based on their willingness and adeptness to serve us. In turn, we guard and protect.

Therein, I believe, is the answer to my quandary. As precious as the ranch is to Ms. Gorgeous, more precious is she to my beloved Tammy Lynn. Her protection is paramount. Clearly, my duty is to accompany and safeguard my 'temporary' human.

Now my only difficulty will be to either convince her that it's best I'm at her side or to ensure my presence is detected too late for her to prevent my accompanying her. Since she doesn't know me sufficiently well to fully appreciate my value, I do believe I shall take the less obvious route. While she gathers whatever she needs from inside, I'll scout around to locate and investigate this work truck and hope that it's both accessible and more comfortable than it sounds.

I do believe this must be the vehicle in question, behind what the humanoids refer to as Barn One. It's a bit dusty but not nasty, has a scratch or two in the bed which I accessed with an agile leap. However, there does not appear much in the way of comfort or camouflage back here. Hmmm, luck is with me. This front window is lowered just enough for my strong, yet streamlined build to climb through. And, more luck, although the floorboard is not carpeted, there is what appears to be a stadium throw on the back seat. A little tug and ... there ... it's now on the floor and I am out of obvious sight. In fact, if I nudge my way in just a bit more, I'm fairly certain I'm not visible at all, even should Ms. Gorgeous wisely peer into the back before climbing in herself.

The door opens and there she is. Yes, she leans over for a quick peek before settling into the front. If I accurately recall the drive from town, I believe I have time for a small, rejuvenating nap.

AVERY LOVED the town she'd chosen as her own. There was a quaintness that spoke to that sentimental part of her but also a bustling energy that promised growth and success for the future. Her future. Despite the continued threat of Craig's antics, she felt hopeful now for the first time in a long time. The weight of a bad marriage was lifted.

Parking in front of the sheriff's office, she stepped out and was somehow not surprised to see a sleek black pelt emerge from the back seat before she could close the door of the truck. "Really?" she asked in exasperation.

Two brilliant green eyes blinked, unfazed by her less than welcoming expression. It was too hot to leave him in the truck so Avery scooped him up and carried him inside with her.

Sheriff Farley was waiting in his office as he'd promised to be when she'd called on her drive into town. He lifted his brows at the cat in her arms but didn't comment as he stood and stepped around his desk to give her a quick hug. He closed the door to the open area where the dispatcher and a small scattering of officers were dealing with the mountains of paperwork associated with law enforcement. Despite the busy atmosphere, the place had a sense of order to the chaos. Paper everywhere; dust nowhere. That was Ben's influence, she knew. He came across as a rough and tumble sort of man, but she'd never seen him in a uniform that was rumpled or stained unless the damage had occurred in the line of duty.

Before Craig came along, Ben had asked her out to dinner while picking up his emotional pieces after a tumultuous divorce. She'd agreed on condition they went as friends, sharing the check along with dinner, conversation, and a bottle of wine. That friendship had worked for them better than any romance could have and stood strong to this day. Ben had since re-married very happily.

With the door closed, Avery placed Trouble on the floor. She wasn't entirely sure why she was taking so much care to keep him close and safe. This was surely one cat that was completely self-sufficient. His home with Tammy Lynn was many miles away but he'd brought himself here and Tammy Lynn seemed to have no qualms about his absence.

"Sit down, Avery." There was real concern in the southern

inflection of Ben's gravelly voice. He took the chair beside hers, on the visitor side of his desk. "How are you?"

"Frustrated," she said honestly. "I should be happy and peaceful and I'm frustrated that I'm not – that I can't be. I knew Craig would be angry, even hostile, at the judge's decision but now it seems he's way more than that ... I think he's a very, very desperate man." She described the scene with Markham, concluding, "... and that's on top of the damage to my SUV. I mean, honestly, Ben, bullets?"

The concern in his eyes deepened. "Not just any bullets, Avery. They came from a high-powered rifle some distance away. That wasn't someone who whipped a concealed carry out of his pocket and fired in a moment of anger. It was planned and accurate, assuming the windshield was the intended target."

"So it could have been an accident. Someone shooting at something or someone else and my SUV was just in the way."

"Could have been."

She read his tone. "But you don't think so."

Apparently, Trouble didn't think so either if the restless whipping of his tail was any indication. He aimed that green stare on the sheriff's face.

"No, I don't, not unless they were shooting at Craig while he was hell-bent on cutting your tires," he admitted. "In any case, I suggest you keep your guard up every second."

Her shoulders sagged. "I will, Ben, but this isn't what I need to be doing. I need to get busy repairing the financial damage Craig's already done to the ranch, not worrying about what additional mischief he's planning."

Ben rubbed his clean-shaven jaw. "Avery, I'll tell you, I'm not so sure the damage to your SUV was Craig's doing, at least not from an intentional standpoint. From what I've been hear-

ing, I'd say Craig's gotten himself in pretty deep debt, maybe
with some pretty nasty people."

"Just what is it you're hearing?" Avery heard the trepidation
in her own voice. "What kind of nasty people?"

"High-flyers ... big league gamblers. You knew Craig
frequented the casinos quite a bit?"

Avery nodded. It was no secret around town, either, she
knew. Frustratingly, she'd had to pay Craig's delinquent
accounts with more than one local tradesperson until her
attorney had secured a legal separation in advance of the actual
divorce. That document had allowed him to post in the paper
on her behalf stating she was no longer financially responsible
for Craig's debts.

"Well, seems he's been playing with money that wasn't his
to spend, trading on what he hoped to get from the divorce
settlement. That fancy trainer at your place this morning? His
employer called me about five minutes after you did. Wanted a
deputy to escort the rig back out to the ranch to 'claim his
property'. Somehow thought I'd be impressed with his credentials. He's got a better grasp of the situation now and I hope
he's too smart to do anything illegal, but we can't count on
that. And there's no telling who else is out there that Craig's
made some kind of deal with. Craig's in over his head, Avery,
and he's made some really bad characters really angry."

Panic hit Avery deep in her gut. "So what are you saying?
I've got to worry about real danger, physical danger, to the
ranch, to Leanne and Tucker as well as Carlee and the horses?"

"I'm afraid that's exactly what I'm saying. You've got my
personal cell. Don't hesitate, not even one minute, to use it if
something doesn't seem right, feel right, smell right. You *call*
me." His words were emphatic.

Avery felt sick to her stomach as she stood to leave the

office. Bending, she scooped Trouble up in her arms once more. "When can I have my SUV back?"

"As soon as it's repaired. We've found all we're going to there. I called the dealership and they picked it up with orders to replace the tires and windshield and front seat. They're to have it detailed inside and out. I let your insurance agent take some photos while it was here and everything's approved, said she'd get the paperwork out to you in a day or two. They'll call you when it's ready."

"Oh, Ben," her voice caught, "that's above and beyond. I appreciate it so much."

"And I'm not done with this investigation, Avery, I promise. Now you let me know at once if anything suspicious happens. No matter how small it seems to you."

Ben hugged her again on her way out, a friendly, reassuring hug that did nothing to reassure her. Nothing at all.

AND WASN'T that just cheery, but – of course – nothing I didn't already suspect. I had Craig Danson pegged for a tosser from the moment I spied him threatening Ms. Gorgeous. I tend to agree with the good sheriff's evaluation of things, as little as I like it. There is evil afoot and that makes my presence all the more requisite. I had wondered at the start if perhaps I'd misread the situation – an e-mail exchange between long-time friends can be totally ambiguous with all those happy faces or frowny faces instead of real words – and that, perhaps, Ms. Gorgeous had not really needed my able and expert assistance. But it's clear, now, that her woes were in no way resolved with the thud of a gavel and the granting of a divorce.

I must somehow ensure she shares what she's learned here with Mr. Military. He has resources that can complement my natural sleuthing abilities.

. . .

OUT ON THE SIDEWALK, Avery checked her phone. Nothing yet from Dirks. She hesitated, tempted to check with the dealership, though it seemed unlikely they could have her SUV ready that afternoon. Besides, there were things she needed to pick up at the feed store as well as from the hardware that were better suited to the work truck. She could have everything delivered, of course, but her nerves were jangling and she needed the normalcy of running errands, of taking care of business. Her business.

She was greeted warmly at the feed store and felt completely comfortable putting Trouble down to roam on the wide-planked wood flooring. The earthy scent of feed, stored hay, and gardening supplies helped settle her nerves.

"What are you needing today, Ms. Avery?" The young woman was summer college help for Barton Feed, but Avery had always known her to represent the interests of the owner well. Kelly was casual in denim but her tee was neatly tucked into the waist of those jeans. Avery envied her the easy, breezy attitude of youth, but not the remembered burden of working her own way through an education.

"I don't need much," Avery admitted. "Carlee will be placing the regular order tomorrow, I think. I mostly just wanted to stop in and see what you have new by way of tack. I do need to pick up a couple of wheelbarrows. I've got the truck so we'll just load them in the back."

"I heard about your car," Kelly said sympathetically. Her glance was curious but she didn't press when Avery simply nodded in response. "What style of wheelbarrow did you want?"

"The oversized hard plastic we got last time works really

well. It doesn't rust out like the metal ones always do. I'm just tired of us having to share between the barns and I'm hoping I have Barn Three full and in business before the end of the year."

"Well, you're in luck. We've got three in stock, right now." While Kelly picked up a radio from the counter and spoke to someone in the yard, Avery crossed over to the wall of tack bright with rhinestones. "I need you to load two of those heavy-duty wheelbarrows into Ms. Danson's truck. Yes, the black ones." She listened again to the other side of the exchange. "Thanks, Jerrod."

"What else can I get for you today, Ms. Avery? Something with glitter and shine?" Kelly's tone was hopeful though she'd know from experience that wasn't the style typically delivered to the ranch. Carlee held to the durable, good quality leather equipment the store kept on hand or special ordered for the ranch.

"Not for me, but sometimes I think something sparkly would be real pretty on Jack."

"Maybe for his Christmas present this year," Kelly joked.

"Could be," Avery gave her quick smile, "but that's all for today. I need to get back and I still have to hit the hardware. And, for the record, I've taken my maiden name, Wilson, back as part of the divorce proceedings."

As Kelly readied her ticket for signature, Avery looked around for Trouble. He sat near the door, watching the opening, for all the world like a guard dog. The thought amused her but then she recalled that she might well need a guard dog before this was done – for the horses though – not for herself.

Kelly handed her the ticket and said, "I got an e-mail today. Our new calendars should be in this week."

Avery was surprised. "Do they always come in this early?"

"The first order, yes. We always end up making several re-orders and I expect we'll sell even more this year. I think when everyone sees the beautiful photographs of the horses of Summer Valley Ranch along with the lovely pond scenes from the McPherson place, these will go *really* quick."

Avery smiled. "I love that old McPherson pond and the horses were particularly cooperative with the photographer, though Carlee had to do some real clowning around to get both Jack's ears forward at the same time."

Kelly chuckled. "Well, we all still wish you and Carlee hadn't insisted there be no facial shots of the two of you. You're both so beautiful – you definitely rival the horses!"

"That's sweet of you to say, Kelly, thank you. Do be sure to call me when they come in. We'll buy several dozen to give as gifts to our clients. Good advertising, you know."

Avery felt good about helping the local merchants any way she could. That was the main reason she'd agreed to have the ranch featured. She honestly didn't need the advertising. Summer Valley was already growing *almost* faster than she could keep up. But neither she nor Carlee had been keen on being in any of the photographs and were insistent that the horses, not themselves, be the focus of any of the shots.

"Come on, Trouble," she said when she reached the door. "We've got another stop to make. Maybe by then, Mr. Hanna will have let me know what he needs for the camera system."

As careful as she was to call him Mr. Hanna, even to the cat, Avery knew she'd already begun to think of Dirks in much more familiar terms. She even liked the sound of his name in her mind.

CHAPTER SIX

*D*irks stepped down from the ladder and contemplated his progress. Angling one camera toward the barn's main entrance was helpful but there wasn't adequate wiring to allow him to move the other cameras to more strategic locations. He measured the distance by the simple method of walking the route and calculating feet per stride. It was crude but effective. He added that total to the text message he'd begun along with some necessary connectors, not yet hitting send as he hadn't scoped out requirements in the two remaining barns.

His handy sixth sense warned him he wasn't alone in the barn but there wasn't a corresponding tingle along the back of his neck. He made no move toward his concealed carry as he stepped around the corner.

Tucker, tall and lanky, was squinting up at the camera Dirks had shifted. "Good idea, that. You planning on moving the others?"

"Yeah, but I'll have to wait until Ms. Wilson returns from town. I want to move a couple to the other barns."

Tucker frowned. "Avery went by herself?"

Dirks studied him, trying to judge his age. Early thirties, maybe mature twenties. "She did. That worry you?"

"Shouldn't it? That son of a bitch she married shot her windshield out, didn't he? Who knows what he'll aim at next. Or what other badass he's pissed off."

"We don't know for sure whose bullets those were ... unless you've heard from the sheriff." Dirks doubted any solid proof would connect the vandalism to Craig Danson. He wasn't even convinced that Craig's finger had been on the trigger, at least not the physical trigger of the gun. Craig had maybe incited the incident, just as he'd precipitated Markham's ill-fated trip to the ranch earlier. Dirks didn't credit him with macho enough to put a bullet into her vehicle in the middle of town.

"Carlee told me it had to be her dad. She should know." Tucker sounded slightly defensive and Dirks took a closer look at the younger man and recognized a gleam in his eyes that was at least infatuation, and possibly some stronger emotion, connected with his mention of the young woman.

"Likely she should and perhaps does but it's always a better bet not to assume anything when a threat of danger is involved. If you guard in only one direction – because you think you know – you leave yourself wide open on several other fronts."

Tucker hunched his narrow shoulders. "Avery said you were military."

Dirks smiled inwardly. As if the word military explained everything about him to the young man. After nearly three decades of active service, Dirks had accepted a desk job. He considered it a weak moment when he'd been recovering from a second injury with the first barely healed. At the time it had seemed ideal, no one shooting at him, no one's life depending upon him, traveling around the many states that he had loved and served and sacrificed a pint or two of blood to protect. All he had to do was review, visit and certify equestrian and other therapeutic complexes across the country as approved to offer services to veterans whose wounds crossed the gamut from loss of sight and limb to brain trauma and PTSD.

Even so, if his first job involved bringing to ruin the most attractive woman he'd seen in all his travel across the globe, he'd be looking to pick up a gun again. Summer Valley Ranch had been approved by his predecessor who hadn't been considered a singular success in his role. Dirks wondered if Avery Wilson was one of the man's failures. Someone was guilty of fraud. One possibility was Craig Danson, the other was Avery. Her team, Tucker among them, certainly wouldn't agree with that possibility but Dirks couldn't afford to ignore it.

Like most people, Tucker didn't have a clue what the term military conveyed, including the search for truth, whatever the cost. Dirks hoped he never did, never had to, but all he said was, "Yes, I am. Are you busy right now? Do you have time to check out the other barns? I could use your help."

Tucker straightened, clearly pleased to be asked. "Yeah, I've had my last client for the day. I've got a couple hours before I need to do anything else with my horses."

My horses. Dirks liked hearing that sense of ownership, that tone of affection. It boded well for the success of Avery Wilson's venture. And then he wondered why he cared. The fact that he did bothered him. A lot.

After walking through the remaining two barns with Tucker and stepping off some additional measurements, Dirks added to his text message to Avery, hit send and then found himself waiting for her response. Tucker had taken himself off to collect some boards and nails and tools to build temporary bases for the cameras Dirks planned to move. Dirks found himself glad the younger man wasn't there to see him staring at his phone like some teen waiting for a response. Decisively, he slipped the phone into his pocket. He had no idea how often Avery Wilson checked her messages or if she kept the volume down to minimize distractions. He was, however, certain she'd check before she headed out of town to see if he needed anything to help keep her horses safe. They were definitely her priority.

Tucker returned pulling a utility cart stacked with boards and tools, and they worked companionably for a little while. Dirks wasn't surprised to find Tucker less than talkative but it was an easy silence broken only by necessity for the work involved. Leanne stopped by after her last client of the day to see if they needed help but didn't seem disappointed to be told they were good. Tucker asked her to make a round of the barns and paddocks.

"Sure thing," Leanne agreed easily. "Then I'll see if I can unearth some of the cots and blankets we use for kids' camp. I need to go home to check in with Jason but I'm coming back here for the night. Hopefully all of this will settle down soon." She grinned. "I haven't seen the appeal in sleeping under the stars or in a barn since I was twelve or so."

"Kids' camp?" Dirks asked into the quiet that followed her departure.

"Yep. Avery started it her first year. I think it was mostly to help Carlee. She was just a kid then and it was right after her mother's suicide. I wasn't here for the first camp, but I was for the second and I've helped with all of them since then."

"This was the first place you ever worked?"

"First and only. I started coming every afternoon when I was in high school, traded cleaning stalls for lessons because my folks didn't earn enough for things like that. In college I worked weekends and evenings to pay for tuition. I knew from the start Avery would make a success of this place. When I got my degree, she hired me straight on."

"Yeah?" Dirks paused before he hammered the next nail. "What's your degree?"

"Veterinary medicine." There was enormous pride evident in the answer.

Dirks lowered his hammer and scrutinized more closely the young man he'd recognized as intelligent but hadn't given nearly enough attention to as someone with drive and ambition. He was also struck by the realization that Summer Valley Ranch had the resources to afford an on-staff veterinarian.

Tucker grinned. "I know. I look like a kid. I hear that all the time. It actually helps out with some of my younger clients who open up to me more than they normally would."

"Do you have a practice? Away from here, I mean?" Dirks was more than curious about the arrangement.

"Nope. Could have I guess, but Avery pays me well. Raises are small but regular and I know business here is only going to get bigger and better. Right now, I stay busy and earn my salary giving lessons along with the foaling and taking care of minor injuries here and there. I do help out some of the neighboring farms if the vet in town is tied up with an emergency but I don't charge them for it. That's just part of being good neighbors in a close community. As a matter of fact, I plan to make some rounds this evening after the horses are fed and settled. I want to ask a few of those I've helped to keep an eye open for strangers wandering around."

Dirks resumed work and put the last nail in place. "Sounds like you've got a good future mapped out right here."

"That's the plan." Tucker stepped back from the ladder as

Dirks descended. "Once these barns are full and Barns Four and Five are built and filled with horses, Avery's going to build a real clinic. We'll need it by then. She's drawn up the design already, has an apartment for me up top." He spoke quietly, without any conceit, though Dirks suspected not many vets his age had a practice that included housing along with salary.

Dirks nodded. "This is going to be quite a place, I think." It was already.

"So, you're going to approve us for the veteran's program?"

It was like a punch to the gut, being reminded that he had no reason yet to trust Avery Wilson. "I haven't come across any reason not to," he said cautiously. But the truth was, his reason for being there had somehow gotten diverted by the events that had transpired in the last twenty-four hours. And by a pair of beautiful green and gold eyes. He'd need to conclude his investigation soon and determine if criminality, negligence, or something else was behind bills received and payments sent by the managing office on behalf of veterans who'd never received any of the benefits of the program from Summer Valley Ranch.

Dirks was glad when a quiet ping from his phone gave him a reason to redirect the conversation. "Ms. Wilson has purchased the fiber optic cable I need for the last runs. She's headed back to the ranch."

Tucker started gathering up tools. "I'll be back later this evening and can give you a hand with running that wire. Lighting's plenty good in the barn for just about anything we need to do."

Dirks nodded. "Sure thing." In the meantime, he needed to get back on track with determining the guilt or innocence of one Avery Wilson.

. . .

EVEN WITH THE lengthy days of summer – which Avery often wished were switched about so that winter rather than summer had the extension of daylight savings time – she needed her headlights by the time she turned onto the ranch drive.

Her first thought was one of relief to see Carlee's vehicle parked in its usual place. Her second was an unwelcome leap of her pulse as Dirks pushed away from the paddock post where he'd been leaning. She watched as his long stride carried him toward the ranch truck. He reached her before she had time to do more than open the driver side door and step out. He'd been waiting and watching for her, that much was clear.

"I see Carlee's home." The inane comment seemed better than staring silently into those dark eyes that regarded her with startling intensity. "Is she okay?"

She found the slight quirk of his lips remarkably sexy.

"Hard for me to tell. She's either not one for conversation or she doesn't have much she wants to say to me."

Avery went for what she hoped was a casual smile. "Don't take it personally. She's an excellent conversationalist but not much of a talker, if that makes sense." The smile faded. "And all of this has been more than a little hard on her."

"She's a real athlete, though. She's put two horses through their paces since she got back. They were a bit unruly but she handled them expertly."

"Uh-oh – she doesn't paddock ride much – usually only when she needs to work off steam. I'd guess she's not happy with the outcome of her talk with Craig."

"Not much chance that was going to go well, anyway, I'd think." Dirks stepped back slightly and Avery realized just how close he'd been standing to her in the shadows beyond the paddock lights. And how right it had felt that he be that close.

She cleared her throat but her voice still sounded a bit husky to her own ears when she told him, "I found everything you thought you'd need."

"Good. Let's get the truck unloaded, shall we?"

IT'S TO BE HOPED *that Mr. Military has made significant progress in safeguarding things here while we were in town. I must inspect his handiwork at the first opportunity although I suspect it will be impeccably done. Whatever his stated purpose – or his true but more subversive one – in being here, I sense he would throw his life on the line, as it were, to protect and serve. Failure is not an option, and all that. He would, no doubt, consider any harm to this facility while he is present a failure of monumental proportions.*

While the bipeds have their exchange of the mundane, cable produced, examined and pronounced just right ... blah, blah, blah ... I shall have a look about. At some point, these two humanoids may realize, accept and act upon their mutual physical attraction. Alas, for them, it is equally possible they will not. Regardless, I haven't the time or inclination to witness either eventuality except as it pertains to the resolution of the threats facing Ms. Gorgeous.

At a glance, this is not the most complex case I've taken on. Strong female weds inferior male whose true colors come to light over the course of time. Strong female discards and divorces. Inferior male attempts to take by stealth or force what he has not earned. And yet, because I am an enlightened and self-aware creature, I must acknowledge that there is something I'm yet missing in all of this. There's a nuance that tugs at my highly developed analytical skills which warns I must blend the apparent with the cryptic to arrive at the truth. To use a rather hackneyed truism, I remain convinced that things are not entirely as they seem.

I may have been remiss in not digging deeper into the tragic deaths of Mr. Danson's daughter and wife. Accidental drowning? Suicide? Perhaps. Yet perhaps not, two deaths in quick succession do seem too much of a coincidence. Was there motive for murder in either and is the remaining daughter now at risk? Digging through online news archives seems a good task to accomplish in the sweltering heat of tomorrow's midday. For now, I'll traverse the perimeter of the ranch proper, the better to sniff out any human predator. Though what my Tammy Lynn calls heat lightning flickers in the distance, I don't believe I will be at any risk of a drenching. After that, however, well ... a feline detective of the first order must have adequate shut-eye for cognitive thinking.

Hmmm, now there's an oddity, one of the young equines is snorting at the water trough. I'll just jump up to the ledge that surrounds it to make a closer observation. Uh-oh. That's not good. A dead bird floating. I wouldn't want to drink that nastiness either. And enough of an oddity to make me want to look further. Each paddock and pasture has its own water trough, sized to fit the number of animals it accommodates.

Fortunately for me – and conveniently for the humans, of course – the water troughs are all on the barn side of fences. All speedily checked.

Worse and worse. A dead bird could have occurred naturally but a deceased rodent in the next? I think not. Time for the humanoids to realize what's been done and get this mess cleaned up.

AVERY LOOKED down at the sleek, black cat with his claws in the hem of her jeans. He'd been twining through her legs and 'talking' to her more and more urgently while she helped Dirks lay out the fiber. She knew he had to be hungry and he sure wasn't much for the dry cat food she kept fresh for him in the kitchen. Unlike the horses, her own mealtimes were never on any kind of schedule and she didn't want Trouble's needs neglected because she'd gotten busy on some task or another. She knew he ate from the bowl from time to time but he preferred to wait until there was opportunity to join in her meal – at least the menu items that appealed to him.

"You were the one who decided to stow away on the ride to town, mister. Leanne or Tucker possibly would've taken pity and fed you if you'd been here. I'll be done here shortly and we'll eat."

In response, Trouble walked his front paws up the denim of her jeans, stretching his full length along her leg.

"Just a few more minutes." Avery reached down to rub the cat's ears and found her hand snagged lightly by an unsheathed claw. "Hey," she said softly, "what's up with you?"

As those intelligent green eyes stared up into hers, she accepted that the feline didn't have his stomach on his mind for once.

Dirks seemed to have reached the same conclusion as he said, "I think we'd better see what this guy wants."

Trouble dropped to four paws at the statement and once again had Avery wondering - truly wondering - if the cat, rather than acting on intonation as most animals did, understood their actual words. It should have been an eerie thought but somehow it wasn't.

She supposed it would have looked odd to an observer for the two humans to fall in step behind the cat, picking up their pace as – after a glance back to ascertain their obedience – he began to trot toward the closest field. Fortunately, none of her team was around to witness.

Moments later, she forgot how silly they might have appeared as she stared in horror at the dead animal floating just below the surface of the water. Not a bird, her mind registered. That would have been a concern but it did happen from time to time. They kept bleach handy because diseased birds sought water and sometimes perished in their attempt to drink. But never had she seen a rat drown in one of the troughs.

"I need to check the other fields," she said numbly.

Apparently satisfied he had their attention focused in the right direction, Trouble no longer attempted to lead or corral them but kept pace as she and Dirks walked in silence from one pasture and one trough to the next. She was sickened as they found one dead animal after another floating in water that was critical to the horses' well-being.

At the last tub, she turned to Dirks and said slowly, "This doesn't fit. Nothing fits together. It's almost as if I'm dealing with two different threats."

Dirks nodded. "This is more along the lines of childish temper. Like your tack being slashed by your ex. Nothing as dangerous as bullets fired."

For a moment, she wanted to agree but it was worse than Dirks, who didn't know the world of horses, could realize at first glance. "This is very dangerous to the animals. Horses won't drink contaminated water. That's why I won't use self-watering systems though that technology has become much better in recent years. We check each water source every single day."

"So this was done at some point during the last twenty-four hours?" Dirks sounded dubious.

"Maybe less than that but I'll have to check with Leanne and Tucker. In the summer, they sometimes check morning and night. Whoever did this put every horse out here at a real risk of a blocked gut and colic. Colic kills more horses than probably any other health issue. And that – the threat to the horses – is the part that just doesn't fit."

Dirks raised his brow questioningly as Avery hesitated. She suspected her next revelation might give the kiss of death to her dream of adding a veteran therapy program to the ranch lineup. "Sheriff Farley says Craig has angered some really bad, really dangerous people. He's desperate to pay what he owes them. He may be a threat to me because he'd always hoped he could later convince Carlee to help him out with money, but he needs the horses. He needs the cash they represent. I just don't see contaminated water being something he'd risk, not even to strike at me."

GOOD GIRL. That was information Mr. Military needs so that he's not chasing a rabbit down an empty hole. There's much more to all of this than even I initially surmised. However as the next step here – as I understand it once the dead varmints are removed – is to sanitize the tubs with great quantities of bleach, I believe I shall absent myself. The strong odor of bleach has a devastating effect on my sense of smell and that would interfere greatly with my pleasure in my next meal which, alas, appears will be delayed even longer.

AFTER HELPING Avery disinfect and scrub the water troughs, Dirks went back to work on the wiring while she refilled each with clean water. He heard the sound of Tucker's diesel returning so wasn't surprised when the young man rejoined him. He filled the younger man in on the dead creatures that had been deposited in every water trough and – recalling what Avery had said about the health threat to the animals – wasn't at all surprised by the low, vicious curses the vet uttered.

"Sorry, but that's pretty low to a snake's belly," Tucker concluded.

"Agreed." Dirks climbed down from positioning the last camera. "I don't suppose your rounds with the neighbors turned up anything."

"Actually, yeah, but nothing I can take to the sheriff as a problem. Guy on a fancy motorcycle, lots of chrome. Heard mention of him at two different places."

"Motorcycle?" Something tugged at Dirks' memory.

"Unfortunately, one said Harley, one said Goldwing. Go figure. At least they now know to be on the lookout and paying attention to the details. Strangers attract attention in an outlying rural area like this." He shot Dirks a look. "You have at any rate. And Markham was noticed as well but mostly because of that ridiculously fancy rig he was driving."

They shared a smile but it was brief and Dirks' next question was dead serious. "If someone wanted to scare Ms. Wilson – really scare her – where would they strike?"

"Carlee or Jack," Tucker said without hesitation. "Carlee's pretty savvy and she'll be watchful and cautious. And Avery will be just down the hall from her and even more careful. But I'll be sleeping – and sleeping lightly – within hearing of Jack's barn tonight and Leanne plans to be right at his stall door."

Dirks suspected he, himself, wouldn't be sleeping much at all. Not until Avery and her ranch were out of danger.

CHAPTER SEVEN

A very awakened to a feeling of absolute panic and for a moment sat up waiting and listening. As remnants of dreams of menace brushed through her mind, she forced herself to control her breathing which helped slow the rushed pumping of blood through her veins. Soft morning light had begun to filter through the light curtains at her windows proving it was later than she usually slept yet she didn't feel rested.

Moments later, coffee mug in hand, she stood in front of the small but crystal clear monitors grouped on her kitchen wall. Instead of the interior of foaling stalls, they were now focused outward toward the barn doors, all still solidly closed. She disliked, intensely, the need to keep their working horses up at night and knew she could not let this go on forever. Still, knowing them securely inside, had allowed her a few hours of actual sleep. It was, she mused, a good thing that none of the pregnant mares were close to term. And, anyway, only mares Tucker believed were 'at risk' were ever brought in for foaling.

Avery kept her animals as close to their natural element as she possibly could. In truth, over the years, the foaling stalls and monitors had been used more often for injury or illness than for foaling. And, thank goodness, both injury and illness were rare. Vaccinations were kept current, feed was strictly regimented, and new horses were quarantined before being assimilated into pastures with the others. Illness did happen, though. There was no way to prevent the disease-carrying opossums and other rodents from contaminating the pastures.

That led her back to the tainted water troughs and the staggering reminder that the danger which had woven its way through her dreams in the pre-dawn hours was a real and tangible threat.

Sighing, she pulled her thoughts from the silent monitors to the view beyond the glass door leading to her garden. The first hint of sunrise edged the horizon, a faint tinge of pink brushing what promised to be a clear sky. When silken fur glided against her bare calf, she glanced down at the black cat who had invaded her life along with a militaristic human. Both were easy on the eye, but – also unfortunately – both were very much alpha males. Not what she would have wanted or needed pushing into what she'd planned to be a quiet life devoted to the equines and the people who needed her help. But now? She leaned her head against the cool glass of the door.

Somehow, she had to return her ranch to normal operation but her hope that Craig would 'give up and go away' had been supplanted by the realization that he had introduced some unknown and potentially treacherous elements into her life. Ben's warning, like his concern, had been crystal clear. Not just Avery herself, but her precious horses and perhaps the young woman she loved like a daughter, were all at risk.

Still, she couldn't spend every moment fretting. She, as well as Tucker and Leanne, had appointments with clients most of the day and they needed to spend some time with the yearlings.

After a quick check of her phone calendar, she sent a brief text to Dirks that she'd unlocked the garden door for him to access the coffee pot and headed to the shower.

Thirty minutes later she emerged to find him comfortably at home in her kitchen, sliding a second perfectly cooked omelet from skillet to plate. She assumed it was the second because Trouble appeared to be enjoying the first. The black cat deigned to lift his head to give her a rather accusatory glance. She surmised he remained completely unimpressed with the rather expensive cat food she'd purchased for him.

She looked back at Dirks and wished she didn't enjoy the sight of him standing there quite as much as she did. "Good morning."

He handed her the omelet. "Good morning to you. You didn't sleep well." It wasn't a question.

Ouch. "That bad, huh?" But she didn't really have to ask. Her mirror had shown her the dark circles under her eyes as she'd skimmed her hair back into a pony tail to keep it from twining into ringlets by mid-morning.

Dirks smiled and she wondered rather inanely how a man with a high-ranking military career and all the burdens that entailed could have such pleasing laugh lines at the corners of his eyes. Those eyes seemed to be studying her appreciatively, despite the evidence of her restless night. Instead of answering her question, he asked about her schedule for the day.

"We've all got rather tight appointments today and tomorrow. Leanne's and Tucker's are all with clients. I have some clients later but also some workouts on horses that don't need to be idle too long." She didn't add that she needed to make up for the lost time spent with her attorney and in court and simply dealing with the drama of Craig. She needed the routine, needed her horses, craved the quiet structure of an orderly life, craved, too, to hear that she would be approved for the next step in the future she had planned for the ranch. "I suppose you have research to do, papers to fill out, all of that."

As a ploy to determine which direction Dirks would rule, it failed as all he did was nod and agree he had things to take care of as well.

They ate in surprisingly companionable silence until her phone rang. She glanced at the caller ID before answering. "Mr. Girard, good morning."

DIRKS TRIED NOT to eavesdrop but Avery was listening so intently and looking sadder by the minute. Sad but not alarmed, so his first protective instinct relaxed at the realization this was not some new threat.

"Of course, Mr. Girard, you're welcome to bring Michael to say good-bye. We'll miss both of you. Yes, it does sound like a wonderful opportunity, those kinds of promotions don't get handed out every day."

Dirks refilled her coffee, adding the unrefined sugar and dash of cream she preferred. She gave him a hint of smile but it was clear her mind remained with the conversation.

"I'm glad you're going to continue with riding lessons for Michael. I agree they've done him a world of good and he's already got such quiet, skilled hands. He's made tremendous progress."

She twisted her mug. "Yes, as a matter of fact, I *have* heard of Marbleson Farms, they're a reputable facility. No. I'm sorry but you have it right, I don't sell my horses."

Dirks watched her eyes as she finished the conversation and looked up at him. The sadness lingered as she sighed and said, "I've got to pull my team together for a joint decision."

"Should I leave?" he asked.

For a moment, she just studied him and he wondered what she was thinking, but then she shrugged. "It doesn't matter. It isn't a secret. I just need their input."

He leaned back in his chair as Avery made quick calls to her team, telling himself he was only interested because of its bearing on his investigation. Everything he learned about the operation of the facility could have bearing of some sort or another.

Avery made a second carafe of coffee in the few minutes it took Carlee, Leanne and Tucker to reach her kitchen. Without answering any of the bombardment of questions as each came in the door, she moved them to the dining table so they could face each other as Tucker, the last to arrive, stepped into the house.

Taking a deep breath, Avery explained the phone call she'd received, finishing by saying, "Mr. Girard plans to buy a horse for Michael. I expect Marbleson Farms is completely capable of helping them select a safe animal."

Tucker nodded, his blue eyes glinting behind wire-framed glasses. "Alabama? On the Eastern Shore of Mobile Bay? They're more than reputable. I've actually been there a couple of times. It's a cool place. I'd be more than willing to waive the fee on a pre-purchase exam."

Avery smiled but Dirks noted the shadows hadn't left her eyes. "I'm sure that would be appreciated and very helpful."

"But unnecessary, right?" Leanne had her elbow propped on the table, chin in hand, a keen insight lighting her features.

"Perhaps, but that depends on what each of you has to say about my thoughts. You know how hard it was for Michael to learn to trust Silver Dollar. And, naturally, Mr. Girard is concerned about the hardship of this move to a new town on the boy. Coupled with new surroundings, starting over with another horse could prove a real setback for him. But we don't sell horses here at Summer Valley."

Carlee was second to catch on. She nodded slowly and her lips curved in the closest Dirks had come to seeing her smile. "Ah ... a gift."

But it was to Tucker, Dirks noted, that Avery turned for final confirmation. The Connemara was in his barn, was his charge, as was young Michael. Dirks supposed he would know best of anyone if this would be right for Silver Dollar as well as for the little boy.

Slowly Tucker nodded. "It's a good decision," he said simply. "I'll haul our girl there whenever they're ready for her, meet with the barn manager and make sure everyone knows what they need to know to keep her well and happy."

Avery drew a deep breath and let it go on a sigh. "That's good, then. For both of them - for Michael and for Silver Dollar. The only stipulation I'll make with Mr. Girard is that actual ownership of Silver Dollar remains with us. When it's time for Michael to step up in size or her to retire, she comes back to us for a well-earned old age in comfort."

A FEW HOURS LATER, Avery watched as Michael slowly exited his father's truck, reluctance apparent in every line of his young body as he walked toward the paddock where Tucker held Silver Dollar's lead line. The Connemara stood quietly watching and waiting as she'd been taught to do with her young charge. Most of their horses were encouraged to walk toward the clients, but the team had realized early on that it caused Michael discomfort so the ball, so to speak, was always in his court.

Michael's father moved to stand beside Avery as his son entered the paddock and carefully closed the gate behind him. Avery smiled at the man briefly but immediately shifted her attention to the boy and the horse and the young vet.

"He knows he's come to say good-bye," his father told Avery quietly. "He's decided not to ride today. He just wants to be with her."

Michael stopped some few feet away from the pretty gray and Tucker spoke to him so quietly that Avery had to listen closely to hear.

"Good morning, Michael."

The boy nodded without speaking. He rarely spoke and, on those rare occasions that he did, it was to the Connemara and sometimes through her to communicate with Tucker. It appeared to Avery that his entire body leaned ever so slightly toward the little horse, but his feet remained anchored in the soft dirt of the paddock.

"Silver Dollar and I heard you were going to a grand new home," Tucker said the words almost in a croon. "You'll be close to the beach, there. Did you know that Connemara's like Silver Dollar are island ponies?"

Again, Michael nodded, this time taking a half step toward the mare.

"I think it'd be unfair if this girl didn't have the chance to get closer to the water, don't you? And I think she'd be much too lonely without you if we were to keep her *here* while you're *there*. She loves you, you know."

Michael's father laid his hand on Avery's arm where it rested against the fence. "What? What's he saying?"

Avery turned to face him then, saw the hope and the fear. "I don't sell my horses, Mr. Girard, but I find I must sometimes give them where they're needed most. Your son needs Silver Dollar and I wouldn't be a bit surprised if Silver Dollar didn't need him just as much. She's timid with most of our clients but she's been nothing but confident with Michael."

Avery looked away from the tears in the man's eyes as she fought her own. The sight of the child with both arms now wrapped around Silver Dollar's neck was a bittersweet happiness. Bittersweet that modern medicine could not cure Michael, but happiness that his progress proved there was hope for his future. And happiness, too, that her team had been able to give him a gift and, in giving, prevent a heartbreak that would have been very real for him.

She felt the intensity of a stare on her and glanced around to find Dirks watching her with an unfathomable expression. He was probably wondering why she would give away a part of what she had fought so hard to keep, but – if that were the case and he didn't understand – nothing she could say would help to clarify.

THINGS HAVE CERTAINLY BEEN VERY, *very busy this morning. It's been hard to keep an eye on every quarter. Even a feline as adept and agile as myself can hardly be in multiple barns and paddocks at once. One can only hope that Mr. Military is as watchful as I believe him to be, although his focus does give the impression that his thoughts are rather single-mindedly with Ms. Gorgeous. It's telling, though, that the lady in question seems singularly oblivious to the fact.*

I'd hoped to spend a bit of time on the computer but Carlee is hard at work on a list of purchase requests she gathered from Tucker and Leanne for their respective barns. Ms. Gorgeous added an item or two and off Carlee went. Even an hour later, my peek in the window showed her still hard at work, though she'd moved on from vendor websites to a complex spreadsheet. Accounts payable most like. Keeping up with the paperwork necessitated by a venture such as this would require great diligence.

With Mr. Military keeping his gaze upon Ms. Gorgeous as she grooms, exercises, and cools one equine athlete after another, I've taken several turns through the barns. The cameras are handy at night when access to the barns is limited, but I don't see them as having much value with so many non-ranch persons, clients as they're called, in and about. Yet all remains quiet.

Ah, there comes Carlee now. I'll just hang about until I'm sure she's done in the office. It would be tiresome to have my own computer work interrupted but I would definitely have to yield to her stronger claim to the resources should I detect her return.

DIRKS WAS SURPRISED when Carly newly emerged from the house, joined him at the fence. She hadn't shown any interest in making him feel welcome or initiating small talk. Even so, she propped a worn but quality work boot on the lower fence rail as if she planned to be there for a while.

Since he'd been given the opportunity, he took it, introducing a topic he knew would get Craig's daughter talking. "The mare she gave away this morning, the Connemara, was she a rescue horse, too?"

Carlee gave him a quick glance, as if wondering that he felt the need to talk to her. "Yes, but not from a kill pen. Some freaking Californian with more money than sense decided it would be lovely to own a pony from Ireland so she bought Silver Dollar and had her shipped over. Stupid bitch didn't realize there would be several weeks of quarantine and testing for diseases once Silver Dollar was on American soil or that the expense of it would be out of her bank account. She got bored before the end of the quarantine period and left Silver Dollar to her fate. Somehow the pony got hurt during the quarantine and the authorities couldn't find anyone to adopt her and take on the vet expenses necessary for her treatment. Avery got wind of her just days before she would have been put down. We drove cross country to get her with Avery checking in with the officials every few hours to make sure every shift and every person there knew we were headed that way so they wouldn't go ahead with the killing."

"That was a long drive to pick up a horse that might not have worked out."

Carlee shrugged. "It wouldn't have mattered. That wasn't why we went. But Silver Dollar was a good addition to the ranch and she'll be hard to replace. Still, Avery did the right thing and we're all glad for that."

Like Dirks, her attention was still fixed on Avery who had brought the fast canter of a short, stocky horse to a sudden stop and now had him spinning circles with only the lightest touch of her feet to his sides, her hands perfectly centered and still on the reins.

"She's working it off." When he didn't respond, Carlee gave him a sideways look and elaborated. "It's what Avery does when she's worried or stressed more than she can handle. She gets on a horse and makes each one do what they were trained to do. And she always finds that thing that they love during the training, that one thing that they're best at doing. But it's still work for them and for her."

It was, he recalled, almost verbatim, what Avery had said about Carlee herself. "Is that what you were doing yesterday afternoon? Working it off?"

"A bit I suppose, but mine was more anger than worry."

So Avery had gotten that aspect of it right as well. The two women knew each other well, but he supposed that was to be expected.

"I won't have him torment her like this," Carlee expounded. "He was stupid and it cost him. He can get over it or not but I won't let him make her life a complete misery."

"Strong words from a daughter."

Carlee turned to face him, propping her elbows on the paddock fence behind her. Dirks would have thought the pose deliberately provocative had her lips not remained pressed thin and her stare challenging and even a little hostile. He surmised she was unaware of the cleavage showing above the top button of her faded blue shirt.

"I'm *her* daughter, too, maybe even more than his. He hasn't been much of a father in the past few years. I'm just another means to an end to him."

"What do you mean?"

At his question, her expression became more guarded. "It doesn't matter. All Craig, and *you*, need to know is I'll do whatever I need to do to keep Avery safe and this place safe *for* her."

"You see me as a threat?"

"Not at all," she said dismissively. Carlee pushed away from the fence and walked away, her hips swinging with what he acknowledged was an unconscious femininity. She'd clearly exhibited no desire to entice him with either her conversation or her walk.

WELL, well, well. Now wasn't that an interesting exchange. There seemed some point to Carlee's conversational gambit but I'm not at all sure I know just what that was. Judging by Mr. Military's expression as he watches her depart, he is as perplexed – and as unimpressed – as I.

CHAPTER EIGHT

*A*very unsaddled then finished cooling Jingle. The hard work of the morning had helped ease the sense of doom she'd felt hanging over her. There was nothing more soothing to her than the familiar tasks that she loved. Unfortunately, the bit of peace she'd gained had been eroded by the sight of Carlee's departing saunter - and Dirks staring after her. She hadn't missed, either, those few minutes when the two had been face to face in deep conversation. Carlee's back had been to her, but Dirks' expression had been one of intense interest in whatever thoughts she'd been sharing with him. Avery didn't allow herself the luxury of analyzing why that nipped at her. It didn't matter. She couldn't let it. Dirks was there to do a job, then leave.

It stung that the job he'd come to do was that of judging this place that she loved so much and into which she'd poured her heart, soul, sweat, and tears. Not only judging the buildings and the horses, but her and the team who'd worked so hard right along with her. And it stung all the more that it seemed to be taking him such a long time to make that decision. He'd

only been here a couple of days, true, but he had to have done
his homework before he got this far. Anything less would have
been a wasted trip. She couldn't imagine one Dirks Hanna
wasting effort in any direction.

Jingle nudged her and she rubbed his neck affectionately
before walking him back to his stall. "You're right," she
murmured to the horse. "Carlee's a grown woman. Her business is her own." Even if Carlee decided to get something
going with Dirks Hanna. Or if he decided to get something
going with her.

Giving Jingle a handful of treats, she kissed his forehead,
hung his halter on the hook outside his door. Then she
stepped around the corner to his older sibling's stall. Jangle,
the seven-year-old son of a thoroughbred mare, was his exact
opposite in looks. She and her team marveled that every one of
Jack's offspring carried the physical genetics of the dam but –
more importantly - the mental and emotional characteristics
of Jack. They learned quickly, loved to work, and were blessed
with a natural affinity for people who needed them. Every one
of them had shown his amazing ability to connect with
damaged humans. And, so far, none had been born a filly
which was an oddity in itself.

Jangle was close to sixteen hands with the lean muscles of
his thoroughbred mother but none of that breed's potential for
flightiness. He was as solid as the rock he looked to be. Avery
ran her hands along the leather of the bridle, then the stirrups
and front and back girths. It was as automatic for her to check
for signs of wear on saddle leather as it was to breathe. They
couldn't afford to take chances with the safety of any of their
clients, some of whom were just at the beginning of their horse
experience. She and her team cleaned and maintained all of the
tack meticulously but Avery insisted upon a full check before

any clients were mounted. She did the same for herself, almost religiously, to set that good example.

She positioned several low jumps before snugging the cinch and swinging into the saddle, aware of Dirks still there, still watching. She wasn't used to an audience and found it more than a little disconcerting. Even so, she carefully put Dirks' presence from her mind and gave her full attention to Jangle. He was a joy to ride. Jumping would never be her preference in riding, but the gelding loved it and she'd learned to handle the low jumps for his sake.

She took the small hurdles all slow and easy, letting Jangle set the pace, letting him choose when to soar over each. Her job was simply to stay out of his way. Unlike Jingle, who still needed her help, this sibling knew what to do and when to do it.

It wasn't until the third round of jumps, that she felt something slip in the saddle beneath her. Her heart dropped at the unexpected sensation of insecurity. She sensed when Jangle felt it, as well, but it was too late for either to react. They were in the air and all Avery could do was try her best to stay centered until he landed. She quickly realized she wasn't going to be successful. Her thought as the ground flew up to meet her was that at least they were clear of the jump.

The landing took the breath from her and, for a moment, she was completely dazed as she stared up at blue sky. She heard Dirks' shout of concern, and wanted to tell him not to startle the gelding, but there was no breath in her lungs for the words.

Then Dirks was crouched over her, looking into her eyes and telling her not to move. She would've laughed if she could because moving wasn't an option until she could breathe again.

When her breath did come back to her it was almost as

painful as having it knocked out. Almost. She pushed to her elbows.

"I need to get up." Her voice sounded weak even to her.

"You need to be still until I figure out how badly you're hurt."

Ignoring Dirks, she sat. "Bruised, maybe. Where's Jangle? Something happened."

At her movement, the gelding stepped toward her. He'd stopped in his tracks as soon as she landed. Dirks reached up to take the reins so the animal couldn't come any closer.

"Whoa, fella. It won't help if you step on her." He gave Avery his arm to brace herself as she pulled to her feet. "You're a hard-headed woman."

She didn't hear any admiration in the comment so accepted it for the scold it was without responding. When she reached for the reins, Dirks released them. She watched as he picked up the saddle and carried it over to the fence rail. When he had his back to her, she bent forward at the waist, pulling in air, but she kept that show of weakness brief. While Dirks was absorbed in studying the saddle, she checked Jangle, carefully walking alongside him. He didn't show any sign of injury from what could have been an awkward landing. Only when she was satisfied with his well-being, did she follow Dirks to the rail where he examined the English saddle she'd been using.

He glanced up at her approach. "Do all of the horses have their own saddles?"

That seemed an odd question to her. "Most, yes, because they have different jobs. Sometimes we have to swap out for rider size. Often we can just adjust stirrup lengths, but if a rider needs a larger or smaller seat, that can't be adjusted." She studied the saddle, trying to see what he saw. "Why do you ask?"

Dirks' expression was grim as he asked, "Who else was likely to ride in this saddle today?"

"I'd have to check the calendar to see who was booked. Otherwise, just me or Carlee. Leanne's never gotten comfortable riding English even though Jangle's in her barn."

Since Dirks hadn't answered her question, Avery moved in closer, knowing she wasn't going to like anything she saw and she was right. The leather she'd checked so carefully was intact, but the steel girth ring was broken through.

"I don't understand," she said bewildered. "This isn't an old saddle. And I've never seen that happen before."

"It was filed thin." Dirks turned the backside of the metal piece toward her. "See on either side of the break? You can tell some kind of file was used to wear through the metal."

"A rasp," Avery said numbly. "Most likely a farrier's rasp."

"Is that something you keep here?"

"Yes. We don't do our own horses' feet but occasionally we have to rasp and pull nails from a shoe until the farrier can get here, just to prevent additional damage from a partially pulled shoe."

Avery stared at the damaged ring, feeling the heavy thud of her own heartbeat. She wasn't concerned with the risk to herself but the thought that someone would put a client – a client likely recovering from previous injuries – at risk like this made her nauseous. That took a very sick sort of person.

"I don't know what to do." The comment slipped out before she thought. Never would she have revealed that kind of weakness and uncertainty to him. Or anyone else.

Dirks turned to look at her and the harsh angles of his expression eased. "You're going to call the sheriff and warn your team. I'm going to make some calls of my own." Almost as if he couldn't help himself, he brushed at some sand on her face. His touch was light, gentle. "Are you okay to take care of your horse?"

Fighting the impulse to lean her cheek into his touch, Avery straightened her shoulders. "I'm fine." And she would be. She was used to doing what had to be done and what had to be done was rarely quick or easy.

She felt Dirks' gaze on her as she walked away. She tried not to limp but she could already feel the stiffness that would get worse before it got better. Her lips twisted wryly. She didn't suppose her stride looked nearly as attractive as Carlee's had just a short time before.

HERE I'D THOUGHT *things couldn't get much uglier, but it seems they definitely can. Dead critters in a few water troughs is a mere prank next to what just happened. Ms. Gorgeous could have been crippled or killed under the hooves of an animal that size! His gentleness couldn't have saved her and he truly is a gentle giant. Some of the other equines are a bit cheeky and that requires watching. It may seem like great fun to chase a black cat detective through a darkened pasture but it's not fun to be on the receiving end. It was, in fact, rather demeaning to have to literally run for my life but such was the position in which I found myself last night while doing a bit of recon. Very young equines have a peculiar sense of play.*

But, this — a saddle deliberately sabotaged and failing during use — is extremely dangerous. Not child's play at all.

And, unfortunately, I find myself almost in the same predicament as Ms. Gorgeous in not knowing what to do next. The cameras are only going to be useful if someone is trying to break into one of the barns at night. I can only hope we get that lucky as these midnight rounds are getting tiresome. We need a break soon. I think I shall hang with Mr.

Military a bit, see if he has any ideas that I can put to good use with or without him.

Ah, there he is, pacing the wide front porch – verandah my Tammy would call it – and talking on that cell phone of his. I do wish these humanoids would realize how difficult it is to eavesdrop. The distance to the ground is difficult enough. Being forced to keep up with the strides of an agitated human male while listening in is beyond ridiculous.

"You're right, this is important. I know I don't often ask for favors. There's a reason for that as you damn well know. Pay back is always hell with you."

Ah, a chuckle, that's encouraging. I thought this was a disagreement of some sort.

"Yeah, work your magic. The sheriff's on it, but, I'm not sure what he'll share with me even if he does manage to dig something up. I need to know who her ex is in debt to and how much he's in for."

Whew, he's stopped pacing for a moment. The conversation will be a bit easier to follow.

"No, I wouldn't lay odds on her guilt or innocence over the missing checks but there's something going on here a hell of a lot bigger than that. It seems straightforward enough that her ex got himself up to his eyeballs in some kind of gambling thing. He obviously planned to pay it off selling the ranch and the horses. The judge's ruling in the divorce put an end to any hopes he had of that."

He resumes his pacing. This restless energy is uncharacteristic of what I've observed since his arrival on the ranch.

"Don't worry about how I feel. It won't change the outcome of my investigation here."

My, my I do believe I detect a bit of attitude from Mr. Military.

Whoever he is conversing with has touched a sore spot and I daresay that spot is Ms. Gorgeous.

"Can't disagree with you on that. If he got her deep enough in debt, she might have signed off on those fraudulent checks and split the difference with Cassidy on our end."

Oh, I say, that's not right! Fraudulent checks? Surely he doesn't suspect Ms. Gorgeous of wrong-doing! Now I am on the wrong side of both Mr. Military and whoever he's talking with.

"BS on that. I'd rather pay you in dollars. Yeah, yeah, I know - you'll get it back in spades. Just come through for me on this. I've got the ranch covered but I need boots on the ground elsewhere. One more thing, check on a Burris Tarent for me. I don't know how he plays into all this, but I need to know if he's a real bad-ass or just a wannabe. Hey, and thanks, okay?"

All right then, so Mr. Military is calling in reinforcements. That's a good thing. His suspicions of her, however, are a very bad thing. I'll have to do what I can to alleviate this misperception. Surely he can see that Ms. Gorgeous is not the Bonnie to her ex-husband's Clyde.

DIRKS KNOCKED on Avery's garden entrance long past lights-out at the ranch. As soon as she opened it, he said brusquely, "You shouldn't be opening the door this time of night without checking to see who's on the other side."

She shrugged. "If you didn't want me to answer, you shouldn't have knocked. But I saw you headed this way through the office window. I've been going over more of the mountains of accounts Carlee makes me read and e-mail approve for her. Besides, Trouble went to investigate without yowling so I knew it had to be more friend than foe approaching."

Dirks suspected from her smile that she wasn't really sure she could count him as a friend or even neutral. As smiles went, it was wary and weary and barely friendly but at least she wasn't glaring at him. He'd have to be happy with that.

He nodded pointedly at the glass of wine she held in her hand. "Got more of that?"

Although she seemed momentarily surprised, she moved back from the door. "Sure. Come on in."

He stepped in and pulled the door closed behind him. They stood for a heartbeat just looking at each other and the silence of the moment enveloped him. He liked the way she looked with a plush bathrobe knotted tight around her waist. He especially liked the way she had her hair piled on top of her head, tendrils still damp escaping and caressing the skin of her neck. Whoa. Damn.

Avery was the one to break the silence and he suspected it was altogether deliberate. "White or red?"

"Either."

She paused in the process of taking another wine glass from the cabinet and gave him a long look. "Would you rather a beer? Most people who don't care if they're drinking white or red would rather not be drinking wine at all."

"Beer, then," he said, "because you're right on that." He took a seat at the granite bar without being asked.

She handed him a cold bottle and an opener. "What are you doing here this late?"

Her tone was blunt but not insulting so he decided to go with it.

"Checking on you." It was the truth – just not all of it. He drank from the bottle. The beer was dark and expensive and damned good.

Instead of sitting beside him, she leaned on the countertop

opposite him and sipped her wine, watching him over the top. A faint frown touched her forehead. "I'm fine."

"You were lucky."

"I suppose." Instead of taking another drink from the glass, she put its moisture beaded surface to her forehead. "Lucky." She gave a small laugh that held absolutely no humor. "This time."

"That's pretty much my point. You may not be again. Your clients, as you call them, may not be."

"I know this looks bad for your review but I swear I'll get all of this settled soon."

"How are you planning to do that? Pay off Danson's gambling debts?" He was pushing and he knew it.

"I won't do that." She sighed. "And even if I would, I probably couldn't. If the sheriff is right, I'm afraid they're much bigger than anything I could come up with."

Dirks took another swallow of beer, savored the taste of it. "And so, what now?"

"Now, I just keep doing what I do."

"You'd be wiser to take some time off, cancel appointments for a little while. Things are dicey and seem to be getting dicier."

Her eyes widened and he felt like he was drowning in the green-gold depths of them. "Cancel appointments? I can't do that!"

He wondered at the hint of desperation in her tone and said reassuringly, "Just for a week or so until we can figure this out." He hadn't meant to say 'we' and had a moment's gratitude when she didn't pick up on it.

"When I said I can't, I meant just that," she admitted reluctantly. "Summer Valley isn't sinking by any means but Craig did put me, put the ranch, in a bind. Tucker and Leanne need their salaries and I have feed to buy and bills to pay. I can't do all that without income from clients coming in and I can't afford to lose those clients permanently. Many of them are referred by physicians. They need this place, what we offer. If they can't get it here, they'll have to be referred elsewhere. I'd owe them that. There are other reputable places not that far away. I've already talked to Leanne and Tucker and Carlee. We'll all be extra vigilant."

Dirks shook his head. "What if that – being vigilant – isn't good enough to keep you, them, and whoever the hell else, safe?"

She placed the wine glass carefully on the granite. "Look, I don't beg ever. I work and sweat and bleed if I have to but I don't ask for what I don't earn. Just don't write off Summer Valley Ranch, please, not yet. We have so much to offer the veterans who have given everything to our country."

The words came as if wrung from her and he could tell the cost to her pride. He wanted to reassure her but he couldn't. "No decision yet." It was as much as he could offer. And he could tell by the disappointment in those beautiful green eyes that it was no reassurance at all.

CHAPTER NINE

*a*very closed the door behind Dirks firmly. No matter the outcome of Dirks' investigation, she would find a way to do what she felt driven to do. Just as she'd found a way to do everything else of importance to her. And she'd do it alone. Too late, she'd realized that Craig was a deterrent rather than a help to things that mattered. She'd trusted him once. Trusted him implicitly. She wouldn't give that kind of power to any man ever again.

She couldn't help her brother, couldn't even find him, but there were other veterans who needed her, who would allow her and the horses into their lives. Those she could, and would, find a way to help whether she was approved to participate in the government's program or not. Maybe not on as large a scale, but everything and anything she could do would count. Not Dirks Hanna or anyone else could stop her there. It might hurt that he thought her unworthy, but it wouldn't stop her.

As she emptied her wine glass and placed it in the dish washer, she felt Trouble twining around her ankles. She stooped to give him a rub but her fingers barely brushed his fur as he walked from her to the glass door that led to the garden. She'd need to close the solid inner door before she turned in for the night, but she liked having it open more often than not, liked the night sky and the sense of space. There'd been a time she'd been secure enough in this haven she'd created to leave it open as she slept, that glass the only barrier between herself and the outside world. She didn't feel that safe anymore.

The realization made her restless. When Trouble turned back to her again, she suspected he felt as agitated as she. She glanced at the monitors and found the view they gave of the barns reassuringly quiet. At least that view should have been reassuring. She felt as uneasy as Trouble looked.

The cat gave a plaintive yowl and she shook her head. "You just came in, fellow. Let's get settled for the night." Even as she said the words, she realized she hadn't yet heard Carlee come in. The young woman had her own entrance to the house. They'd created a separate living space, small but comfortable, even adding a tiny kitchenette though Carlee preferred to share meals with Avery. Usually Avery could hear the sound of her moving about or perhaps it was more that she sensed another presence. But not tonight.

Avery didn't like to hover but the temptation to check on Carlee was strong. She'd finish her office work, first, she told herself. By then, her step-daughter would likely be home so she'd give it at least that long. Carlee was a grown woman, after all. The fact that recent events were unnerving didn't change that reality.

The damaged saddle heaped on her dining room floor was all the reminder she needed of just how unnerving those events had proven. Ben Farley was sending someone to pick it up for evidence first thing tomorrow. He'd promised to have it dusted for prints but she and the sheriff both knew there'd be nothing to find that would incriminate anyone. The only prints on that saddle would belong to people who had no reason to wear gloves or wipe the saddle clean of any trace they might have left behind.

She battled her inner, and Trouble's outer, anxiety another hour before she tried Carlee's number. It rang the requisite three times before going to voice mail. Avery didn't leave a message. Carlee would get in touch with her as soon as she saw the missed call. She'd always been good about that, even as a teen-ager, certainly in the years that she and Avery has become a team.

After a quick check confirmed that Carlee's car was not where she normally parked, Avery made herself accept that Carlee had gone out for the evening and might or might not return that night. Pulling on a pair of jogging pants, she hit the elliptical. As hard as she had worked today, stress was over-riding any benefits from the activity. A work out was the only thing that might combat the ill-effects of tension and her fall. She could definitely not afford a sleepless night.

When her cell phone finally rang, she nearly fell off the exercise machine reaching to answer it.

"Carlee." She didn't try to hide the relief in her voice.

Silence, then, "No, this is Leanne."

"Sorry, I didn't look at the caller ID." Avery held her disappointment in check. "Everything okay out there?" Leanne had insisted upon spending the night with Jack again, just as Tucker was on a cot close to the field of yearlings. Avery suspected those efforts were either for nothing or unnecessarily risky but she hadn't been able to dissuade them.

"Avery, I'm not there. Carlee didn't tell you?"

Avery rubbed at the sudden tension between her brows. "I haven't talked with Carlee. Tell me what?"

"She sent me home, said I hadn't been married long enough to be spending my nights in a barn alone. But, Avery, I'm worried. She didn't answer my text message so I called and she didn't answer that either. She promised she would – it's the only way I agreed to let her do this. I'm already on my way but ..."

Even as Leanne talked, Avery had been pulling on her socks. "I'm going to the barn. I'll find her." She clicked off, not bothering to answer when Leanne rang her right back. Leanne would only want Avery to wait until she could get to the ranch, and Avery had no intention of doing that.

Avery grabbed a lightweight hoodie from the basket in her closet and headed to the mudroom where her boots waited. Trouble trotted through the darkened house at her side.

For one brief moment, she thought of calling Dirks for backup but her feelings were still stinging from their last exchange. Instead, she called Tucker who answered on the first ring. "What's up?"

"Go to Barn One. I'm looking for Carlee."

CARLEE'S VEHICLE was parked in the shadows close to the side entrance of the barn. Tucker waited for her there and shook his head. "Everything's quiet inside. Carlee isn't there."

The fact that Carlee's transportation was there, but not Carlee, couldn't be a good thing. Before Avery could voice that concern, Trouble yowled once then streaked past both of them. Avery's reaction was gut-based and immediate. She couldn't recall the exact moment she'd come to trust the cat's instincts or knowledge or whatever it was that propelled him in a given direction. She only knew that he'd displayed an uncanny accuracy for detecting trouble long before the humans around him.

Avery broke into a run right behind him, disregarding the night shadows that made speed hazardous. The flashlight that Tucker snapped on did little more than disorient her with its bobbing, shifting beam. She heard Leanne's truck sliding into the gravel at Barn One, the slamming of the truck door, and Leanne's voice calling to her. She saved her breath for running, knowing Leanne would find them soon enough.

Trouble moved quickly along the fence rail that ran behind the barns, passing the wide gates of the first two pastures. At the farthest gate, he stopped briefly and yowled again as if urging them to catch up before he shot forward toward the two and three year old horses. Typically, they huddled together, taking comfort from each other as they slept. They were still gathered, but milled restlessly about.

Avery lost sight of Trouble momentarily. "Carlee?" she heard the panic in her own voice and forced herself to take a deep breath, before calling out again.

"There!" Tucker said, lifting his flashlight. "I see green cat eyes gleaming."

EASY DOES IT. Thank goodness for smart humans. Avery tells Tucker to turn off the flashlight and warns both him and Leanne to move slowly so as not to spook the young horses. They seem as large as adults to me but I sense their immaturity. Carlee is sitting up but not moving. She may be hurt or just dazed but she is much too close to those sharp hooves. These young equines are already disturbed. Any sudden movement could send them into a panic. My speed and agility could put me over the fence in a trice, but Carlee might well be trampled.

There now, Ms. Gorgeous is kneeling beside Carlee. While the humanoids evaluate Carlee's need for medical attention, I'll do a bit of investigating on my own. Hmmm, nothing to tell by the appearance of the ground except that there seems to have been a scuffle of some sort. Unfortunately, the ground is much too hard and dry for anything as clear as footprints. Not to mention the fact that the young horses have been stomping about. It will be a wonder if none of them has trampled Carlee already.

Ah, what have we here? Some sort of halter it appears but nothing like the quality that Ms. Gorgeous purchases for her ranch. Instead of leather stitched to solid metal connections, this is made entirely of rope with its own lead line built in. Interesting and really a quite clever device. I believe Mr. Military must see this and, it comes as no surprise to me that he has already arrived on the scene.

"CARLEE, ARE YOU HURT?" Avery crouched down, careful not to bump against her step-daughter. She looked across Carlee to Tucker who was level with her on the other side. "Tucker, we may need an ambulance."

"No," Carlee said at once but her voice sounded weak and thready to Avery's anxious mind. "I'm fine. Shaken a little and pissed a lot, but fine. He shoved my face in the dirt before he took off, probably to make sure I didn't get a better look at him."

Tucker growled and rocked back on his heels. "I'll kill the bastard for that."

"At least the pasture babies are safe. The jerk jumped the fence so I know he didn't get any of them."

"Did you see who it was? Could you describe him?" The sound of Dirks' voice so close startled Avery but she realized almost at once that it shouldn't have. He had an uncanny ability to track misfortune.

"I wish. I'm not even real sure it was a guy, but I think so, broad shoulders and all that."

Carlee's voice seemed stronger, now, Avery thought, and even more irritated. But, still, she'd taken a hit and could have injuries more serious than she was aware. "Maybe you shouldn't talk right now. Let's at least get you inside and comfortable. I want to see you in the light."

"I probably look like warmed over death with a few scrapes and bruises and a covering of dirt thrown in, but I'm fine, Avery, I promise. I'm just glad I got restless in the barn and stepped out for some fresh air. The first inclination I knew that something was up was hearing the colts snort and blow. I thought maybe a coyote had gotten into the field."

"Avery?" Leanne's voice pulled her attention from Carlee. "I think you need to take a look at what the cat's found."

But it was Dirks who reached down and took the rope halter from between Trouble's sharp teeth. He held it toward Avery. "Recognize this?"

"No," she said slowly. "It's definitely not one of ours."

Anger burned through her at the realization of what he held. There was no doubt in her mind now. Someone had actually tried to steal one of Jack's babies and may even have succeeded if not for Carlee. There was also no doubt in her mind that Tarant was behind this. Markham wasn't the type for stealth-in-the-dark activities, but Tarant probably had many on his payroll who had both the temperament and the skills. If Tarant wanted a fight, he was going to get one. She'd make damned sure of that.

DIRKS FOUND himself amazed at the way Avery held to her routine the next day, even after all that had happened. Most women – hell most men – would be in stress mode. If Avery was stressed, he couldn't tell. If anything burned in her this morning, it was probably a lingering fury.

Once Avery was convinced Carlee wasn't seriously injured, he'd seen the anger take over. In full view and hearing of every one of them crowded into her kitchen the night before, she'd pulled up Craig's number on her cell phone. Her warning, more of a promise than a threat to Dirks' mind, had been issued in clear, concise terms.

"I didn't expect you to answer, Craig, not when you saw my name on your screen, and that's fine, but I know you'll listen to this message. You need to hear, know, and understand something. You'd better call off your dogs - Tarant and any others - and make them believe that nothing on this property belongs to you. If anything happens – if Carlee, if any of my team gets hurt or any of these horses are taken – you're going to pay way more than any debt you owe them. In fact, you'd better pray that none of my horses even come down with a cough, because I'm going to blame you and I'm going to come looking for you. Bet on it."

When she clicked off, she'd glared right at Dirks as if daring him to comment. He hadn't. Nor had any of her team, though they probably wanted to applaud her as much as he did.

He watched her now as she methodically groomed a strong-looking horse that stood quietly under her attention. Dirks didn't doubt she was aware of his presence, but she didn't comment on the fact or so much as acknowledge him. She talked softly to the animal the whole while, resolutely ignoring the fact that Dirks was watching her every movement. When the light red coat gleamed to suit her, she went over the saddle touching every piece of it with meticulous care before swinging it up on that muscular back.

As she pulled the girth snug, an SUV pulled alongside the paddock in front of Barn Three. Dirks watched a sturdy, young woman in scrubs step out of the driver's side and walk around to open the passenger door. A too-thin, young man eased his way out, leaning heavily upon a cane until he was upright, after which he used it to find his way forward. His eyes were open, but Dirks realized at once that they were sightless.

Avery left the horse ground-tied and met the young man at the paddock fence. She smiled at him warmly. "Sergeant Mallette. Good morning."

"Good morning, ma'am. How are you?"

"Happy that the sun is shining and all my horses are healthy."

"How is Applejack today?" Dirks could hear the eagerness and affection in the soldier's voice. "Ready for a ride?"

"That one's always ready. He's tireless. And, yes, he's ready for you. All saddled."

"One day I want to be able to saddle him myself." Though Dirks couldn't hear even a hint of self-pity in the young man's voice, his own throat tightened. Men like Sergeant Mallette had given way too much, way too young. What a small thing that would seem to most riders, the ability to saddle their own horse. Maybe even a burden rather than a blessing that they could do so.

"And you will," Avery said evenly. "Think how far you've come in these few weeks. You can ride without me, unsaddle him and even finish cooling him without me. Just a bit longer and I promise you'll saddle by yourself."

But Dirks suspected that wouldn't happen until Avery was sure the sabotage had ended and the saboteur was behind bars.

Avery moved to the center of the ring, standing tirelessly while the horse and rider circled her slowly. The soldier's balance was steady and Dirks knew how difficult that balance astride a horse must have been to develop without sight. He'd seen others struggle just on their own two feet once they'd lost the ability to see. After fifteen or so minutes, Mallette lifted the reins which cued the horse to a slow jog. Dirks wouldn't have called it a trot but definitely more than a walk. After another fifteen minutes, the soldier reined him back down to a walk and turned him in the opposite direction and started over again.

Dirks' gaze stayed as much on Avery as the soldier. She talked encouragingly to him as often as she was silent. Dirks never heard the least hint of weariness or impatience at the slow pace of the session. Nor did her smile, genuine and pleased, once slip.

After a bit, he supposed curiosity got the better of the nurse as she moved to stand beside him. "I haven't seen you here before. Are you a student?" Her glance was bright and friendly, her freckled face pleasing with a cheerful expression.

"No, I'm just visiting. Are you with the VA?"

She pulled a face at that. "No, thank the Lord. I work at the regional hospital. I bring Sergeant Mallette here on my own time between shifts."

That caught Dirks' attention. "That's good of you."

"Little enough. I lost my husband to an IED three years back. I do what I can for those who actually do make it home. A little bit like Ms. Avery, I guess. I don't know how much money she could be making with the time she donates to the veterans. She's trying to get in some government program that will pay her back for her time and maybe let her take on some more but last she mentioned it, the government was taking its usual slow crawl to get to her application. Even if it works out, I suspect she'll always give time to some that might not be covered even by that."

Dirks turned his attention back the woman in the center of the ring with way more to think about than he'd expected to be given. He tried not to read into Avery's face what might not be there, but he couldn't deny the joy shining in her eyes, the fiercely hopeful expression on her face as she watched the soldier. Dirks had fought the attraction he felt for her, knowing he had to be objective, knowing he had to see her clearly enough to know if she was capable of subterfuge, of pocketing money intended to help wounded veterans.

But now? No way, Dirks thought, no way in hell could he believe she'd risk everything she'd created here for a few fraudulent dollars. No way would she jeopardize her dream of helping the men and women who put their lives on the line every day they were away from their families. Whatever was happening, she was the victim and not the catalyst behind the events.

And somehow, he had to figure out the who and the why behind what was. Craig was the easy answer, almost too easy. And sometimes the easy answer was the correct one, but Dirks would dig and dig deep – deep enough to be certain the answer he found was the true one.

CHAPTER TEN

*T*hings are heating up and not just between Ms. Gorgeous and Mr. Military. Dad talks about feeling things in his bones and the young whippersnapper that I confess to have been, believed he meant the aches and pains of old age – not that I'd ever been so unwise as to voice such a thought! As I've followed closely in his paw prints and matured into my profession, I've come to understand what he was truly describing was that knowledge of things deep inside. Bone deep.

The danger is increasing but so is the troubling suspicion that I am somehow missing a key factor. That is a failing I've come to associate with my well-meaning, but less brilliant, humanoid counterparts. Typically, my work is more to ensure they understand and act upon my dazzling deductions. With this case, I must now dig much deeper to unearth a truth that is proving frustratingly elusive.

I admit to the possibility that the weak-spined ex could be the culprit behind all of the catastrophes but I cannot overcome the fact that I've not once scented his recent presence around any of the barns or paddocks. It lingers in some places, most recently and most strongly in the guest quarters he purportedly used throughout the lengthy divorce *proceedings and the main house as well, though fading there. I've even caught a whiff or two around the tack rooms, particularly where Carlee sat amidst the destruction of some expensive tack. With that taken into consideration, I must decide whether or not I can accept that the thus-described spineless ex could so influence the increasingly nasty turns of events or accept that he is a victim of his own stupidity with those events no more than the domino effect of that stupidity.*

At the center of the danger is Ms. Gorgeous, around whom everyone seems to be hovering this morning. Mr. Military has yet to take his eyes from her though she seems oblivious to his stare as she watches the young soldier who, though sightless, remains determined to learn new ways to enjoy his life. Tucker has edged over from his work once or twice to check on the woman who seems more friend and mentor than employer, as has Leanne. And here is Carlee, yet again, hovering and casting anxious glances toward Avery. If possible, Carlee seems even more agitated now than last night after her own brush with danger.

Hmmm, I wonder the reason for her frown as Carlee glances down at her ringing cell phone. I believe I'll step a bit closer as I can't hear what she's saying from here. In true detective work, eavesdropping is less a character flaw than a necessity.

"I wouldn't consider Avery's voice message a threat, if I were you. More like a promise." *Carlee is quite definitely brassed off. Her voice sounds dire and her pacing, as she listens to whoever is at the other end of the line, brings her closer to Mr. Military.*

"What did you expect her to do? Let you take everything she's worked so hard to make here and squander it on your bad habits?"

Uh-oh, Carlee's rising tone has drawn Mr. Military's interest from Ms. Gorgeous.

"I *have* tried to help you, Dad. I don't know what else to

do. I can't support myself and you and your gambling too. You've got to stop! Stay away from here, just stay away."

Well, it would seem Carlee has realized belatedly that she holds Mr. Military's complete attention. She turns away and lowers her voice, wiping at what I suspect are tears in her eyes. Fortunately, she seems oblivious to my own stealthy move to keep within hearing of her conversation.

"What do you mean you're afraid? Of who?" *Carlee pauses, no doubt listening to her father's reply.* "Jesus, Dad! Okay, yes. I'll meet you but it won't change anything. I can't help you with this."

There's no mistaking Carlee's agitation as she slides her phone into her pocket. This does not bode well for anyone.

I wish Mr. Military had heard more of that conversation but at least Ms. Gorgeous remains focused on her client. My lady doesn't need anything further to distress her and it would appear Carlee plans to place herself in the line of fire with her worry for her father.

"What's next on your agenda?"

Avery pulled her gaze from the young sergeant as he carefully unsaddled Applejack. She glanced briefly at Dirks, before returning her attention to her client. It alarmed as much as irritated her to realize that she found Dirks more appealing each day. "I've got a contractor coming out to talk with me later today."

"Contractor? Are you starting another barn?"

"No. It's a project I've had in mind for a long time. The problem is the work's already started but this guy is dragging his heels about finishing. I've asked him to meet with me but I've got a few hours before he'll be here. I'll probably put that time into paperwork."

"I've got a better idea. Let's go into town for some lunch. It will do you good to get away from here for a couple of hours."

For a moment, Avery just stared at him. Was he ... what? Asking her for a date? Wanting to grill her again? Rather than stand there and wonder, she asked bluntly, "Why?"

His smile was killer - at least for her - she admitted to herself.

"Just because," he said, his tone light and easy. "We've got to eat. We both have time. You can tell me about this new project you've got going."

Telling herself she was bat shit crazy for so much as considering it, she found herself nodding assent all the same. The idea appealed to her. Dirks appealed to her, damn it. "I'll have to get things cleared away from this session and Applejack back in his stall. But ... okay."

Bat shit crazy became a mantra said under her breath as she waited patiently for Sergeant Mallette to curry and brush Applejack, as she scheduled his next appointment and then said good-bye to him and the nurse who volunteered to drive him faithfully each week. She wondered sometimes if the young woman had feelings for the soldier, feelings that went beyond being a Good Samaritan. But it was none of her business and she had plenty on her plate without worrying whether or not two hurting souls might find real and lasting joy in each other.

She had to wonder if she truly had lost her mind as she returned to the house, not just to brush the dust from her clothes and grab her purse but to change into something a bit nicer, a bit more flattering. *Bat shit crazy* she thought again as she dusted some blush across her cheeks to take the pallor away and added just a bit of color to her lips.

When she was done, she just stood at the bathroom sink

and stared at herself in the mirror. She didn't look old, she acknowledged, but she felt old. Craig had made her feel unattractive, something brushed aside and far less appealing to him than his addiction. It might almost have been easier if he'd had some grand and passionate affair, left her to be with another woman. She wasn't sure why that was so but it seemed to her that at least being set aside for a living, breathing creature was something she could understand. He hadn't cared for his string of flirtations any more than he'd cared for her. They, like she, had been found less enticing than a game of blackjack.

And as she had that thought, she had another just as quickly. It no longer hurt. All that Craig had done or said in the past years had lost the power to hurt. She smiled at herself in the mirror and suddenly felt just a bit pretty again. Lord, it had been a long time since she'd felt attractive.

"Bat shit crazy," she told the woman in the mirror but when she turned away she was still smiling.

It was nice to feel Dirks' hand on her elbow as she stepped up into the passenger seat of his truck and she decided to let it feel good, at least for now, at least for a little while. He'd be gone soon but she could allow herself to enjoy this feeling, however fleeting it might be. Her reality, though, was that while her past life with Craig no longer had the power to hurt her emotionally, his misdeeds could hurt her in ways far worse. She'd have to focus on damage control just to survive, to ensure her dreams and Summer Valley Ranch survived.

"What are you worrying about?"

She glanced across at Dirks and realized that, while he had his seat belt on, he hadn't yet started the truck. "Worrying?"

"That crease is back between your eyes."

"That's called age," she said wryly.

To her surprise, Dirks reached over and smoothed the area between her brows with his thumb. The touch startled her and brought with it a warmth that was completely unexpected. "That," he said firmly, "is called worry."

Taking a deep breath, she exhaled slowly. "A little. Yes."

Avery thought Dirks would question her more, but he simply started the engine and turned his attention to driving.

As they left her ranch and turned onto the main road, she forced her shoulders to relax. Even if this did turn out to be simply a further opportunity for him to grill her for information, she wouldn't let herself be disappointed. She would just view it as another step forward in his decision making. She wanted desperately for that decision to be favorable. It wouldn't stop her if that wasn't the case. She'd find a way to help the patriots who needed it, who needed the solace and comfort and, yes, the healing that horses and riding could bring them.

"It's back." Dirks' quick glance her way held amusement.

"What? What's back?"

"That furrow."

This time she chuckled and it surprised her that she could. "Busted. But at least I quit biting my nails."

"You bit your nails?

"You sound surprised."

"I am actually. I've always attributed that trait to insecurity. You're one of the strongest, most secure women I've ever encountered."

She didn't know what to say to that so she skirted what sounded like a true compliment. "I started biting my nails a couple of years ago, when I was letting Craig make me feel crazy. I quit when I filed for a divorce."

"Interesting choice of words - that you 'let' him make you feel crazy."

For a moment, she didn't answer because she didn't want to get deep into her marriage, into the things that Craig had done, and the despair to which she'd nearly succumbed. Choosing her words carefully to steer past those times and those feelings she didn't want to ever experience again, she finally answered. "Some things, even some feelings, are a choice. It's just that simple. I'll never again let another person have that much influence over me. Emotions are one thing. I may get hurt again. I'll surely have times I feel sad or disappointed, as well as happy and triumphant, but I'll never doubt myself again. I'll never let anyone do that to me. That's a choice."

"Good for you," Dirks said softly.

AT AVERY'S REQUEST, they made a brief stop at the sheriff's office. Dirks liked the man, liked what his initial investigation into the town had told him about the man. Honesty and integrity in law enforcement wasn't a rarity but it was nothing to take for granted either.

Farley was clearly disappointed that he still couldn't offer anything concrete. "I promise I won't stop digging but I can't say I expect to find who actually fired those shots, Avery. I'd be lying if I told you I did."

Silently, Dirks agreed. There was about as much chance of that as finding the proverbial needle in a haystack.

"Did the garage get your SUV ready to go yet? I didn't check with them this morning but Jeff told me they were close to being finished yesterday."

"Unfortunately, no," Avery told him, "they called earlier.

The seat that was shipped to them from New Orleans came in just before closing yesterday evening and it wasn't the right model. They're waiting for the replacement. Once that's delivered and installed, I can pick it up."

"Well, if you need one of us to run out to the ranch and get you when it's ready, just give me a call."

Avery's smile was affectionate and Dirks realized he didn't like seeing quite that much warmth toward the sheriff who apparently was more than a little fond of her.

"I'm sure that won't be necessary but I'll keep it in mind." She hesitated. "You haven't heard anything more about the 'high flyers' you mentioned last time I was here?"

Dirks suspected she would've worded that question much less vaguely if he hadn't been there. He knew she didn't trust him completely and he couldn't blame her for that. She had to feel that anything he knew and heard could be used to deny her application. What she didn't realize was that not being approved for the program would be the least of her problems at that point.

"Nothing. I haven't heard a word." The sheriff didn't seem too happy about it either. "Nothing else has happened at your place, has it?"

"Nothing else? Other than dead animals in water troughs and a saddle damaged with intent to get someone hurt, maybe even killed, and Carlee being knocked down by someone trying to steal a yearling, you mean?"

Farley scrubbed his hand over his brow. "I'd lock him up if I could, Avery."

Her expression softened. "I know that, Ben. I don't fault you for any of this. I just don't know what to do about it."

"All you need to do is keep watching out for yourself and I'll keep sending a patrol car through as often as I can."

But Dirks could tell neither the sheriff nor Avery believed, any more than he did, that those measures would be a deterrent to whoever was behind what was happening. At this point, he suspected that not even locking Danson up as the sheriff wanted to do would alter what had been set in motion.

DIRKS WAITED until they'd finished a meal that was well-prepared and all the more enjoyable for the company he was keeping before he said the things he knew would return that furrow between Avery's brows and maybe even tempt her to bite her nails again. He might have waited even longer but his thoughts were too close to the surface, as close to the surface as his growing feelings for the woman across from him.

"You're staring at me," she told him.

"You're beautiful." And that was the absolute truth.

"It's not that kind of a stare."

"Busted," he tossed her own word back to her, "but you are beautiful."

She blushed and the look was good on her but she was as strong as he'd told her she was and not to be distracted. "Let's go back to the 'busted' part. What is it you're *not* saying?"

"I've started an investigation into your ex's activities."

"Why?" she asked clearly dismayed. "I told you he has nothing to do with Summer Valley any more. The property, the horses, everything is one hundred percent mine and what I want to do, what I *will* do, for the veterans has nothing to do with *him*."

"But he's put you, and the horses, at risk."

"That's my battle."

Not alone, he wanted to tell her. He was wise enough to refrain.

"All *you* need to do," she persisted, "is determine if I'm solvent - which I am - and whether I'm capable of meeting the needs of wounded veterans - which I am. If you can't see that by now, I don't think there's anything left I can show you to prove it. That frustrates me."

"I've seen what I need to see to know that." He felt a pang at the way her face lit at the words.

"So you'll approve Summer Valley for the equine therapy program?"

He was glad they were through eating because he knew she wouldn't have kept her appetite with what he was going to tell her next.

"There's a problem."

Her shoulders dropped ever so slightly but he saw it, saw the brief flash of happiness in her eyes fade.

"Okay." That one word was all she said but her expression said volumes more.

"Summer Valley Ranch was approved for the VA's equine therapy program nearly a year ago," Dirks admitted.

Avery stared at Dirks, her expression one of total disbelief. "That can't be. I've been waiting forever just to hear back on my application."

"During the past year monthly checks have been sent, signed, and cashed for daily equine therapy for four different veterans who don't exist."

"You're not making any sense."

But Dirks saw a flash of some hidden something in those beautiful eyes that suddenly made him doubt, made him wonder if his attraction to her had caused him to make a mistake. But he'd started on this path, and even if it led someplace he didn't want to go, he had no choice but to continue the discussion.

"The person on our end has been terminated and charged with fraud."

"And on this end." She was watching him steadily, with that same unreadability he'd seen in her the first time they'd talked, the first time they'd shared a meal. And he realized that had only been a few days ago. Despite his feelings for her, he forced himself to remember that he'd known her barely a week. The fact that he'd researched her, dug into every facet of her life for several long weeks didn't make for knowing a person.

"That's why I'm here."

"Well," she said and though her tone remained calm and even, he could hear the underlying bitterness, "I'm sure you've plundered through all the dirty laundry of my life with Craig. You'll know those checks didn't come to me, haven't been deposited to the ranch account or my personal account."

Spine straight, she placed her crumpled linen napkin on the table. "I'd like to go back to the ranch now."

Still wondering if his emotions had control of his good sense, Dirks reached across and took her hand to keep her from getting out of her chair. His orders were to keep the details of their investigation from her but if she were guilty, she already knew them. If she wasn't, if she was the victim of her ex's guilt, his investigation had just turned an unexpected corner. "The funds were mailed to a post office box in Alexander City, made out to you, signed with your signature. After our guy was identified, that post office box was closed."

Every bit of color drained from her face. "You're crazy or you're lying."

"You know I'm not. I wouldn't say it if I couldn't prove it."

She snatched her hand away and got to her feet. "One thing you can't prove is that I signed those checks because that never happened. I'll get my own ride back to the ranch. I don't want to talk to you or be around you, not right now."

Dirks watched as she exited the restaurant with a quiet dignity that pulled at him, made him regret having been the one to tell her why he was really there, regret having hurt her. One thing he didn't regret was being the one sent to investigate her. He might later, if she really was guilty as his superiors were convinced, but if she wasn't guilty after all, he was going to be the one to prove her innocence.

He supposed she'd go straight to Sheriff Farley to get that ride back to the ranch, but he didn't take any chances with her safety. He paid the check quickly and followed her. From across the street, he watched as she and Farley exited the sheriff's office together before he got back in his truck and trailed them back to the ranch.

CHAPTER ELEVEN

*A*very felt as if she'd been slapped. She'd walked the few blocks back to Ben Farley's office without even noticing her surroundings. She was grateful the sheriff hadn't asked a single question when she stepped back into his office and asked if one of his deputies could take her home. He'd simply picked up his western style hat and walked her out to his patrol car.

Ben remained mercifully uninquisitive, commenting upon the opening of the new barbershop in town, the weather, anything except what had caused her to leave Dirks alone someplace in town and find her own way home. He pulled to a stop in front of her house and got out with her. Shooting a warning glance at the truck and driver that had followed them back, Ben gave her a hug. "Do you want me to run him out of here?"

Avery followed the direction of his gaze to Dirks' truck. She hadn't been aware that he'd been that close behind them but she couldn't have said she was surprised by the fact either.

"Unfortunately, it isn't that easy. He's government and he

hasn't done anything wrong – at least not according to the law."

"Makes me no mind, Avery. You want him gone, he'll be gone." Ben smiled faintly but his eyes held a glint of steel. "I like him well enough, but you've got a place in my heart and always will."

"Same here, Ben," she said huskily. "I'll be okay. Thanks for getting me home."

"If you need me, call me. I'll always come. You know that."

"I do know."

She watched as the sheriff got back in his car and pulled away. He stopped briefly and put his window down to say something to Dirks. She couldn't hear and didn't care. The feeling of numbed disbelief had given way to a burning anger. And it didn't help that the anger was directed more at herself than anyone else. Apparently, Dirks was just doing his job. If she was a casualty, well, business was business.

Although she could feel his gaze on her as she walked back into her house to change, she was careful not to even glance at him. So much for feeling attractive, for *being* attracted. She had a ranch to run. Sooner or later, she and Dirks would have to talk again, she knew. She was under investigation and if she ran him off, the government would just send someone else.

The government. Realization hummed through her veins. That she was under scrutiny of federal authorities scared her. It was one thing to be judged fit or unfit to be part of a VA program. Being judged guilty or not guilty, subject to being charged with fraud against the federal government, was another thing entirely. A truly frightening thing.

The whole time she changed back into jeans and tee shirt, her mind spun with the implications. She knew she was innocent. Still, if Dirks was right in everything he said – and there was probably little possibility he wasn't - it meant someone had forged her name and taken money intended to help wounded veterans, maybe even set her up to take this fall.

That last thought had her pausing as she unpinned her hair and pulled it through the back of her ball cap.

That someone could only be Craig but her mind reeled to think he'd been either that desperate or that determined to destroy her. But if Craig had meant to set her up for jail and take control of the ranch, why hadn't he? Cold feet? Or was it only and ever the money? Only and ever his gambling debts driving him? And how could she prove his guilt and clear herself?

Sighing, Avery pulled on her socks and boots. Dirks had made it clear that he believed she was the guilty party. Or had he? She got to her feet then just stood, thinking. Dirks hadn't said 'signed by you'. He'd said 'signed with your signature'. She wasn't sure if there was a difference in his mind. He hadn't espoused any belief in her innocence, just stated the bare facts and rather baldly at that. Even if there was a difference in his mind, the only difference would be in whether or not she went to federal prison for something she hadn't done. It wouldn't change that she had almost trusted him, almost let herself feel something for him. Never again. She'd trust herself, her horses and the team that had proven their loyalty to her over and over again.

The thought of prison terrified her, the thought of what would happen to her horses in that eventuality, brought a cold clamminess to her skin. She had to force herself to breathe against the weight that pressed down on her. No, she wasn't going there again, either. She wasn't, wouldn't be helpless. She'd already proven she was a fighter and she'd fight this with her last ounce of strength and willpower. She would *not* be a victim, not to Craig or anyone else.

"Meow."

Avery glanced down in surprise. "Trouble. I didn't hear you come in." Scooping the cat up in her arms, she took comfort from the warmth of his body, the feel of his sleek fur against her arms. She still wasn't sure why he'd shown up in her life and he might be hers for only a little while, but she'd enjoy him until he decided it was time to return home to Tammy Lynn.

CARLEE STEPPED into the kitchen from the garden door just as Avery walked through from the hall. "Hi," Carlee said, studying her closely. "I was just checking on you."

"I'm fine." Avery did her best to smile normally. "Any reason I wouldn't be?"

Carlee gave a laugh that didn't sound the least bit happy. "It just never seems to end, does it?"

"Has something else happened?" Avery felt her heart clutch.

"No, thank God. I'm just feeling edgy, I guess."

Carlee was normally such an undemonstrative person that it caught Avery off guard when the young woman stepped closer and leaned her head against Avery's shoulder. She gave her stepdaughter a light hug and was neither surprised nor offended when Carlee moved away again almost at once. Craig had told her once that, after Caren's death, Carlee's mother had ceased to show any sign of affection to either her husband or her remaining daughter. Carlee had withdrawn more and more and it was still rare for her to initiate touching any human though she was openly affectionate with the horses and Avery had long suspected she had some feelings for Tucker that she was careful to hide when he was watching.

"Jake Everett is supposed to be here in about half an hour. Hopefully I'll find out why he's dragging his feet over the fenced riding path."

The project she'd mentioned to Dirks, and never had the chance to elaborate on, was a safe place she'd designed for sightless clients to ride with some sense of independence. When finished, it would be a riding path with tall, sturdy fencing, lined on the inside with thick shrubs. It would be a means for those without sight but who wanted a sense of independence, like Sergeant Mallette, to ride in safety. If they inadvertently guided their mount too close to the fence, their knees would hit heavy shrubbery rather than unyielding posts and boards. When finished, the route would wind over a full five acres of level ground. With a raised platform, she'd be able to see the rider at all times and reach him - or her - within minutes if need be.

"I'll go with you to meet him," Carlee said.

"Well, you're always welcome but I can deal with whatever is keeping Mr. Everett from completing his work here. If I have to, I'll fire him and find someone else to finish the job. I don't care if it *is* mid-stream of the project."

"I'm going." Carlee was adamant. "He might not take kindly to being fired."

Avery shook her head in exasperation. "Carlee, I'll be fine. Again, you're welcome but there's no need."

Carlee ignored that. "We can take the ranch truck." She hesitated. "Maybe later we can go for a ride. Just us."

And that was when Avery got it, saw the uncertainty, the hint of insecurity. Carlee had clung to her side when she and Craig first married, transitioned to a poised young woman in the years after, but returned to a more fragile state as Craig had slowly deteriorated, destroying Avery's trust and their marriage. Carlee would never cling but it was clear she needed to be close to Avery for now.

"A ride sounds wonderful, Carlee." Avery didn't have to pretend her pleasure at the thought. It would be good to get away, just enjoy the horses as the afternoon faded and the blistering heat eased.

Carlee grinned. "Good. Now let's go tackle Mr. Everett. Figuratively, that is," she added with a wink.

JAKE EVERETT STEPPED out of his truck as they approached. He leaned one hip against the hood and watched as they climbed down from the ranch truck and walked toward him. Behind him five acres of the flattest land on her ranch had been studded with tall, sturdy posts waiting for boards to be run at several different levels.

"Mr. Everett," Avery offered her hand and, though the man took it, she could both see and feel his reluctance to do so.

He was a lean man, weathered by the work he did in the sun and the wind, the heat and the cold. His company had a solid reputation for delivering quality work on time. Avery knew because she'd vetted that company well and selected it, and him, with care. It had surprised her when he and his crew had simply stopped work mid-stream without so much as a word to her. She'd waited until the work was a month past due before contacting him, more because those final days of court had drained her than for any patience on her part. She'd paid half of the total up front, trusting that Jake Everett would live up to his promise. What he'd done so far was quality work, but now she needed it finished.

Because the man didn't show any inclination to address the problem, Avery decided to take the bull by the horns. "I appreciate you coming out to talk with me. I would've appreciated more if you'd finished the job on time like you promised."

He flushed a dark red. "And I would've appreciated not being put in the position I'm in with the lumber yard."

Avery realized that what she'd taken for embarrassment was anger, pure and simple. "What do you mean?"

"Ma'am, half that material you ordered - and then had hauled away from the lumber store without paying - has nothing to do with what I'm doing out here for you. I've built a reputable company with hard, honest work. I don't want my name associated with anything less than honest dealings."

Avery felt a slow burn heat her from the inside out but she could feel Carlee bristling beside her and placed a hand on the girl's arm. "Mr. Everett, I don't know what you're accusing me of or what you're talking about. I've paid for everything that's been delivered, everything you've put in the ground and what's laying there stacked, ready to be put up. Just like I paid you up front, believing you'd do a good job."

"And that's just what I've done. A good job. And I'll finish once you're square with the lumber yard and I can look Stu Sykes in the eye again."

"Who?" Avery stared at him in complete bewilderment. "Who is Stu Sykes?"

"Owns a lumber yard near Jackson's Gap."

Carlee wasn't being silent. She shook off Avery's hand and stepped forward with a fierce glare. "I don't know Stu Sykes and I've never placed an order with that lumber yard. That is *not* where we got the posts *or* any of the rest of the material. We got everything here in town, local. Just like we buy everything else. *Local*. I paid for it myself and watched it being unloaded."

Jake Everett rubbed the back of his neck as he looked from one to the other. Clearly, being on the receiving end of the wrath of a young woman wasn't his idea of a good time. He focused on Avery. "If you buy everything local, why'd your husband call and ask me where to get the best deal? Hell, I even told Stu he could let the man send someone to pick it up - that I didn't have a doubt in the world you'd put the check in the mail that same day like he promised."

Before Avery could even open her mouth, Carlee said the dirtiest word Avery had ever heard her utter.

"I'll pay Mr. Sykes tomorrow. From my own account. You just finish this job like you promised and you'll get paid the second half of the money like you were promised." Carlee swung on her heels, then swung back. "I'll tell you one thing, Mr. Everett, you're no more a man than my dad. A real man wouldn't have just walked away from a commitment. A real man would've had the brass to come speak his mind up front instead of waiting for his client to call and ask what the hell was going on. Avery is the most honest woman you'll ever meet. She pays every bill *before* it even comes due. Ask anyone in town. You and your Mr. Sykes are dumb as dirt to take the word of a jerk you don't even know, over the phone and hand him thousands of dollars' worth of material."

Carlee stalked away, leaving Avery to stare after her a moment. She glanced back at Jake Everett and almost apologized before deciding Carlee was right. He hadn't been man enough to call her and give her a chance to explain or deny. "If you plan to finish the job, be here first thing tomorrow and every day after until it's done. The first day I don't see you and you don't call and say why, I give the job to someone else and they get the rest of the money."

Carlee was crying without making a sound when Avery reached the truck and climbed behind the wheel. "I'm sorry."

"Carlee, you have nothing to apologize for, and no, you won't pay this Mr. Sykes. I'm going to take the man a copy of the notice my attorney put in the paper when I was granted a legal separation. He can go after Craig for the money if he wants to. Neither you nor I are responsible. And if I never see another man, it will be too soon," she smiled a little and added, "except Tucker." Then she started the engine and put the truck in drive. "Now let's go saddle up."

ALL OF THE things Avery wouldn't say to Carlee were spinning through her mind as she drove back toward the barns. What Craig had done made no sense. What on earth would he do with posts and lumber? He could have absolutely no use for fence material.

As if reading her mind, Carlee said. "He sold it. Probably had someone - probably whoever picked it up - ready and willing to pay a fraction of what it's worth. Quick cash. Damn it!" Carlee's clenched fist pounded her thigh and she repeated with even more emphasis, "*Damn* it!"

Avery gave her stepdaughter a quick glance and sighed at the expression on her face.

"You don't own this, Carlee, and neither do I."

"He's my dad."

"And I was his wife. Doesn't make us responsible."

Carlee smiled ever so slightly. "Doesn't make us 'dumb as dirt' as Misters Sykes and Everett either."

"Exactly right. Now let's just give all of this a rest and enjoy the rest of our day, okay?"

The   tension   in   Carlee's   shoulders   eased   visibly. "Yeah. Let's."

I REALLY DO NOT *like that Ms. Gorgeous and Carlee are out alone and it's more than clear that Mr. Military isn't any happier about it than I am. He watched with a scowl as they rode out on some singularly large horses. They are not feisty equines, it's true, just large. In fact, the one Ms. Gorgeous calls Jack, the one she saddled, is a gentle creature, but still they've been gone some time now and Mr. Military is almost making* me *nervous with his stalking about as he watches the horizon for their return.*

The sun is getting low along the horizon and while the clouds are a glorious crimson as if lit from within, that gorgeous sunset isn't what is holding Mr. Military's attention any more than it is mine.

Although I've heard a coyote or two and even a wild cat of some sort, it's not four-legged creatures that concern me. There is evil afoot here. It's fortunate that I noted a shotgun slid into the leather scabbard on Carlee's saddle. No doubt she's as excellent a shot as she is an equestrian or she wouldn't bother with the weaponry but that is only a small consolation. One must wonder if she could shoot her own father if he proves to be the one behind the evil happenings.

I do acknowledge it's doubtful he poses any physical threat. I believe that threat comes from men he has made very, very angry.

At last, they're making their way over that last hill. And not a moment too soon as the sun is slipping farther and farther and the shadows are deepening. Perhaps the equine have vision as excellent as mine but I prefer not to have Ms. Gorgeous' safety hanging on that possibility.

. . .

"TROUBLE, THAT IS ONE HARD-HEADED WOMAN." Dirks propped a foot on the lower rung of a paddock and watched as Avery and Carlee rode into the barn and began the task of unsaddling and grooming.

Carlee had acknowledged his presence with a quiet greeting as they'd passed by him. Avery had simply given him a cool glance which had Carlee studying her curiously.

Dirks bided his time until they were finished with their mounts, then gave a hand as they, with Leanne and Tucker, fed and hayed the horses. Whether that helping hand was wanted or not, he couldn't have said and didn't much care. If Avery had said anything to the others about their conversation at lunch, he couldn't tell. The three of them acted the same as they always had, comfortable in his presence, accepting he was there and not likely to go away until his investigation was finished. Only Avery continued to give him a chilly shoulder. She wasn't blatant about it. But he knew.

When everything was done that needed to be, he fell into step beside her as she walked back to her house. Carlee had stayed behind, talking with Tucker about one of the two year olds he thought might be ready for some additional handling. Dirks had learned that all of the youngsters knew how to lead and would allow themselves to be brushed and combed by the time they were two-year-olds and none would be ridden until they were three but it seemed there was plenty for them to learn in between the leading and the riding.

Avery didn't acknowledge his presence. Dirks didn't bother to speak. He didn't need to remind her that he strode close at her side. She knew perfectly well he was there.

It wasn't until they reached the door that she stopped and turned back to him. "Go away."

"You're just putting off a conversation that's going to be had."

"It's not going to be had tonight. I'm tired and I'm not going to talk to you now so go away."

Dirks sighed. "I'm not the bad guy, Avery."

"You're not the good guy, either." It was a stark reminder of his purpose in her life.

Dirks didn't try to stop her as she went inside and closed the door firmly behind her. "Damn it," he said softly. He turned to go and nearly stumbled over Trouble who was sitting at his feet staring up at him with what seemed to be an accusatory expression.

Dirks gave a grunt and stepped around him. Tomorrow, Avery would have to talk with him. The only problem was Dirks didn't have a clue what he was going to say to her.

CHAPTER TWELVE

$\mathcal{A}$very woke feeling heavy-lidded and weighted down. Somewhere in her dreams she'd lost the peace of mind she'd gained by the simple act of riding with Carlee along the slopes and ridges of the valley. She had been invigorated by their discussion of future plans for Summer Valley and possible expansions of existing programs. Unfortunately, Avery could no longer put aside the reality that she was being investigated for fraud by the government. It was a reality she had not shared with Carlee. In one sense, they were truly partners, but in another they would always have that mother-daughter relationship. Avery saw no need to distress Carlee more than she already was just as she suspected Carlee had shielded Avery from some of the uglier things her father had said over the course of their separation and divorce.

Sighing at the inevitable, she dressed and found her boots. She'd send Dirks the usual text about coffee and breakfast but if he stayed more than another day or two, she planned to purchase a coffee pot and cookware for his bungalow. She wished she'd done that already because she definitely did not feel like facing whatever he felt he needed to say to her. On a whim, she grabbed her own coffee before she hit send and headed out to the barn. It was an evasion tactic but she felt entitled all things considered.

The air had that slight morning coolness which she knew would dissipate as soon as the sun hit the tree line. Still, she enjoyed it while she could, settling in one of the canvas chairs they kept throughout the barns for just such moments as this, at the beginning or end of a busy day. Jack thrust his head over the stall door and nickered at her as she stretched her legs and crossed them at the ankles in front of her.

"Good morning to you, too," she said softly.

As he nickered again, more urgently, she chuckled. "I'm going to finish this cup of coffee then check the chalkboard but I suspect you've all been fed."

"You're right, he has," Leanne said stepping around the corner, "but that won't stop him from begging."

Some horses would quit eating when they were full, some would eat and then eat again if they could and, just like the consequences of the wrong feed or poor quality feed, over-feeding could be devastating. Colic or founder too often ended in death. Founder could leave a horse crippled and in a lifetime of pain which was why her crew was extremely careful to check and double-check on feeding before covering someone else's barn.

And Jack was in Leanne's barn because he, of all of the horses, had the strongest affinity for those wounded in mind as well as body. That characteristic passed down to his offspring was a large part of what had made Summer Valley Ranch successful in the art and practice of equine therapy. And that was where Avery's heart had turned and she knew it was where it would remain. She could have made a comfortably good living providing nothing but riding lessons for youngsters but that first foster child, abused physically and mentally, had set her and Jack on a different course.

It had taken time to build their clientele, to vet riding instructors with other facilities, until she could successfully, confidently, refer those happy, healthy children and adults who simply wanted the opportunity to learn to ride. Now, so many physicians and counselors referred patients to her, she couldn't take all of them without another barn filled with horses that were suited to the task. Someday, hopefully soon, she'd have that. Meanwhile, she managed to find a way to take the ones that seemed to need her most, conferring with the referring professional, reading through summaries of treatment released to her by the patient or their primary caregiver.

Avery looked up from her reverie to find Leanne still standing and watching her. She tilted her head in silent question.

"You don't look like you slept well," Leanne said bluntly.

"I know." No point in denying the fact. She'd seen for herself the shadows under her eyes as she'd combed her hair and pulled it through a ball cap.

"Anything I can do to help."

"Shoot me."

"Well, now *that* would solve everything." Leanne's tone was dry.

Avery chuckled. "Sorry. Just tired of dealing with the mess I made of my life. But I'm off my pity pot. I've got a couple of clients this morning but there's something I need to take care of later. I'll let you know when I head out."

"Do you need me or Tuck to go with you?"

Leanne had asked the question with studied carelessness but she appeared troubled and Avery realized it was a look she was seeing too often.

"No, just a paperwork issue I've got to take care of."

"Something you're not letting Carlee handle?"

Avery realized her light explanation had done nothing to erase Leanne's troubled expression. Paperwork was Carlee's venue and they all knew it.

"Carlee's got a full plate. It's end of month close-out and she mentioned a trip into town to pick up a few bales of alfalfa until our shipment arrives. Besides, the worst of this trip is the drive time out by Jackson's Gap." That was pretty much a flat-out lie but Avery considered it a necessary one. There was no danger in what she was doing or where she was going, just an unpleasantness that was hers, not Carlee's, to manage.

Leanne didn't look entirely convinced but she nodded and turned to go. After a few steps, she glanced back over her shoulder at Avery, her expression almost fierce in its intensity. "And you didn't make a mess of your life, Avery. You fell in love and you trusted a man who wasn't deserving of either your love or your trust but that's on him – not you."

Avery watched Leanne stride away and sighed. She appreciated the sentiment but suspected she should have been wise enough to discern that Craig wasn't the man she thought him to be at the start. Clearly, her judgement hadn't been what it should have, not then and - apparently - not now. Her attraction to Dirks was assuredly ill-advised. A man who would dig until he decided whether or not she was guilty and too bad if the verdict wasn't a good one for her. Nope, her judgement wasn't to be trusted at all, not where men were concerned.

"At least not human males, right, Jack?" She rose to scratch lightly behind his ears then walked out into the heat of the morning. It was time to start her day. She returned to the house, ready to deal with Dirks once and for all, but, judging by the nearly full pot, he'd decided to ignore her routine offer of coffee and the use of her kitchen. Wise man.

DIRKS HAD DECIDED to steer clear of Avery though the ping as her text came through tugged at him on a visceral level. Reluctantly, he'd set the phone aside without answering. A trail bar and bottle of water would have to suffice. Avery needed a cooling off period. He did, too, but not for the same reasons. He'd been on his laptop half the night, digging deeper and deeper into the past and present of Craig Danson, and he'd resumed that search long before getting Avery's text.

Her ex was a piece of work for sure. On the surface, he was a man in debt up to his eyeballs with all the typical trappings of that status. Gas card limit maxed out, hefty credit card balances for the most expensive men's clothing and liquor stores, a bank note he had no apparent means of paying for the exact amount of the deposit he'd made on a ritzy apartment the day after Avery's divorce was granted.

Below the surface was an uglier story. Avery had mentioned 'high flyer' when talking with Farley the day before. It wasn't all that difficult for Dirks to delve into the local casino's financial records. What he found made him wince. Craig liked to play blackjack for some pretty high stakes and he didn't win very often. But Dirks knew perfectly well that what was recorded was the tip of an iceberg laden with 'chips across the table' depths. The casino seemed legit in their record-keeping but there were ways for less than honest players to keep cash exchanges out of sight and off the record.

Dirks hadn't had much reason to investigate gamblers before but he knew someone who would have. He noted a couple of the names and shot off a quick e-mail to Trey Hyatt before collecting his truck keys, sunglasses and cap from the small table that stood near the door. He made the trip into town at a casual speed, his thoughts divided between the road ahead, his investigation, and his feelings for Avery. Heading straight to one end of the tree-lined street in front of the courthouse, he stepped out of the truck knowing that his boots and jeans were sufficiently worn that he wouldn't stand out from any other citizen with business in town.

He didn't expect to have any new insight but, as he walked, his gaze scanned both sides of the street. There were numerous places a man could have waited in the dusk and taken an easy shot, before disappearing without notice.

Dirks reached the spot Avery's truck had been parked but walked past without hesitating. There was nothing to see there now and his morning stroll hadn't revealed anything that he didn't already know.

The diner he'd spotted on his initial trip into town was bustling as he stepped inside. Noting the sign which had been turned from *Please Wait to Be Seated* to *Take a Seat*, he made his way to a booth near the back.

A waitress with neatly pinned hair slid him a one-page laminated menu. "Good morning. What can I get you to drink?"

"Just coffee, please."

"Do you know what you want or do you need a few minutes?"

Dirks flipped the menu over from the lunch selections to the breakfast items on the back. "You can add a BLT to that coffee."

"You got it," she said with a quick smile as he handed the menu back to her.

The coffee was strong, the bacon crispy, and the waitress wasn't nosey so Dirks enjoyed the meal. He was on his second cup of coffee when his phone alerted him of incoming mail. It was a two-lined response to his earlier query. "These are not people you want to take out to dinner. File to follow."

With a sigh, Dirks finished his coffee, paid his bill, and retrieved his cap from the bench beside him. He'd read the file Trey sent on his laptop when it came through but he didn't need it to know Danson had brought a pile of bad down on everyone around him.

Still leaving his truck where he'd parked it, he walked the short distance farther to the sheriff's office. Farley was stepping out onto the sidewalk and stopped when he saw Dirks. He pushed his hat back a little further on his head and acknowledged Dirks with an unsmiling nod.

Dirks felt sure the sheriff wasn't a fan of his after whatever Avery had told him yesterday but he didn't much care and didn't bother with niceties. "Are you keeping an eye on Danson?"

"I pretty much keep an eye on everything and everyone in my town." Farley's tone was mild, a lot milder than the hard gleam in his eyes.

"Well, someone sure seems to be getting by you on their way to Avery's place pretty often."

Farley rubbed the back of his neck and looked down at the sidewalk a minute before looking back at Dirks. "Hanna, if you want a fight, I can give you one, but I don't think it will help anything that's going on out there. I'm madder at myself than you are about that and if I had to guess, I'd say it's about the same with you."

Dirks took a deep breath and let the tension slide from his shoulders. "Yeah. I want to take a punch at somebody right now but I reckon it's not you. I've got a friend taking a hard look at the men Danson's been mixing with at the casino. I'd like to hear what you know."

"Probably not enough to help, but I'm willing to share if you've got time to take a walk."

Dirks fell into step with the sheriff and asked. "How long have you known Craig Danson?"

"Just since he married Avery. He seemed like an okay guy for a long time, not a go-getter, mind you, but decent. He set up office as a financial adviser for a while here in town but I don't think trade was real brisk. He closed the place after the first year's lease was up and Avery said he was working from the ranch. Guess that's a business you can keep pretty much online. Must have been fairly successful, though."

"Based on ...?"

"Drove some pretty sporty cars over the years and sent Carlee to a very good university. And Avery's way too smart to take care of a man who can't take care of himself."

"You don't think he bought those cars with the ranch money he was helping himself to?

"Avery told you about that, did she?" Farley shot him a sideways glance before adding, "No, that came later. I'll admit I did some digging when I started hearing rumors about his gambling. Not from Avery, mind you. She's a woman who keeps things to herself until she can't. He was making money, at least for a while. Just not from the locals."

"These guys Danson gambled with and owes money to - are they local?"

"No. Best I can tell they're from up around Birmingham. Fly in and out on a chartered plane. Pretty much always come in together. Don't frequent the women. Don't drink. Just gamble and leave."

"Any indication of cheating?"

"Not that I know ... and I would. I golf with the manager there on a regular basis."

Dirks mulled that over, making sure he didn't have any other questions that the sheriff could answer for him. Their conversation, which they'd kept in low tones, had been interrupted frequently by residents greeting their sheriff and giving Dirks the once-over. They'd walked through most of the town streets and would soon be fairly close to where Dirks had parked his truck.

"I guess Carlee's running errands."

Dirks looked up and followed the sheriff's glance across the street where the young woman was stepping out of an office supply store. She met their gazes and strode across the street toward them. She nodded at Dirks and smiled at Farley.

"Hey, Ben. Things okay with you?"

"Fine, Carlee, how about yourself?"

"I'm good. I checked with the garage and Avery's SUV is almost ready to go, said for sure by six o'clock closing. I'm going to leave my car parked beside the library. Don't tow it off, okay?"

The sheriff chuckled and shook his head. "It'd be safe from me but why don't you let me have a deputy run the SUV out there on their next round your way?"

"Well ..." Carlee smiled and shrugged "I've got my eye on a few things in town that won't fit in my trunk."

"Okay, give me your key and I'll make sure your car gets home safe."

"I'll take you up on that, but I'll bring the key and the car around to your office later. Got some places left to go for now.

And I appreciate you keeping a watch on the ranch and Avery."

"On you, too, Carlee," the sheriff reminded. "And that won't ease up until things settle down."

Carlee took her leave, acknowledging Dirks with another nod. He suspected she was as unhappy with him as Avery was.

As she walked away, Dirks commented, "She and Avery are close."

"They are that. I suspect Carlee would fight tigers for Avery. Her father's behavior can't be anything but an embarrassment to her."

Dirks took his leave of the sheriff, knowing he'd learned all he was going to and knowing, too, that nothing he'd heard was going to be of much help, just as the sheriff had said. Time to head back to the ranch and hope Trey had sent that file on the gamblers.

Time, too, to have that conversation with Avery she'd been avoiding.

AVERY PARKED the ranch truck in front of Sykes Lumber Yard and put the windows down. As she turned the engine off, Trouble stood and stretched. "I can't imagine why you insisted on coming with me," Avery commented. "I've never in my life known a cat that liked to ride in a vehicle."

But then, she had to admit, she'd never known a cat quite like Trouble. Taking a deep breath, she opened the door and slid from the truck seat. She pulled the photocopy she'd made of her attorney's newspaper notice from her purse then realized she couldn't leave her purse in the truck, not with the windows down. And she couldn't put them up and lock the doors with Trouble inside. Not in this heat.

"You're a lot of trouble," she said, "and no pun intended."

Trouble merely observed her through green eyes narrowed against the glare of the late afternoon sun. The drive had taken her longer than expected. Her GPS hadn't accounted for the poor condition of the roads.

"Stay put," she told Trouble, knowing he probably wouldn't and there was nothing she could do about it.

Slinging her purse straps over one shoulder, she closed the truck door and walked to the front entrance. The cavernous room she entered appeared to be part office and part show-room with samples of hardwood and natural stone countertop displayed. Apparently, Sykes believed in diversifying his business enterprise. There were three different desks but none of the leather chairs were occupied.

"Hello?"

Silence answered so she crossed to the wide doorway at the back of the showroom and found herself in a warehouse of sorts. Following the sound of voices, she made her way to the other end where two men in jeans and a woman in leggings and long, sleeveless shirt watched as a semi was being loaded with lumber.

They didn't seem to have heard her footsteps above the sound of the forklift so she lifted her voice a little and said, "Mr. Sykes?"

The thinner, older man turned toward her. "Yes, ma'am, I'm Mr. Sykes. Can I help you with something? I'm sorry none of us were up front. Excuse me a minute." He turned from her to the woman. "Sharon, you need to get back to your work area."

The woman – actually more like girl, Avery realized as she turned around – rolled her eyes at him but did as she was told.

She shot Avery a grin that said the girl didn't hold her responsible for being sent back to work.

Sykes turned his attention back to Avery. "Now, ma'am, what can I do for you?"

"I'm Avery Wilson - previously Avery Danson."

And just like that, his demeanor changed from helpful to border-line hostile. "You brought my check?"

The younger man turned around at the words and Avery could see the family resemblance between them.

"No, I'm afraid I don't owe you anything."

"Now see here," he stepped closer. "Your husband sent a truck out here to pick up several thousand dollars' worth of my lumber."

Avery stood her ground. "Ex-husband."

"Not at the time, he wasn't!" His face took on a dark red tone.

She handed him the photocopy she'd brought. "You'll want to read this."

He read it and glared at her. "Won't stand up in court."

"Yes, sir, it will. I have an excellent attorney."

"I'll make you and him sorry," he threatened.

The sound of a warning yowl echoed eerily through the warehouse.

"What the hell was that!"

Avery sighed as a second yowl, closer, bounced off the walls. "That would be Trouble."

She watched as the black cat made his way closer. His back was arched and his hair bristled.

"Well, get him out of here. The next time you see me will be in court."

"I'm confident I won't ever see you again, Mr. Sykes, not

once you show any attorney you engage that piece of paper. They won't waste *their* time, even if you want to waste *yours*."

With an air of calm she certainly didn't feel, Avery turned and retraced her steps through the business, scooping up the black cat as she went. Her knees were trembling, but she was careful not to show it. Not for the world would she let the man take it for fear, instead of the anger it was.

CHAPTER THIRTEEN

*D*irks couldn't decide if he should feel irritated or reprieved when he returned to the ranch and Avery was nowhere to be found. What he did feel was a hum of tension along with a thread of self-awareness because he recognized that tension reflected equal parts disappointment and concern. Nor did he fool himself that his concern for her safety was due to no more than a bone-deep military training that gave him a sense of responsibility for civilians in general.

Telling himself he was an idiot for being glad that one black cat was missing as well – after all, how much protection could a cat provide - he settled in to read what Trey had sent. Superficially, there was nothing that would alarm the average reader. Craig had been playing with a tight trio of independently-wealthy high rollers. That appellation - independently wealthy - should have implied that winning or losing wouldn't necessarily be a big deal, right? It was all about the game. But Trey had dug deep. With deepening misgivings, Dirks read on through the misfortunes that had plagued a long line of fringe players. Some had been *lucky* enough to win large amounts from them, others unlucky enough to lose sums they couldn't repay. Dirks flipped through pages of newspaper photocopy, a drowning on a boating excursion in the Keys, here, a hunting accident in Texas canyon country, there, and even a suicide or two.

The accompanying report had been written in Trey's sparse style and, really, he didn't need to use many words. Trey knew Dirks was more than capable of reading between the lines. Danson had put himself opposite some really bad guys, himself and anyone associated with him.

Restless and mad as hell at a man too stupid to know what he'd done, Dirks reached for his cap and strode out toward the paddocks.

Tucker was leading a horse back to the barn as a small car pulled out toward the open road beyond the ranch. Tucker greeted him with a smile that faded quickly. "You don't look happy."

"Understatement."

"Anything I need to know?"

Dirks hesitated then shook his head. "Nothing you don't already, really. Danson's an asshole."

"No argument, there. After I put this fellow up, I'm headed out to check the progress on the enclosed riding path. The contractor finally showed back up to work. Want to tag along?"

Restless and, admittedly, curious, Dirks nodded and fell into step with Tucker.

As THEY BOUNCED along what was little more than a cow path, Dirks asked, "What, exactly, is an enclosed riding path?"

"Well," Tucker scratched his head, "I don't really know how to describe it. I don't have anything to compare it to. It's an

Avery invention. She got the idea from Sergeant Mallette who keeps pushing for her to let him ride outside the paddock."

"That's the young man who lost his vision overseas?"

"Yeah, an IED." Tucker's tone was grim. "Stinkin' shame."

"It always is," Dirks agreed. "So young Mallette wants to extend his boundaries."

"And Avery is determined to help him do that. She set aside five acres and hired one of the local contractors to enclose a walking trail. Took us several nights to lay out the design to make the best use of the acreage because she wanted it to be something that would give the rider a sense of open spaces, not just a bigger circle than the riding paddocks they're usually in when they ride. There couldn't be any angles to give a horse reason to stop, so it's all curves."

Tucker stopped the truck close to several large trees that Dirks thought were some kind of oak but not the huge, live oak that covered so much of the South. The sun was large and red and almost riding the horizon. Before them were a half dozen or so tanned, leathered workmen in well-worn jeans and tee shirts and what seemed to him like a maze of fence posts, hundreds of them, with no particular pattern.

As they climbed out of the truck and walked closer, Dirks could see the railing that was going up. Instead of three evenly spaced rows of railing similar to that around the riding paddocks, six boards were being fitted top to bottom in the middle of the span. And, instead of being placed on the outside of the posts for a nice, neat look, they were being nailed on the inside. Dirks opened his mouth to ask about the oddity then realized the safety of the design. A rider without sight would not find his boot hung in an unexpected and potentially dangerous position against a fence post. Avery was taking no chances with the well-being of Mallette, or any sightless riders who placed their trust in her. She wasn't building for beauty but for safety.

Tucker shook hands with one of the men, greeting him by name, and slapping an arm lightly to his shoulder. "Dirks, this is my cousin, once or twice removed. Hadley Small, Dirks Hanna."

Dirks held out a hand and found the man had a grip that matched the muscles bulging from his forearm.

Hadley, it turned out, was foreman for the group. He glanced at his watch and called it a day. He walked back toward the trees with Tucker and Dirks even as he kept an eye on his crew while they gathered up their tools and placed them in the job boxes attached to the work truck.

"I'm glad to see you and your men back at work here," Tucker said.

"Yeah," Hadley agreed, "me, too. Close to home for a change. What happened here, anyway? Jake just pulled us off out of the blue and sent us to another job two counties over. I asked him more than once about coming back to finish but he wouldn't even talk with me about it."

"Just a misunderstanding," Tucker said, but his voice was grim.

Hadley nodded. "It happens," he said easily, "but I'm glad we're going to finish what we started. I don't like leaving things undone. Besides, I like Ms. Avery and what she's got going on out here. I wish my sister, Jean, lived closer. Her second kid was just diagnosed with autism. She's got him in a really good program where she is, but I think this thing with the horses could help, too."

"Jean moved to New Orleans when she got married, didn't she? I'll ask Avery to check out some riding facilities in that area. She's got a bunch of contacts," Tucker offered. "I won't keep you from supper, Hadley. I just wanted to make sure work had started again. Looks like y'all are making good progress, too."

"The railing won't take as long as the fence posts," Hadley assured him.

The two chatted a few minutes before Hadley rounded up his crew for the trip back to town. Tucker and Dirks pulled out right behind the work truck.

As they rode back to the barn, Dirks asked, "What was the misunderstanding?"

Tucker told him about Craig's sleight of hand with the lumber while Dirks listened in silence. "I expect that much material cost a pretty penny," was all he said.

"Close to eight thousand, according to Carlee," Tucker agreed.

"Seems like a complicated ruse."

Tucker shot him a look. "Yep, but it worked."

Dirks didn't answer. Apparently, it *had* worked but something felt off about the whole thing. There seemed a pretty big risk to Craig of finding himself in some real legal trouble since he'd identified himself openly to the owner of the lumber yard. Dirks didn't like the sense of growing desperation that implied.

Tucker stopped the truck in front of his barn and Dirks followed the younger man inside to help with the evening feed. He missed his gym time though there was plenty to do around here to at least stretch his muscles, if not really work them. Morning and evening push-ups did that but he was getting bored with that routine and craved the weights in his basement gym.

As they fed and hayed horses, Dirks was increasingly aware of Avery's absence and the slowly gathering dark. He heard

Leanne before Tucker did, probably because he was listening so hard for the sound of an engine to signal Avery's return.

"Tucker! Tucker, where are you?"

Before either could respond, Leanne ran breathlessly into the barn her face filled with fear and fury. "Carlee's hurt. She was bringing Avery's SUV back to the ranch and someone ran her off the road just past the old Roberts' place. Deliberately – that was the word she used. The vehicle rolled and she hit her head. She thinks she lost consciousness for a while but her voice was weak and I couldn't hear everything she was saying. Then she disconnected and I can't get her back."

Dirks' first thought iced the blood in his veins. Avery was somewhere along that same road with a person who clearly intended to do her harm.

Tucker wheeled to run and Dirks grabbed his arm. "With me," he said, taking charge because that's what he did. And Tucker, looking shell-shocked and frantic, nodded.

Dirks turned to Leanne. "Do you have a gun?"

She nodded, her face white. "I do and I'm good with it. What the hell is going on?"

"I'm not sure, but keep whatever firearm you have on you and loaded until we get back. If Avery takes another route and misses Carlee and us, keep her here whatever it takes. Call 911 to make sure emergency service is headed to Carlee, then call the sheriff's office to send someone out here until I get back. Tucker and I will make sure Carlee is safe." He wasn't sure if her startled glance had to do with the avalanche of orders, the fact that he thought a loaded gun was a necessity, or the familiarity with which he'd spoken of Avery. No 'Ms. Avery' or 'Ms. Wilson' now.

With Tucker giving directions, Dirks drove with the speed and skill he'd learned in emergency training, navigating sharp curves as easily as straightaways. He didn't like the fact that the light was fading, partly due to the time and partly to the overhang of clouds. "How far is this place?"

"Ten miles or so." Tucker was clearly worried. "It's not the route I usually take. It's shorter in distance but the road isn't nearly as good." He was silent a moment, then repeated what Leanne had said. "Deliberately. But why? None of this makes sense to me."

No, Dirks thought grimly, violence was pretty senseless to most rational people. "Just how well do you know Craig?"

"Better than I want to."

Dirks thought that was a cryptic answer and shot Tucker a sideways glance. "Meaning?"

"Craig always seemed a pretty good guy in the early years when he and Carlee first started coming here and later, but distracted, you know, like he didn't see anyone but his daughter. You could tell Carlee was his world and she was just a crushed little girl grieving for her mama and sister. But even once he and Avery got married, he didn't have much to do with me, or Leanne when she came on board. When things started going bad, though, he wanted to hang out more at the barn, staring at the horses and telling me how much all this was worth and how hard he'd worked for Avery to have her dream."

"Did he? Work hard, that is?"

"I'm not saying he didn't, but it wasn't at the barn or anything to do with the running of the place. The really hard, physical part - that was all Avery's sweat."

"When he was talking about his hard work was he sad, angry?"

"Mostly a little drunk and kind of sloppy with it – not falling down drunk – just, well whining, I guess, and not realizing how weak he sounded."

Dirks thought about that without answering. That was his impression of Craig. Weak. The kind of coward who'd take a man's money and send him to pick up a horse that wasn't his to sell. Perhaps, if he'd had a little to drink for courage, even frustrated enough to put bullets through the windshield of a vehicle he already knew was empty. But did he have the nerve to run another vehicle off the road, thinking it was Avery taking her SUV back to the ranch? Yeah, maybe, but maybe not.

Would Markham have hung around to do that? To what purpose? To scare Avery into letting him take the young horse his boss was determined to have? Again, maybe, but something wasn't adding up for him.

A strand of wire fence flashed on their left and Tucker said, "This is the edge of the Roberts' place."

Dirks took his foot off the gas. "Watch to your right," he directed tersely. And Dirks watched his side of the road.

An instant later he saw headlights angled away from them. "There, on the left."

In a sharp bend just ahead, the SUV was sideways some distance from the graveled edge of the road. Dirks deftly swung to the shoulder of the road but barely had the truck in park before Tucker leapt out. Dirks hit the flashers and followed suit. In the distance a siren wailed.

As he followed Tucker, Dirks swiftly made note of several factors. There wasn't really a ditch which was probably a good thing. Otherwise, the SUV would most likely have flipped even harder during the rollover. Also good was that no trees crowded the edge of the roadway as was so often the case. The vehicle had stopped on its own rather than by slamming into the unforgiving trunk of a tree.

Tucker looked up as Dirks reached the car. "She's hurt and

the door's jammed." There was over-whelming fear and frustration in his voice.

The window was down and Dirks could see Carlee's head leaned against the seat. He moved in close and spoke her name.

Carlee opened her eyes and gave him a wobbly grin that faded quickly as she murmured, "Glad it was me and not Avery." Dirks slipped a penlight from his pocket and her eyelids lowered as the light flashed across her face. A nasty purpling bruise already marred her temple and cheekbone. She'd need x-rays and observation at a minimum. He swept the light across the side of the SUV quickly, noting the dints and scratches from the rollover. Dirks didn't ask her any of the questions crowding his mind. Time for that later. The sound of sirens was reassuringly close now.

"Carlee." When she didn't respond immediately, he spoke her name more sharply.

She opened her eyes. "I'm here. Hurts."

"Where?" Dirks held her gaze with his as the ambulance slid to a stop on the road beside them.

"Head ... neck ... shoulder. Everything." Speaking was clearly an effort for her.

As the first EMT reached them, Dirks told him, "Driver is conscious and coherent but she took a hard hit to her head and her door is jammed. What kind of tools do you have?"

The EMT called back to his partner and within minutes the door was opened and they were crouched beside Carlee assessing her condition with Tucker hovering, still visibly anxious.Dirks waited patiently for the EMTs to finish their initial assessment and communicate with the local hospital. When they backed away to set up a stretcher, he moved in aware of Tucker pressed close to his side.

"Carlee, I need to know. Was this an accident?"

Slowly, she rolled her head side to side, wincing at her own movement. "No, he made a pass, too close. I swerved, but held the road. So he turned and came back. Nothing accidental about that."

"He?" Dirks kept his tone calm and non-judgmental but he was seething inside.

"Maybe. For sure a pick-up ... black Ford ...," her voice was slurring now. Carlee's eyes drifted closed. "... and the motorcycle ..."

Dirks had seen no sign of any other vehicle. "What motorcycle, Carlee?" But Carlee had slipped into unconsciousness.

Dirks and Tucker watched as the skilled rescue workers carefully maneuvered Carlee onto the stretcher.

"Craig drives a black Ford." Tucker clenched his hands into fists. "I'm going with her. Then I'm going to kill that son-of-a-bitch."

Dirks didn't censure the threat. He was feeling pretty violent himself. "I'll bring Avery to the hospital after I make sure the sheriff can place someone to guard the ranch for a few hours." Dirks intended to have someone he trusted to help with security by morning but it would take a little while to get them mobilized.

As he watched Tucker climb into the back of the ambulance over the half-hearted protests of the EMTs, he realized this job had just taken a real personal turn for him. He knew he'd have to deal with the repercussions of that at some point. For now his only focus was Avery's safety and the safe-keeping of the animals and place she loved.

BACK AT THE RANCH, *at last. What an exhausting and unpleasant day. I must, however, confess to the truth that I elected – and was not the least coerced – into accompanying Ms. Gorgeous. But, truthfully, what else was a cat to do when she seems clearly willing to put herself in harm's way without a thought to the consequences? Nor can I so much as chasten her over the habit.*

This is not the first time I have found it a serious impediment that humans and felines do not share a common language. While my superior intellect allows me to understand them, alas, their somewhat less sophisticated brains do not give them the same ability. And even when they speak, it is too often of banalities that suffice nothing. Even more frustrating of late, is that the equine housed in these facilities cannot communicate with me in the least. I think they have knowledge that would be of distinct help in identifying the hooligan responsible for these unfortunate occurrences.

And, of course, we must come straight to the barn. Not so much as a saucer filled with milk am I to have until Ms. Gorgeous knows her beloved equine are still safe. Though, to be honest and fair, that was an exquisite lunch I had. The lovely lady has somehow discerned my preference for lightly grilled fish.

"There you are! Why haven't you answered your phone? I've been scared sick for you!"

Oh dear, judging by the alarm in the young Mrs. Leanne's voice I suspect it is a good thing I had lunch at all. Dinner may well be unfortunately late.

AVERY LISTENED in stunned silence as Leanne explained what had happened. The young woman had been pacing in front of the barn with a shotgun. Before Leanne had even finished speaking, Avery turned on her heel to get back in the truck.

Leanne grabbed her wrist. "Avery, you can't. Mr. Hanna said you were to wait here."

"*Mr. Hanna* can go to the devil. I've got to get to Carlee!" No doubt, she sounded as frantic as she felt. Her heart literally pounded against the wall of her chest. "She'll be terrified and she could be -" Her voice just quit on her midsentence at the thought of losing the young woman she'd come to love as a daughter.

"Listen to me. I just got off the phone with Tucker, just this minute. They've taken her for x-rays of her neck and back, just to be safe, but Tucker said she can move arms, legs, fingers and toes and she was speaking coherently and seemed stronger. In fact, she was arguing with him and the nurses about needing to get back here to the ranch, to you. To take care of you, Avery. Tucker's got her, I promise, and," Leanne's voice turned even more grim if possible as she added, "you and I have to take care of things here."

CHAPTER FOURTEEN

*A*very's gaze scanned the pasture ahead of her. Everything was still and quiet, except for the occasional call of a night owl. She gave a quick glance over her shoulder as she began her second round of the inner perimeter fencing where groups of horses had gathered together for the night. Ridiculous as it might seem to some, the knowledge that the black cat trailed steadily at her side gave her a sense that the cat had her back. Now and again, he trotted lightly ahead but he always circled back and around her. Someone might step out from behind a stout tree trunk up ahead, but she felt certain Trouble would know and warn her if anyone tried to sneak up behind.

Her last text from Tucker had been reassuring. Between each round of tests, Carlee started another argument with the hospital staff about needing to get home. Avery's last response had been "Sit on her if you have to but she's not to leave".

She and Leanne had separated, each walking the same route in reverse, through the barns and then around the pastures. They crossed paths for a second time in front of the huddled yearlings where Avery stopped in her tracks, struck by a sudden thought she felt incredibly guilty about not having before that moment.

"Leanne, is Jason okay with you being here?"

"Jason had reserve duty this weekend," the young woman said easily. "He left a few days early to spend some time with his mom and dad."

Remorse bit sharply at Avery and she sighed. "So he doesn't know you're risking your safety for me? Is that what you're not saying?" She knew she should send the young woman home but suspected she'd get absolutely nowhere with that argument.

Leanne's response proved that point. "This place is my livelihood and my second home, Avery, and you're way more than my employer. Jason knows I can take care of myself just like I trust him to take care of himself. I'll tell him everything when he gets home but I don't want to distract him by telling him via cell phone because he'd want to be here – for both of us."

"And I appreciate you, I really do, but God knows I don't want anything to happen to you."

"I know you don't, and I feel the same in return and - heaven knows why - but I'm glad that damned cat is marching along with you. You're the target. We both know that, you and the horses. Anything happens to me it would just be collateral damage so to speak. I'm willing to take my chances to help keep you and them safe. You'd do it for me."

Avery couldn't argue because it was true. Of course, she would. All she could do was nod, eyes stinging and emotion constricting her throat. God, what a nightmare this all was.

I DARESAY anyone wishing harm upon any facet of Summer Valley

Ranch would find themselves facing two determined women with loaded firearms. As a matter of fact, right about now, Ms. Gorgeous looks very much as if she were wishing for something or someone to shoot.

Ah, the sound of a vehicle approaching has reached their awareness moments behind mine, but then they lack my highly developed sense of hearing. Should humans ever develop the extreme faculties of the feline species, they would be lethal indeed. Unlike myself, the ladies doubtless do not yet realize there are two vehicles, rather than one, and the second of those is Mr. Military. Both my female warriors are easing cautiously toward the drive that fronts the barns, guns at the ready.

No blue lights flashing but it is a sheriff's car at the fore. I suppose that is the equivalent of the cavalry arriving but I would put all of my money on Mr. Military should a true battle ever ensue.

AVERY HELD her gun with barrel lowered as a deputy stepped out of each side of the patrol car.

"Evening, ladies." The driver of the car tipped his broad-brimmed hat. "Sheriff Farley sent me and Ray to watch out for things so you could get to the hospital." He was young, clean-cut and solemn. Whatever he may have thought about facing two women with shot guns was concealed behind a neutral expression.

His partner, older by at least a decade, eyed their weapons warily and leaned against the hood of the car, letting the younger man keep the lead.

"Have you heard anything, Matt?" Avery had known him too many years to stand on ceremony or be intimidated by his official demeanor.

"About Ms. Carlee?" The younger man's lips curved just the smallest bit. "Just that she's bending the ear of any and everyone standing between her and leaving that hospital. Better them than me. Rather take my chances with whatever's going down here. Ms. Carlee's one determined young lady when it comes to this ranch and you."

Avery drew a deep breath. It was small reassurance but she'd take what she could get. Then she tensed as another set of headlights swung toward them.

Before she could swing her gun up into position, the deputy spoke quickly. "That'd be Mr. Hanna. He followed us out after talking with the sheriff. Said he'd take you into town once we were here."

"You'll be here all night?" She needed that reassurance. Needed to know Jack and his offspring, as well as the many talented and useful rescue horses that depended upon her, would be safe.

"Yes, ma'am. Mr. Hanna plans to have security in place come morning but we're here until then."

Avery shot the deputy a look but held any comment for Dirks who had apparently taken a great deal upon himself. She had not, would not, forget that he was investigating her. Had not, would not, forget his lack of trust in her.

Even with that, she couldn't deny the leap of her pulse as he stepped down from his truck and walked toward them with that long stride.

"Deputies." His greeting was for them, but his gaze was for Avery alone. "You'll take it from here?"

"Yes, sir. We're here until Sheriff Farley sends replacements or calls us in because you've got it covered."

Dirks, nodded in response, his glance like a feather touch on Avery's face. "You ready?"

"Yes," Avery said, meeting his look evenly, before turning to Leanne. "Go home and get some rest. Or, better yet, why don't you stay here since Jason's not home? At least you'd know the deputies were just outside."

Leanne shook her head. "I'll be fine at home. No one's after me. Collateral damage only, remember?"

Suddenly unutterably weary, Avery told Dirks, "I'm going to take a last look at Jack before we go."

Feeling his eyes on her back as she turned and scooped the black cat up in her arms, Avery kept that back straight and her stride long and even, pretending with every fiber of her being that she didn't know how keenly Dirks Hanna was watching her every move.

She'd surprised the cat with her action. She felt it in the immediate stiffness of his muscles. Trouble was just not your cuddly housecat. To her surprise though, he relaxed against her as she walked into the barn. But he'd matched her minute by minute through the long day which suddenly seemed never ending and she suspected he was as tired as she. She scratched his head lightly, and again he surprised her, this time by arching his body and pushing ever so slightly against her fingers. She wondered if he were truly showing pleasure at the touch or just accepting her need for the contact. For just a moment, she cradled him close as she stood in the hallway of the barn, watching as Jack put his head over the stall door to nicker a greeting.

She gently placed Trouble on the hall mat and moved closer to rub Jack's forehead, smiling because the huge horse pushed against her caress more vigorously than the cat had done. But Jack was hers, after all. He didn't just allow her attentions, he demanded them as his right. It amazed her that some people did not realize domesticated animals craved a kind touch as much as most humans did.

For a brief moment she wrapped her arms around Jack's

neck, knowing she would risk life and limb to keep him safe, always. Stepping back, she smiled tiredly down at Trouble who sat watching them both with a somewhat aloof gaze.

"Come on, mister, let's get you settled in the house while I grab my purse." She turned to leave but Trouble didn't move. Avery stopped and looked back. "Hey, Trouble, come on. You know I don't have a kitty door."

With a deliberate look from her to Jack and back again, Trouble jumped onto the canvas chair just outside Jack's stall. As Avery watched, the sleek black cat settled himself into the crouched position of a cat relaxed but ready to move fast if speed was needed.

"You're something, aren't you," Avery said in wonderment.

Trouble blinked without moving.

"Thank you," she whispered, then left the cat to guard the animal she loved more than life.

DIRKS WONDERED if the cab of his truck felt as close, as intimate, to Avery as it did to him. He also wondered, with a touch of bitter amusement, if she'd cooled off any since their last conversation, a conversation that now seemed eons ago instead of little more than a day. From the way she sat, slightly turned so that he was presented with little more than her shoulder, he'd guessed she hadn't.

Dirks had learned long ago that the best way, sometimes the only way, to get through a thing was to make a way, particularly when it wasn't going to present itself on its own.

"You may as well know I've pulled in a couple of favors. I have a security team set to arrive by daylight."

She shifted slightly so that she was facing straight ahead and shot him a glance.

Bingo. At least he had her attention, although that might not prove to be a good thing.

"I've got money. I can pay for my own security."

"Not these guys, you can't. They don't work for civilians."

The glare she gave him was incredulous. "That sounds like something more unethical than what you've accused me of doing."

He glanced from the road to her for a brief second. "First, it would only be unethical if government money was paying for their services. Second, I haven't accused you of anything. I gave you the facts of my investigation and I'll work just as hard to prove you innocent as guilty."

"I am innocent and I don't want any favors from you. I'll reimburse you whatever this costs." Her voice was as fierce as the expression on her face.

Dirks shrugged. "Fine, if you've got a cabin in the mountains they can use for a month or two this summer, they'll be just as happy to use yours as mine."

The irritated sigh she expelled brought a curve to his lips but he was careful not to let it become a full-fledged smile.

"Look, if we can have a truce for just a little while, I'd like to talk about what happened to Carlee this evening."

"Leanne said some jerk ran her off the road. God, she could have been killed." Dirks noticed her hands clench in her lap before she added, "And it very well could have been, likely was, some thug associated with Craig's gambling debt."

"Carlee said the vehicle was a black Ford pickup. Tucker suspects it might have been her dad. Farley's going to bring him in for questioning. If he can find him."

Avery turned to face him at that. "No." Her voice was emphatic. "There's no way Craig would do that. He adores Carlee. He would never hurt his own daughter."

"She was in your SUV, remember?"

That seemed to give her momentary pause, but only for a moment. Avery shook her head in obvious bewilderment. "Things just don't fit. How would Craig know Carlee – or I, if he believed it was me – would be on *that* road at *that* time of day unless he followed Carlee from town? That road isn't the most direct route back to the ranch. And if he *did* follow her then he'd know it was Carlee and not me."

"Do you never come that way?"

"Yeah – sure I do – sometimes. There's a really nice fruit and vegetable stand about midway. At least once a week or so one of us, Carlee or I, will make a run to stock up. It's a pretty drive and actually not any farther, just slower because of all the curves."

Dirks sorted through events of the day in his mind. Both Carlee and Avery had left the ranch that morning, Avery in the ranch truck, Carlee in her car. Craig was most likely avoiding town and any face-to-face with either of them – or the sheriff. The spine of his back didn't seem his strongest point, but then neither was his character. After Markham's failed visit, Craig was also likely watching the ranch as much as he could, trying to figure out his next plan so he could easily have seen both women leave the ranch and followed them. After that, all he had to do was wait at some point, just outside of town, for Avery's return. He'd have no reason to associate Avery's SUV with Carlee driving, rather than Avery. And Dirks strongly suspected that the side pass at the SUV had been more spur of the moment than an actual plan.

If Dirks had to guess, Craig was running on nerves and panic, out of money, out of a plan, and doing his best to avoid the bad asses he'd let loose upon himself. He wasn't sure he completely bought in on a Craig set on murdering Avery. She seemed to be his golden goose. He had no legal claim any more but there was Carlee, still, as a tie between them, and he suspected Craig wasn't thinking all that straight about now.

He said as much to Avery. They had almost reached the turn in to the hospital when she finally spoke, and all she said was, "I don't know. I just don't know."

The little-girl-lost quality of her voice tugged as hard at Dirks emotionally as her earlier kick-ass stance, caught in the headlights of his truck, legs braced, and shotgun cradled in her arm had yanked at him physically.

He angled smoothly into a parking slot near the main entrance, hearing the release of Avery's seatbelt almost before he had the truck in park. Acting on feeling rather than thought, he caught her hand in his before she could hit the door latch. The action – his hand on hers – caused her to turn in surprise, eyes wide and lips opened to question or protest or curse. He had no idea which.

Before she could do or say anything, before his mind could convince him of the greater wisdom in restraint, Dirks captured those open lips with his, tugging her gently closer with his hand. To his wonderment, instead of snatching that hand away, instead of pulling back, she leaned in. He deepened the kiss, feeling things he hadn't felt for a woman in a long time, emotions mixed with purely physical lust.

His free hand cradled her face and he fought the urge to do anything else with that hand, to explore other aspects of the woman who was an unexpected wrecking ball to his senses – at least for now.

When Avery slowly pulled away, he let her go, released her hand.

Her eyes, which had fluttered closed under his kiss, were

wide again. She touched the hand he'd held to her lips, then said faintly, "Well ... damn."

She fumbled to open the door behind her, eyes still locked with his, until she turned and stepped down out of the truck.

He followed her across the parking lot, fighting a grin. Yeah. Damn.

AVERY WATCHED CARLEE SLEEP, firmly pushing thoughts of Dirks and the kiss they'd shared out of her mind. That kiss, and her reaction to it, was for later. Much later.

Avery had tried to make Tucker go home, back to the ranch for rest, but he'd refused. Heading with Dirks to the hospital cafeteria and twenty-four-hour grill was as far as he was willing to go from Carlee.

Her step-daughter, no, not step-daughter - *daughter* - child of her heart, even if not her body, seemed restful but Avery's stomach was in knots once more. How could she protect her? How could her father have put her at risk?

Nurses came and went, barely making a ripple in Avery's awareness. After a battery of tests and scans, the doctor had given an all clear the previous evening, no back or neck injury, no brain trauma. Doubtless sore muscles, aches and pains to go with the bruises, but otherwise okay. Carlee had made him promise she'd be released after the night of observation he insisted upon. He'd promised on condition that Carlee showed no signs of concussion through the night.

Still Avery could not overcome the bone-deep fear that gripped her, not even when Carlee opened her eyes and smiled. "You look a mess and I'm sure I look a hell of a lot worse." Her voice sounded a bit groggy but her gaze was clear.

"Carlee, I'm so sorry."

"Don't. Avery, just don't. None of this is your fault and we both know whose fault it is."

"I don't know what to do to keep you safe."

"It's your safety we have to worry about, Avery, not mine. Whoever was in that truck made a mistake this time, but we might not be so lucky the next."

"I still can't believe Craig did this."

"I can't be sure it was my dad or his truck. Tucker's convinced but everything happened so fast. Maybe Dad wasn't driving, maybe he was, but it's his fault either way." Carlee's eyes were bleak. She closed them briefly and then opened them again. "And I'm sorry about your SUV. I guess it's back in the shop again."

"Yes, and someone is going to have to explain to me why the air bags didn't deploy."

"Actually, it's not all that uncommon. There are a lot of factors that come into play." The sound of Dirks' voice from the doorway pulled Avery's gaze like a magnet. He'd been up as long as any of them, but the dark stubble where he hadn't had time to shave looked like pure, rugged male rather than the mess Carlee had proclaimed her to be.

Avery pulled her thoughts and her attention back to Carlee who had glanced up as the two men came back into the room, but closed her eyes again almost immediately. "Carlee, are you hurting?"

"No, just trying to get my thoughts together. Avery, you've got to change your will so the ranch doesn't come to me if anything happens to you."

"Not going to happen." Avery was amazed at the steadiness in her voice when renewed fury at Craig pulsed through her veins with every beat of her heart.

"You've got to. Something's broken inside my dad's head if

he thinks I'd use your money to help him out of the mess he's in. That would be the only explanation for his crazy actions. Who knows what he'll do next. Or maybe he told those goons he owes that you're the only thing standing between them and repayment. And who knows what *they'll* do next."

"Even if I was willing, and I'm not, who else would I leave it to? I'm the only child of an only child and no surviving relatives."

"Leave it to Tucker or Leanne. You're not going to be safe until he – or they - know he can't get his hands on anything through me."

"Carlee, I'm just not going to do that. You can tell him I did, but you helped make the ranch. It's yours as much as mine."

Carlee just shook her head but Avery could tell by her step-daughter's expression that she wasn't done with this particular argument. That was fine. Avery knew it wasn't an argument Carlee would win no matter how long or loudly she pursued it.

DIRKS STEPPED out onto the curving sidewalk at the front entrance of the hospital while Avery helped Carlee dress for the trip home. The doctor would have preferred to keep her one more night but Carlee was adamant about her release, reminding him of his promise, and he finally conceded to her insistence.

The morning air was still faintly cool, but that wasn't going to last long. Late summer had hit central Alabama with a vengeance.

Preoccupied as Dirks was, his subconscious registered the shiny Goldwing barely a split second before his conscious. The man stowing his helmet ignored Dirks until he spoke.

"You were at the courthouse." Dirks had no doubt. The bulge of muscle across shoulders, neck and back. The dark, buzz-cut hair. Dirks' brain recorded the tiny tattoo on the back of one hand. It was an odd design, apropos of nothing that Dirks could tell. He'd want to look that up later, though he suspected it had little or nothing to do with the matter at hand.

The other man turned, a placid expression belying the sharp gaze. "Was I?"

"And at the scene of a wreck last night."

The expression tightened. "You are mistaken."

No street thug, this one. His speech was smooth with no hint of accent. His clothes mirrored his bike. Expensive.

"I'll be watching to see if you turn up anywhere near Summer Valley Ranch. It would be a mistake on your part."

"Threatening me is a mistake on yours. A much worse mistake."

Dirks watched as the other man retrieved the helmet he'd just stowed and threw a leg over his bike.

Dirks smiled grimly. "As long as I don't see you again there won't be any problem."

Dirks stood back as the motorcycle engine caught and roared. Just as he'd made note of the tattoo, he quickly memorized the tag. He'd share the tag and his concerns with Farley.

The rider didn't look back as he wheeled his bike smoothly into the flow of traffic on the street in front of the hospital.

CHAPTER FIFTEEN

*W*ell, it certainly seems as if young Carlee is not one to go about all pallid and weak in the face of adversity. Likely, she was never one to skive off school as a child. She beat Ms. Gorgeous out the door this morning, stooping to give me a stroke on her way past with that morning cup of brew - joe or java or by whatever name it is called - most all of my humans seem to enjoy. The drink is an enigma to me and I can only suppose the taste is more appealing than the odor which is not unpleasant but certainly nothing equivalent to an enticing dish of cream or broth.

Carlee herself is somewhat of a puzzle as well, or rather I find certain aspects of her behavior to be so. That light stroke along my back, for one, which she never fails to bestow. It is not for show, of that I am confident as there is frequently no one about to witness, such as now. I just would never take her for a cat human, certainly not that Carlee is any way disagreeable toward me for she never is. It's more, rather, that she takes scant – if any – notice of me much of the time. In fairness, I must ask myself if my vanity is slighted that not all humans recognize the depths of my intellect and sleuthing skills. But vanity *aside, the Egyptians knew what they were doing when they proclaimed the cat as the great god.*

Ms. Gorgeous has certainly come to understand and appreciate my abilities and there she is now, moving with that exquisite grace of hers. Ah, and lovely person that she is, her first move is to fill a clean bowl with the sweetest cream. It is this awareness and consideration of my basic needs that seems lacking in Carlee, as it is in so many other humans. Nor does Ms. Gorgeous select just any bowl for my morning repast, mind you, but one of exquisitely patterned and quite delicate china, a fitting vessel for a god. Heh, heh. She is a woman of refinement, one who understands that presentation is essential to the art of fine dining.

Oh dear! I discern the sound of another truck and trailer entering the premises. I do hope it isn't a return of the nasty Mr. Markham. A quick glance at Ms. Gorgeous reassures me on that score. Though she has heard as well, her expression remains serene. At ease, I set my attention to the delectable dish before me. Whatever the humans are about this morning, I have at least these few moments of peace before I once more set my attention to pulling the latest pieces of the puzzle together. It's unlikely that whoever forced Ms. Gorgeous' SUV into a roll-over with Carlee driving is not part of the threats that face Summer Valley Ranch.

Is the ex-husband childishly acting out his anger at having lost the court battle? Was the intent to scare and intimidate or was it a serious attempt at murder? Or was it the despicable Markham, or a hired minion, at the wheel? Should I anticipate a next move as being some threat in the guise of a warning or blackmail attempt from one or the other of them?

Oh, dear, I did not nearly enjoy my lovely cream as much as I might have for mulling over these possibilities. I must more closely guard myself to ensure I remain in the moment when enjoying such elegant repast.

However, now that I have finished, I'll take a pass through the barns. I've no doubt that the security team Mr. Military engaged is as vigilant as any human could be, but they are – after all – only human.

AVERY WAITED as the woman clad in jeans and tee shirt stepped out of the big rig. Her hair was pulled through a ball cap in a loose pony tail. "Malone, it's so good to see you again."

The other woman returned the smile. "I'm glad you called me. The video you sent of the mare was pretty impressive. She has a nice stride and a really quick turn and I know I can trust your judgement on her disposition." She turned a sweeping gaze on the barns and paddocks. "I just love this place. It's so well laid-out. My barns are such a hodge-podge, us throwing things together as we needed them."

Avery laughed. "It was sometimes hard not to do that myself but I stuck to my vision even though it sometimes meant waiting until the money was right to move ahead on the next phase. And how is the rodeo business?"

"Wickedly paced. I made the finals again, hauled twelve outside horses and three of my own. I thought I'd be slowing down by now, but ... busy is better."

Avery had met the woman just a few years earlier. She knew how difficult life had been for her.

"I did much appreciate the note you sent." Malone's voice was quiet and Avery caught a glimpse of the shadows that lingered in her eyes. "Now about this mare."

"She's in barn one." They fell into step together as Avery continued to talk about the horse. "Tucker has given her a clean bill of health, x-rays and all. No sign of bone chips or spurs that would give you any problems later on. I have no idea where she came from or what sent her to the kill pen.

She was a rack of bones with sad, sad eyes but no one who saw her then would recognize her now. This girl is gorgeous."

"Personality?"

"Sweet but not particularly peaceful. She's playful, too much so for most of our clients though a few of the more skilled riders enjoy her as much as I do. More than once, when I'd watch her racing across the pasture, dodging the other horses in some game of her own, I'd think of you. It was Leanne who finally accepted that she needed a different kind of job. All of us agree we could probably find ways and places for her to be useful here but we're not where she'll be happiest."

They stepped into the cool of the barn and Avery led the way to a wide stall. "Meet JJ's Red Jasmine. We call her Jaz."

At the sound of her voice, Jaz immediately abandoned the rubber ball hung from a tether for her entertainment and stepped closer, thrusting her head over the stall door and nickering a greeting.

Malone moved close, rubbing her hand over the broad forehead, clearly delighted when the mare pushed back against the caress in pleasure. "What eyes, what beautiful eyes. Where's her halter?"

Avery chuckled, taking the halter and lead from a horseshoe hook outside the stall. She handed it over and stepped aside, giving control to the accomplished horsewoman she knew Malone to be.

Malone led the mare to her trailer and spent a moment brushing and grooming. "I know she doesn't need it, she absolutely gleams, but I need a moment for her to get to know me and to figure out which saddle will be most comfortable to her."

Avery would have done the same. Saddles were always personal choices of feel and fit for both horse and rider.

After lifting and checking each hoof, Malone saddled the mare with what Avery could see was well-used but meticulously-cared for tack. Minutes later, horse and rider were in the paddock. Malone spent time slowly warming up the mare's muscles before moving her seamlessly from one gait to another. Skillfully, perfectly in sync, they executed a series of side-passes, small circles, spins, and backing. After half an hour, Malone was grinning, her delight evident.

In the time Malone had been working the mare, Tucker had moved to stand beside Avery, then Leanne and finally Carlee. They watched together as Malone walked the mare to cool her out.

"From that expression, I'd say Jaz may just have found her 'forever' home." Leanne sounded delighted.

"Well, at least she'll be off the feed and vet bill." Carlee commented.

"She's earned her keep in the time she's been here," Leanne returned quickly.

Though aware of the exchange, Avery didn't comment on it. Leanne's tone had been a little defensive, perhaps, though Carlee hadn't been caustic in the least. It had been a simple statement of fact. Carlee was the most practical of them and Avery knew someone had to be. She and Leanne were less so but they were still cautious not to overextend the ranch. It was the livelihood, after all, for all of them. It allowed them the opportunity to do what they loved and make a better-than-average living doing it while helping both the humans and the horses that crossed their path. It was a hurtful fact that they couldn't save everyone and everything. It just wasn't possible.

Malone was still smiling as she led the mare toward them.

She nodded when Avery asked if she remembered her team. "I do and it's good to see you all again. What a handle this gal has! Who gets the glory for that?"

Leanne, who'd ridden her most, stepped forward. "She came to us that way. All we had to do was put some weight back on her and rebuild her muscle."

"Well, I'm completely won over. How long has she been here?"

"A little over six months," Carlee chimed.

Malone stared straight at Avery. "I want her, no doubt. I know you don't sell your horses. I remember that from my first trip here and my first rescue, who has won me a ton of money by the way. Still and all, I'd like to reimburse you for what you have in her."

The figure she named had Avery shaking her head. "That's way more than what we put into her and we've enjoyed her while she was here."

"Then you tell me."

Avery cut the amount by more than half, adding. "Truly, though, we don't need anything back. I called you because I thought she'd be a better fit for your world than ours. She's yours for the taking."

"It's more than fair to me. If she doesn't take to barrels, I'll have no problem getting that back for her as a rope prospect. Her build is pure athlete and her mind seems sound. Eager but not agitated. I won't lose a penny but I'm betting my heart she'll love running drums."

"She doesn't have registration papers," Carlee cautioned, "at least not that came with her. All we have is a piece of paper giving ownership to us with her name and description. I suspect she has good bloodline. We just couldn't find any way of tracing them back to her. We don't try with the geldings but we do with the mares in case we want to breed them. It helps to know what genetics to avoid and what to blend together."

"I understand that, there are some lines out there I don't want anywhere in my string, but, really, I don't need papers. I make my living competing, for myself and for others, not buying and selling. A simple bill of sale is all I need."

"I'll get that ready while you unsaddle," Carlee offered.

Avery gave Carlee a smile of thanks, more for not commenting on the unexpected offer of money than the preparation of the necessary paperwork. Leanne probably wouldn't take kindly to a witty zing about recouping expenses for a rescue horse that hadn't been as useful to their program as the others. Avery hadn't a doubt that all of her team were close and definitely had each other's back but they weren't above sniping at each other over differences of opinion.

Avery's gaze tracked Carlee as she walked away. The girl had covered her bruises with makeup which she rarely wore and Avery suspected that was more to keep concern and comments at bay than from vanity. Otherwise, Avery could see no sign of the soreness she knew the girl had to be feeling in her back and shoulders and neck. The doctor had warned that the third day would actually be the worst so Avery would be particularly watchful in the morning. For now, though, Carlee seemed truly fine and Avery let go of a little more of her anxiety.

Avery was on the point of turning back to Malone when she saw Carlee change her angle to intercept Dirks who was walking their way. The sight of him made her heart leap a bit. She'd done her best to put the memory of that kiss from her mind but it had crept in at odd moments and came flooding back now. *I'll work just as hard to prove you innocent as guilty*, he'd said. But would he? Could she trust him? Trust these feelings she didn't want to have for him? Craig had been a bitter, bitter lesson but Dirks was a different kind of man. One that appealed to her on every level, she had to admit.

When Dirks shifted his gaze to hers, she realized she was staring at him. She realized something else as well, Carlee was still facing him and there was something in the line of her body, in the way she leaned slightly forward, and in the tilt of her chin that shot a line of discomfort straight through her as if she'd been caught eavesdropping on a personal moment. She shifted her attention quickly away, not returning the quick smile Dirks had sent her.

When she glanced back a moment later, Dirks was staring after Carlee and she wondered what would be revealed if she could see his eyes. One thing was sure, she would never be in competition with any woman for a man's attention, particularly not with the young woman she considered as much her daughter as any person could ever be.

DIRKS WATCHED CARLEE WALK AWAY, still unsure what that exchange with her had been about. She'd commented only that she'd met his security team, Rick and Jeremiah, but her tone had conveyed that she was unimpressed by their quiet, polite manners. She'd been civil when she asked Dirks if he considered them a match for the trouble hounding the ranch but her expression said clearly that she, personally, did not. Dirks had assured her they were professionals and known only for success not failure. He had no intention of telling her they were retired Special Forces. He didn't believe anything he said would sway Carlee's opinion, anyway.

She made no secret of the fact that she was suspicious of Dirks, his motives, his reasons for being there, and – most pointedly – his interest in Avery. She was protective, fiercely protective of Avery. Dirks didn't find that unusual from all he knew about the relationship between them, but he did find the vehemence of it a little off-putting. He had a sense that there was more than concern in Carlee's attitude toward Avery, perhaps a hint of jealousy and a determination to keep Avery's affection to herself. He would expect that in a child or even a teen, all things considered, but he didn't expect it in what appeared to be a strong and self-sufficient young woman. But he knew as well as anyone that there was a reason for the old adage that appearances could be deceiving.

Putting thoughts of Carlee aside, Dirks walked toward Avery, keeping his stride quiet and easy though his thoughts were anything but. He wanted her. He wasn't supposed to and wasn't sure what to do about it but it was there. He supposed the first necessity – beyond keeping her and everything she loved safe – was proving her innocence in whatever financial shenanigans her ex had had going on for the past year. The second necessity, and it was a necessity to him at least, was to convince her that he was someone she could trust, someone she could count on. That, he suspected, was going to be a hard sell when her last example had been the likes of Craig Danson.

He found no lingering remembrance of their kiss in the cool glance she turned his way as he reached the paddock. In fact, she seemed even more remote now than before that moment of undeniable heat in his truck.

Dirks smiled, nodded, shook hands through the introduction with Malone Summers. Then he hung back, quiet and patient, watching as a pretty mare was loaded onto a long, aluminum trailer. Papers were exchanged as Carlee rejoined the group.

A short while later, Malone Summers pulled out of the

drive. Carlee shot Dirks a look over Avery's shoulder. It wasn't hostile but it wasn't friendly either. For a moment, he wondered if she would deliberately pull Avery away on some pretext but, after a moment's hesitation, she turned and walked away with Tucker and Leanne.

Dirks' patience was rewarded when Avery turned, saw him still standing there, and walked his way.

She stopped in front of him and just said, "Hi."

To Dirks' amusement she seemed as if she didn't quite know what to say now that she had given into the impulse to seek his company, and he was pretty sure it had been impulse. The sunlight caught in her hair, pulling hints of bronze from the coffee-colored curls. He fought the urge to touch an errant tendril.

"Good morning," he said in turn. "I'm headed into town shortly. Need anything?"

"Not that I can think of."

"Mind if I pick up some steaks for that big-ass grill you never use? I'd like to pull my team together with yours for shift turnover every evening until we get things sorted out. Might as well get everyone fed while we're at it."

This time the hint of a smile on her lips reached her eyes, not big and bright like he hoped one day to see but at least it was there. "Sure. I have a few clients until early afternoon but there are peas in the freezer I can put on slow simmer."

"Sounds good to me." And because he couldn't help himself, he reached out to touch her face, just once, very lightly.

DIRKS USED the drive into town to sort through his thoughts. What he suspected, what he thought he knew, what he knew for sure, as well as some facts and figures from files he'd studied and then restudied.

Someone had signed Avery's name to government issued payments for veterans. Craig was the most likely culprit because he damned sure didn't believe Avery had done that. And it was Craig who'd siphoned money on a regular basis through an ATM card, Craig who was in financial straits. Avery, along with the ranch, was solvent but she'd, no doubt, been unable to grow her business as quickly as she likely would have.

He knew Carlee had money from her mother's insurance as well as from her share of the ranch proceeds. Her car payment and cell phone were automatically deducted from her checking account. Occasionally, she bought clothes, mostly jeans and shirts and boots, but not often and not extravagantly. She was as solvent as Avery and wanted Avery to remove her from her will.

Tucker made a better than average living at the ranch and, like Carlee, he saved most of his earnings and lived well within his means. Leanne and her husband were renting a small ranch house while saving money for a home of their own. Still young and childless, they indulged once a week or so in dinner with drinks, beer for him, a glass of wine for her. Their vehicles were well-used and equally well-maintained. No large debt, no large luxuries.

Craig was the financial gap. He gambled wildly and, while he didn't lose big, he lost regularly. Interspersed with the frequent losses were the occasional large wins, probably just often enough to keep him coming back for one more try.

In addition to siphoning money from the ranch until Avery caught him at it, Craig had cheated the owner of a lumber store and taken money for a horse he didn't own. Both actions made him a prime candidate for prosecution. With no reliable means of income, he'd be getting desperate now.

Carlee may not have positively identified her father as the driver who'd run her off the road but her suspicion was more than clear. She believed him at least capable of killing Avery to get his hands on the ranch, the horses, and the money through her. So far neither the sheriff nor his deputies had been able to find Craig for questioning. Was Carlee beginning to wonder if her own life would be in danger if her father became desperate enough and she withheld money from him?

Dirks parked at the edge of town and walked through it as he had only a couple of days earlier but this time with a different end in mind. Before, he'd been hunting for clues to a way to clear Avery's name with the government and ensure she was safe from her ex-husband's enemies before heading back to D.C.

This time, he was contemplating the town through an altered viewpoint, wondering if this was a place he could live with a woman who had built a life and a business here, a business that enabled her to live well and help others – both equine and human. He'd never ask her to leave. He wasn't ready to talk marriage and she wasn't ready to hear it, but if he didn't think this was a place he could make his home, it was a conversation that would never happen. He wouldn't do that to himself or to her.

It was a peaceful place, a pretty place, with parks and restaurants and theaters, with businesses and shops and boutiques, not too far from larger towns with brighter nightlife but not too close to them either. So where, exactly, did that realization leave him?

He'd never been tempted to marry and he wasn't sure why that was. Over the years, he'd had a series of love interests, some more serious than others, but he'd let each slip away and hadn't looked back with more than a twinge of regret. That twinge was not because he'd wanted forever after with any of them but because he'd truly cared about each one - just not enough to propose they tie their lives together forever. And eventually, each one of them had accepted that - some with tears and melodrama, some with a hug and a smile of regret - and moved on to a man more inclined to think in terms of forever.

It was true there were times he wondered what his life would have been like with a son to play ball with, a daughter to take to some father-daughter middle school dance. In the thick of action, though, as he held men dying with whispered regrets and sorrow over a family left to grieve, he knew he'd made the right decision for him. But that was then.

Now? Now was different. Now there was Avery.

He passed the sheriff's office but didn't drop in. He and the sheriff had already talked by phone about the biker, the tag number on his Goldwing, and his odd tattoo. If Ben Farley had learned anything new, he'd know it. He had that much faith in the lawman and suspected the lawman now had that much faith in him. They were on the same side in this quest to return Avery to a place without turmoil and without dread that something or someone she loved would be hurt or taken.

Just as he'd decided to return his truck and head to the local meat market, a young woman stepped out of the feed and tack store, clearly intent on locking up. Dirks was surprised when she called out to him. "Aren't you the guy out at Summer Valley Ranch? The government guy looking at the place for some kind of veterans program?"

"I am." He introduced himself and shook the hand she offered so casually.

"I'm Kelly. Are you headed back to the ranch now?"

"Yeah, I am, after another stop."

"Great. I have some calendars I'd love for you to take to Avery if you don't mind. She doesn't come into town that often - none of them do - and I'm dying for her to see what the photographer did. They're right on the counter. It won't take me a minute to step back in to get them."

She was already unlocking the door and Dirks doubted she even realized she hadn't given him a chance to agree or refuse.

When she stepped back out, she was beaming. She handed him the top one on the stack. "Isn't that place gorgeous?"

He supposed it was, but all he saw was the woman astride a magnificent horse he recognized as Jack, and he knew he'd found his answer. She was half turned from the camera so that the photographer had caught little more than the lift of her chin and curve of her cheek with that tumble of hair to her shoulders. Her back was slim, straight and he could see the strength in her as much as the beauty. Yeah, for her, he'd live here in this pleasant little town - or anywhere else she chose to be.

CHAPTER SIXTEEN

True to her word, Avery had tender peas simmering in vegetable stock. It had been a busy afternoon. She'd worked with three clients, pulled salad greens and vegetables from her garden, showered, dithered over make-up, no make-up, and back again. She suspected the kitchen smelled more like the bacon she'd fried to season the peas than the light fragrance of her soap.

When Dirks opened the back door without knocking, it felt right and she tried not to let that bother her. Just go with it, she told herself as she glanced over her shoulder at him from her place by the stove.

He placed the steaks on the granite counter, followed by a bag of what most assuredly was hand-selected baking potatoes. Her eyes widened at the amount of both. "How many armies are you feeding?"

"Just one small one," he answered with a grin. He stepped closer to peer into the cast iron roaster she was stirring. "Oh, man, I don't know when I last had fresh corn creamed by hand rather than dumped out of a can. I almost swung by the open air market for salad things, but it looks like we don't need them."

She liked his grin, realized she liked it too much so turned her attention back to the roaster of corn. "Need or not, we'll have those salad things, fresh from my back yard, washed, and in the 'fridge. There's beer in there, too, if you're interested."

"I am." He pulled one out, saw the Chardonnay chilling, and asked, "Wine?"

She hesitated ... not a date, not a date, not a date ... then said, "Sure."

Beer and wine and steaks wouldn't make it a date. It was a military strategy session, nothing more. Even so, she sensed the change in him. She just wasn't sure what that change was, what it portended, if anything. They'd shared meals early on – before she realized she was in his line of fire for assigning guilt – but that was then and this was now and now felt very different.

She pretended not to notice as he rummaged through her cabinets, passing up her everyday wine goblets to find what he wanted in a lighter-than-air crystal tinted a rich emerald green.

He pulled the cork on the wine with quiet expertise and poured. When he handed her the glass, he smiled. "Almost the same shade of the green in your eyes."

And her heart tilted. She took the glass he held out to her, their fingers barely brushing, but the touch, soft as butterfly wings, had her heart dropping as if on the wildest roller coaster.

Once Dirks started the grill, the team started gathering. With her part done, Avery took her wine glass to the double-glider, dropped her sandals to the deck and tucked her feet under her. Trouble bounded agilely to the seat beside her and curled up, waiting in anticipation of steak she supposed.

Tucker came first, sniffing appreciatively at the scent of hickory flavored charcoal. "Oh, man, I know that stuff ain't good for you, but it's so worth it."

Dirks just smiled and offered him a beer from the kitchen as if it were his to offer. Avery lifted a brow and smiled as Tucker stepped in and grabbed a bottle and a glass and returned just as quickly. He took a seat on the back step and poured his beer into the glass.

"I don't think grilling over gas is considered any healthier than charcoal," Dirks offered.

Tucker frowned at that, considering, and then shrugged. Apparently, all he cared about in that regard was the steak. "You learn anything new or interesting while you were in town?"

"Not new, but interesting. Just reaffirmed some things in my mind."

Avery wondered what that meant but had no intention of asking him. She thought Tucker might ask but Carlee walked up and, as usual, there went Tucker's attention. She'd smile if she thought Carlee had any real interest in him. As it was, she feared Tucker was in for a real heartbreak if he got any more serious. She hoped he wouldn't. The team worked well together. A failed romance or broken heart could ruin that. And she wasn't entirely selfish in her hope. Tucker didn't deserve heartbreak. He deserved the love of his life to love him back. And there she went again, believing in fairy tales.

Leanne arrived next, her husband with her. "Avery, hey, Leanne said I was welcome to join y'all."

Avery stood and gave him a hug. "You're always welcome here, Jason, and you have as much right as any of us to know what is going on. Especially now. This is probably not what you expected to come home to." She still felt guilty that Leanne was at any kind of risk because of her problems.

Jason had wide shoulders, a full head of dark hair without a hint of curl to it and dimples that Leanne told her he preferred to call creases. Leanne went straight to the kitchen to get them a drink and Jason pulled two of the wooden chairs closer to the action.

For a moment, it seemed to Avery that the atmosphere was turning almost festive, at least until Carlee stepped out of the house with a glass of ice water in her hand. The glance she gave Dirks at the grill was just as cool as the drink she carried as she moved close to Avery.

"Are you still feeling sore?" Avery asked, scooting over to make room. Trouble leapt to the deck, not looking back at the two of them, as he curled his tail around him.

"Hardly at all. Quit worrying." It was an order but Carlee said the words lightly with a smile. She glanced around. "Are we eating out here? It's cool enough for a change."

"I actually cleared the dining table, but we could I suppose."

Before the suggestion could become a debate, Dirks' security duo arrived.

With the potatoes roasting on the grill and the group settled in various places, Dirks took the lead, giving quick introductions to those who hadn't yet met. Avery immediately liked the two men Dirks had brought in but she was uncertain that they could be effective when no one could guess where the next risk lay. She wasn't surprised when Carlee said as much.

"We don't know who or what my dad has turned loose on us or even what he might decide to do next. Jesus, running

Avery's car off the road? There's just no talking to him. I can't get through to him at all."

"When was the last time you talked with him?" Dirks asked.

Carlee thought a minute. "Two days ago, I think. I tried twice today. He's not answering his phone. Guess he doesn't want to hear it was his own daughter he nearly killed."

Carlee's voice held deep bitterness and Avery's heart ached for her. Clearly, Carlee had come to accept Tucker's opinion that it had been Craig who had run her off the road. Avery reached for her hand but all Carlee allowed was one quick squeeze. Carlee wasn't – had never been – what Avery thought of as a hugger. Even so, the fierce pressure of Carlee's hand in hers, however brief, held a wealth of emotion. Feelings Avery knew Carlee would never put into words.

"Even if the truck was your father's," Dirks said evenly, "he may not have been the driver."

Carlee stared at him, perplexed. "What are you suggesting? That someone could have stolen his truck and then tried to run me - or Avery - off the road? That doesn't make sense."

"Depends on who was driving." Jeremiah had a quiet, low voice, but one that commanded immediate attention. Avery suspected he'd never have to shout to be heard. "Your father has made some serious enemies. He owes them money and they want what's due them."

Avery realized what Jeremiah was hinting at before Carlee did and watched as understanding dawned.

"You think someone did something to him? Hurt him and stole the truck?"

Carlee stood and began pacing, nearly stumbling over Trouble in her distraction.

Glancing at Dirks, Avery's heart dropped as she realized

the men suspected Craig was more than somewhere hurt. Carlee was angry at her father now, but Avery had no doubt she would be devastated to lose him. He was her only blood relative since the deaths of her sister and mother. From his expression, Dirks at least thought it might well have come to that.

RATHER THAN RISK being trampled by clumsy feet, it would behoove me to take a turn about the barns and paddocks. Add to that, with the humans all gathered in one place, the villains would have free-rein should they decide on an attack in the next bit. Not that I think they will, mind you, nor does Mr. Military, I'm confident. If he had concerns, he would've taken additional precautions. Still, a bit of extra reconnoitering would not come amiss since the bit of prime steak I'm anticipating is still 'resting' on the kitchen counter. I took a peek earlier and, though I remain perplexed why a dead cow should require rest, the humans in my life all appear to deem that a necessity prior to displaying their culinary expertise.

It's a lovely night, less humid than typical. I can almost catch a scent of autumn on the evening breeze but it's a certainty that there are several more weeks of brutal heat to come. I don't sense any agitation amongst the small herds of the young or the old equine in their respective pastures. All seems definitely quiet there as well as within the barns. It would probably be a waste of time and a bore to make another reconnaissance but the steaks aren't yet upon the grill so I may as well.

There are times that boredom can be appealing and the stroll is good exercise. It's vitally important that I maintain a solid physique as certain aspects of sleuthing can be draining if one is not in tip-top shape.

After meandering along the pastures, I find myself at what Ms. Gorgeous refers to as Barn Three. It's late enough that all of the child-prodigy equine have been fed and, once fed, are snoozing on a full belly.

Barn Two is much the same. Noble heads hang over stall doors, gazing at me rather quizzically as I pass by. Some of the horses doze in a corner, caring less that I'm here for their protection.

All appears as it should be, yet I have this sense of disquiet, that all is not as it should be and, in Barn One, I find exactly the sort of thing I dread to see. A note fastened to a stall front. Not just any stall but that of Ms. Gorgeous' most beloved equine, Sir Jack. Ah well, just Jack as the humans call him, but really, how mundane is that?

I find nothing distressing about the scent, or lack thereof, that clings to the small area that encompasses the stall. It is clear, however, that this needs the humans' immediate attention. These humans leave each other reminders or information upon a whiteboard with colored markers. They do not use pen and paper and thumb tacks.

AVERY LOOKED ALMOST RELIEVED when Dirks decided the grill was ready and refused to talk business for the next little while. He declared the steaks he'd hand-picked were prime beef and not to be relegated to 'back-seat'. Sensing her stress at the turn the conversation had taken, he deftly changed the subject altogether, effectively distracted the entire group by producing the ranch calendars he'd picked up while in town.

He glanced willingly at the pictures on each page, though the only ones that truly caught his attention were the six that featured Avery with six different animals. Even he could tell that her attire had been matched to suit both tack and horse. Sleek sophistication matched to a tall, athletic hunter-jumper. Bling, as Leanne laughing tagged it, when she sat astride a compact quarter horse under western saddle. Jaunty Irish togs as she leaned lovingly against the little Connemara she'd given away to a young boy in need.

But even he had to acknowledge the stark elegance of the

photograph of Carlee that Tucker called to his attention. Her hair was tucked completely under a hat and the photographer had been positioned so that the camera caught only her profile against a darkening sky of sunset plum and lavender. The horse was sleek and muscled, captured dramatically between one movement and the next.

But looking from the photograph of Carlee to the inner-lit beauty that was Avery, he thought 'no contest'. He could see her relaxing into the quiet camaraderie of the group but the respite proved brief. Trouble leapt onto the porch with a yowl, drawing everyone's attention to him. He circled Avery's feet until she stood and placed her glass of wine on a small table.

"What is it, Trouble? What's wrong?"

"Really, Avery," Carlee said with a half-laugh. "He's hungry as usual and smelled the steaks on the grill."

"I don't think so." Avery stood for a moment, just staring into Trouble's green eyes. Instinctively, she stepped down from the porch. "I'll be back when I've checked out what's stressed him."

She seemed barely aware of Dirks' handing over the tongs to Tucker. "They're ready. Get everyone served and we'll be back."

He followed close by her side as Trouble led the way. Her pace quickened and Dirks realized with a silent dread where the cat was leading them. "Jack!" He heard the urgency in her voice but all was quiet in the barn and there was her beloved Jack, safe, his head thrust over the stall door as usual at her approach.

Dirks slowed as he saw the folded paper tacked to Jack's door, just below the handle where the horse could not reach and worry it free. He hesitated then pulled it loose, handing it to Avery who had been solely focused on Jack.

Slowly, she read it aloud. "You will connect with any buyer who contacted you in the past asking to purchase the offspring of Flying Jackanapes and you will now offer them - all of them - for sale. You will receive drop off instructions for the money from each sale. If you fail to sell them or fail to produce the money, the animals will die, one by one. You have 24 hours to offer the first sell, no more, no less."

She looked at Dirks in absolute terror and surprised him, as much as he suspected she surprised herself, by moving into the shelter of his waiting arms. Dirks couldn't help himself as he brushed his lips against her temple. Her action proved that she trusted him, even if only instinctively, trusted that he would help her keep her horses safe. And he would, if it took his last ounce of effort - by God, he would.

"I don't know what to do," she admitted, whispering the words against his chest.

"Yeah, well I do," he said and prayed that she would believe him, trust him.

Carlee stood up as they walked back toward the gathering.

"You found something after all, didn't you?" Her gaze searched Avery's face. "The horses? They're all right?"

Avery handed her the threatening note and Carlee blanched upon reading it. Without missing a beat, Carlee shot Dirks a hard glare. "So much for your crackerjack security team," she said derisively, but her voice softened as she turned back to Avery. "What are we going to do?"

"I've got the beginnings of a plan worked out," Dirks said. "We've got at least a day before there will be another move."

For a moment, Avery thought - feared - Carlee would explode, the anger was so clear on her face. And Avery understood, truly she did. If anything, it would appear to Carlee that Dirks was interfering far more than he was helping, but, unexpectedly, Carlee nodded. "That's probably true. The note says twenty-four hours."

She turned to Avery, studied her quietly for a moment. "You're completely wiped, aren't you?" she finally asked softly. "We both are, I guess. We need a mental break. Let's get away, at least for a bit, maybe trail ride tomorrow, talk through our options and come up with a plan. Do you trust Mr. Hanna to keep an eye on things for a few hours in the morning?"

Avery heard the disregard for any plan Dirks had in the making as well as the challenge. She knew Dirks would have heard it as well, but he responded calmly. "I can handle things here, Carlee."

Avery wasn't sure that Carlee was convinced, but somehow, Avery was.

CHAPTER SEVENTEEN

I remain uneasy about the notion of Carlee and Ms. Gorgeous out in the open spaces of the ranch with no protection and so, I suspect, does Mr. Military. On the other hand, I can understand Ms. Gorgeous needing a 'mental break' as Carlee put it. As weighty as my sense of accountability toward my humans, I can only imagine the strain of having sole responsibility for the livelihood of three full-time employees – with Carlee being family as much and more than employee – as well as the safety of all of these large animals enjoying, as am I, the pre-dawn coolness.

All seems peaceful, at least for now. Mr. Military's security duo has been as vigilant as he could want through the night, but my anxiety increases nonetheless, perhaps due to nothing more than lack of sleep. I've pushed past my own limits, I fear. One last swing through the barn and past Jack's stall and then a much needed power nap. I dare not allow myself more of a rest than that, not until I sort through my disquiet.

Fortunately, all is as serene in here as without and Ms. Gorgeous' favorite chair is looking satisfyingly cozy there at Jack's stall door. All I need is a few moments rest and I shall be ready to go again.

Oh, dear, there is a light on in what these horse humans call a tack room, where saddles and bridles and various and sundry other equipment and supplies are kept. With the memory of the devastation wrought on the evening of my arrival at Summer Valley Ranch still strong in my mind, I move to the doorway on silent paws.

Odd. It is Carlee, who really should be sleeping at this hour, particularly so soon after her nasty wreck. Yet, here she is running her hands over the attachments that make up a saddle, the various straps and buckles and screws. Her expression is intense but not tense. As I watch, she turns from one saddle to another and repeats the scrutiny.

I hear a sound and press against the wall as I turn to look down the long barn hallway. Ah, it is one of our fearsome protectors striding quickly but surprisingly lightly toward the glow of the light. He hesitates as he recognizes one of the denizens of the ranch.

"What are you doing? Is something wrong?"

Carlee's laugh is a brittle sound. "Other than the fact that I haven't slept since this mess with my father started? No, everything's lovely. Avery and I are going riding this morning out in the hills on two of the younger horses. Broke but still fairly green. It's good for them and something we routinely do."

"But?"

"But just recently Avery took a bad tumble because tack had been deliberately damaged. I've found a piece or two since then that I've had repaired. We always use western saddles out in the hills and at four a.m. my eyes opened as I realized I hadn't checked these since ... well since then."

"Everything seems okay?"

"Yes, everything's fine."

He nods, hearing clearly as do I, the dismissal in her tone. He can't know that she has just shared more with him than is typical. In my time here, I've discovered Carlee to be a young lady of surprisingly few words.

As he exits, I glance back at Carlee and feel a distinct and unpleasant shock as she slides first one, then another gleaming rifle into two scabbards and attaches each carefully to the saddles in front of her. Clearly, she expects danger or is at the least direly worried about the possibility. It is only a bit reassuring that her movements are sure and confident. This is not her first outing with rifles.

Carlee seems not to notice me as she strides from the tack room and the barn. I glance at the cozy chair in front of Jack's stall but I've an inexplicable, yet solid, feeling of unease that isn't going to allow for a nap.

AVERY OPENED her eyes to an unexpected sense of well-being she immediately attributed to her decision to take a day for herself. For her and for Carlee. They both needed a time out, away from the ranch and the worries that surrounded them. The thought of being out in the low hills with just the horses was quieting. It was a thing she and Carlee did regularly but not often and they'd made time less often as their business grew.

She trusted, absolutely, that Dirks would keep Jack safe in her absence. That trust amazed her but also gave her an immense sense of relief. And Carlee was right, they couldn't put their world on hold or fall apart in dealing with this new threat. Nor could she be sure this would be the last threat to come at her.

It was time to move forward. With Craig no longer siphoning off income, she believed she could soon see her way clear to either increase their barn crew or turn the three, part-time barn help into full-time positions. There were pluses and minuses to either option and she made a mental note to discuss the opportunities with Carlee during their morning ride.

Avery showered quickly and wasn't the least surprised to hear clatter from the kitchen. She walked into the room to find Carlee, dressed as she was in jeans and tee-shirt, at the stove top, flipping a grilled cheese sandwich. Carlee turned to give her a half-smile. "I knew you'd be up early."

"And yet you're up even earlier. Did you sleep well?"

"Fairly well. You?"

Avery nodded, reaching for a coffee cup. "Surprisingly after last night, and I'm looking forward to this morning so thank you for the suggestion."

"And for insisting?" Carlee asked wryly but didn't wait for an answer. "I've eaten already but you relax a minute with your coffee and breakfast. I'll meet you at the barn. I've settled on the grey gelding. Who do you want to ride?"

"The sorrel mare, Bella."

"Good choice."

Avery was grateful for the breezy tone of Carlee's voice. The combined aroma of coffee and toasted cheese sandwich had her settling in her chair with a sense of contentment, until she noticed Trouble staring at her intently. He meowed. Loudly. She glanced at his bowl but it was full as was the water container so that wasn't his problem.

"What's up, Trouble?"

His next effort was almost a yowl but he wasn't making any move toward the door so she wasn't sure what he wanted her to do. "Are you missing home? I would imagine Tammy Lynn is missing you terribly. Let's give her a call this afternoon, shall we?"

Trouble gave her an indignant glare. Sighing at the vagaries of animals, Avery finished her breakfast and slipped into her boots but when she reached the door, Trouble swatted at her jeans-clad leg.

"Hey! What's up with you, mister?" She reached down to rub his ears and found her hand clasped between the cat's front paws. His claws were sheathed but his pull was insistent.

"Come on, now, Trouble. I need this time off. You know as well as I do that Dirks will keep things safe here."

Avery wasn't much surprised when Trouble wove his way between her legs with nearly every stride as she walked across the yard. She was unsure of the reason for his disquiet but he was definitely discomfited about something. Perhaps no more than the fact that she was going to be out of his sight and protection this morning. She didn't have a doubt but that he'd understood enough of their conversation to know. He was that kind of cat.

When she reached the barn, Carlee had both horses saddled and was standing with them at the front of Barn Three. Out of habit, Avery checked her own tack and found everything impeccably in order just as she expected. The sight of the rifle slid solidly into the scabbard gave her pause. "Firearms, Carlee? We'll be on ranch property the whole time."

"I'm not taking any chances." Carlee's voice was firm. "Too much has happened."

At her feet, Trouble yowled again and snagged a paw firmly into the leather of her boot. Avery looked down. "Let go, Trouble. It's fine." She sighed as she looked back at Carlee. "Okay, then, let's move. Where did you want to go?"

Carlee's shoulders relaxed. "I thought we'd ride the perimeter then end at the twisted oak on the far end, maybe eat lunch under the small grove there. We've had enough rain this summer that the spring should be plenty deep with fresh water for the horses. I've packed a couple bottles of water and sandwiches for us."

I MUST FIND MR. MILITARY. Something is very, very dodgy. There are rifles attached to both saddles but I also glimpsed what appeared to be a handgun in the bag of food Carlee packed before Avery exited her room. That is a lot of firepower for two women on what is supposed to be a leisurely ride. I fear I've overlooked something and, yet, even now, I can't quite grasp the direction from which the danger might present itself.

DIRKS STOOD in the doorway of the guest house and watched the two women ride out. He didn't much like that they were headed out alone but he was smart enough to know he couldn't prevent it. He wasn't surprised when Trouble came yowling to his doorway and slipped inside.

Pouring another cup of coffee, Dirks returned to his laptop. He hadn't slept well and had been up for a while digging through the accumulation of information he'd received that morning.

He tried to ignore the black cat pacing at his feet but Trouble wasn't about to be disregarded. Dirks gathered up his laptop and papers. "Come on, Mister. Let's at least get outside." After a moment's hesitation, he headed to Avery's side garden and the comfortable double-glider.

For just a moment, he allowed himself to focus on his memory of her sitting there the evening before, the late sunlight picking up the lighter tones through the curls that tumbled to her shoulder, catching on the brilliant green of her eyes. "Man," he said softly to himself, "you're hooked." That much, he knew was true, and just as soon as he had sorted out the problems in her life and ensured her safety, he was going to do something about the fact. Maybe she didn't want another man in her life after all she'd been through, but he was damned if he would just walk away without trying.

He settled on the glider, wishing she were beside him. Trouble continued to pace, frequently swatting at his leg in a frustrated attempt to communicate his desire for Dirks to take some action. The problem was Dirks didn't know what action he was supposed to take.

He read, re-read, and filed a few more reports before hitting one with the handwriting analysis he'd requested. A keen sense of satisfaction came with the verification that Avery's signature conclusively did not match that on the checks she had purportedly signed. They were close but not close enough. To his surprise, however, Craig Danson's also did not match. That information was completely unexpected and he wasn't sure what to make of it. He filed that document away as well.

The next report was filled with photographs of Craig Danson. There were a multitude of them over recent months and he scanned through rather cursorily. Then one brought his scrolling to a complete stop. It was the local casino and the photograph was circled in bold red as were the next few. The researcher had realized quickly that the photographs were not of the same person. This Craig Danson, impeccably dressed in what Dirks felt certain was a name brand sports coat and derby hat, looked much younger, though the features seemed uncannily similar. At least what Dirks could see of them. None of the circled photographs had caught him actually facing the camera. Did Danson have a son or a younger brother? No one had mentioned those possibilities to him, not here at Summer Valley or during the course of his investigation. Why hadn't he thought to ask? Avery had told him Carlee didn't have any family besides her father, but maybe she didn't know. Damn it! He wished he'd dug a little deeper.

Dirks stood abruptly, paced, tried not to step on Trouble who remained determined to get him to do something. He returned to study the photographs again, one at a time. There were several, all from casino security, taken at what appeared to be a cashier's cage.

Dirks felt a prickle along his neck. He didn't know the man but he'd seen that face. He entered Avery's house without hesitation, searching for the calendar of ranch photographs they'd all admired last night. He found it on the counter and flipped to the month of September, of Carlee with her hair pulled back and up and tucked under a fedora, her face little more than a profile, turned away from the camera. The barest glimpse, all he could see, of a strong jawline without the softening effect of hair swirling around her jaw and neck. A dark, arched eyebrow. What little was visible anyway. For whatever reason, the women had preferred the horses, not themselves, to be the focal points of the photography.

Not a son or a brother, then. Carlee.

Dirks pulled his cell phone from his pocket and hit Avery's number. The call went straight to voice mail. His gaze moved to Trouble who had followed him in, undoubtedly anxious and trying his best to get Dirks to understand what the cat had clearly already deduced.

"Can you find them?"

Trouble meowed sharply and turned, heading toward the door, obviously satisfied now that Dirks had shown himself at last ready to take action.

Dirks made only one stop. To grab his rifle from behind the seat of his truck.

I CAN ONLY HOPE Mr. Military can keep up with me. I'm fairly confident I know the destination of Ms. Gorgeous and Carlee but we must take a short cut over some tricky territory if we are to get there ahead of them. Fortunately, Mr. Military's exercise routine is daily and strenuous - he's no lay about - and he has a propensity for loaded fire arms that he carries concealed at all times, one at his shoulder, one at his ankle. The rifle, he has retrieved, is just lagniappe.

I'm quite beside myself at the thought we may not reach Ms. Gorgeous in time. Nor am I sure of all the implications but clearly Mr. Military was disquieted by the picture of Carlee. I can only discern that it is from Carlee that Ms. Gorgeous must be protected. The whys and wherefores can come later. Time is of the essence.

THE MORNING PROVED ABSOLUTELY beautiful and Avery felt a peace she hadn't enjoyed in some time. The horses were content to walk when the path was uncertain and trot or slow gallop when the ground was flat. Avery let Carlee choose the pace, confident the young woman would always be careful with the safety of the horses.

"Let me know if you get ready to stop," Carlee said to her. "If you get tired."

Avery shot her an amused look. "We've only been riding a couple of hours and walked as much as anything. This is hardly the pace of our normal day. What about you? Holding up okay?"

"Quit worrying about me, Avery, I'm fine."

"I know, but I can't shake the realization that I nearly lost you, that you could have been killed in that car wreck. I don't want you to push yourself."

"We've both been pushing ourselves for a while," Carlee said dryly.

"That reminds me of something I was considering earlier. I think it's time we thought about adding full-time barn help or doubling our part-time crew. I see plenty of benefits to full-time positions because that would give us an eventual knowledge base for backup and possible training as 'fill-in' instructors."

Carlee pondered that a moment. "On the other hand, we've been able to help some really bright kids get through college without an overload of debt with our part-time work."

"Exactly. And I hate to lose that aspect."

Carlee swatted at a horsefly aggravating her young mount. "What if we mix the ideas? Alan will graduate this semester. What if we take his opening and make one full time position and keep the other two as part-time for now?"

"I like that. It would give us a chance to see how the full-time will work out."

Carlee swatted again. "Let's speed up a bit, put them into an extended trot and see if we can shake some of these horseflies."

Avery pressed her heels lightly but firmly into Bella's sides as Carlee gave a quiet verbal command to the young grey she was riding. When the terrain grew rocky, they pulled back to a walk but Avery was pleased to note the tactic to leave the irritating insects behind seemed to have worked, at least for now.

They walked the horses in silence, each lost to their thoughts, as the hills leveled and the stand of oaks that was their destination became a haze of green on the horizon.

Avery hadn't realized that Carlee had fallen behind her

until she spoke again, so quietly and evenly the words didn't make sense until Avery glanced back and saw the pistol Carlee held trained at her back. "What? What did you say?"

"I said I killed Caren. My mother, too."

For a moment Avery didn't, couldn't, speak. Her mind could not comprehend. "Your sister drowned."

Carlee's expression was serene. They could as easily have been talking about the weather or the ranch. The pistol in Carlee's hand was absolutely steady as was her gaze on Avery's face. Waves of cold swept over Avery. Mind racing, she fought not to let it show. No weakness, she thought, I mustn't show weakness, though she didn't know why not or what difference it could possibly make.

"Caren did drown, yes. I always made sure she was safely seat-belted into her wheelchair. It was my job. Mom said so. Couldn't have her falling out and getting hurt. So I double-checked that she was securely strapped in when I slipped up behind her to unlock the wheels." The corner of Carlee's mouth lifted in a half smile. "Caren never heard me, never knew I was there until I gave her chair a push toward the pool. She opened her mouth to cry out, but I said her name. When she turned and saw me, I said, 'I've got you, Caren. It's okay.'"

Carlee paused and Avery heard the call of a bird, the rustle of a rabbit in the brush close by. "And you drowned her." Even as Avery said the words, she couldn't believe them. Not yet.

"It wasn't hard. Caren trusted me so she didn't call for mom, who was asleep anyway. I'd already sneaked into the house and made sure of that. I was right there, after all. I always had her. When I jumped into the water, Caren thought I was coming to save her. It was easy to hold the wheel chair down long enough for her lungs to fill with water. She watched me, every second, there under the water. Just watched me.

After that, all I really had to do was 'find' her when I came in from ball practice. I did the hysterical thing really well, seems I have a talent for acting." That half smile reappeared fleetingly then Carlee's expression turned cool, unemotional, a look Avery had seen on many occasions and failed to interpret.

Avery was hit by waves of nausea. "Why? Why would you do that? How could you kill your own sister?"

Carlee's gave a casual shrug. "She took up too much of Mom's time. There was so much I wanted to do, places I wanted to go, but there was always Caren, her disability, in the way. Caren was okay but she was weak. I can't stand weakness. That's why I always liked you. You were always strong."

"And your mother?" Avery watched her as she would a rattlesnake, a creature cold and deadly and completely devoid of humanity.

"Mom was even weaker than Caren but in a different way. Drank herself into a stupor every night after Caren died – all because she'd fallen asleep on the sunporch with Caren still outside by the pool. She thought if Caren needed anything, she'd hear her and wake up." Carlee shrugged. "And she probably would have but I couldn't very well tell her. She couldn't bear the guilt and I couldn't take it from her."

"So it wasn't suicide."

"I'm sure Mom wanted to die. She even told me that once. And she would have drunk herself to death eventually. So I guess you could say it was suicide, just daughter-assisted."

"And you're planning to kill me because ....?"

"Oh, I'm not just planning to kill you. I have to kill you. And don't even think about the rifle in your scabbard. Yours isn't loaded. Mine is."

"But why me? Why now? I don't understand. Carlee, everything I have would have been yours." Avery couldn't wrap her mind around anything Carlee had said. The sounds of nature around them that had sounded so sweet just minutes ago now seemed a mockery.

"And so it will be – just sooner. Actually, I was going to wait awhile, but you and Mr. Hanna are getting much too cozy. Do you think I haven't noticed? Besides, you've kept way too close an eye on things since you found out Dad was cheating you and I can't be sure you won't eventually figure out I was too. And if you don't, Dirks Hanna will. He's smart, too smart. I can't risk you changing your will if that happens. I've worked too hard for this place, I've earned it."

"You asked me to change my will." Avery felt as if she'd fallen down the rabbit hole with Alice in Wonderland, to a world where absolutely nothing made sense. She struggled to make logic of what she was seeing and hearing in a person she thought she knew as well as she knew her own self.

"Well, yes, but I knew you'd never do that. I wanted you to believe I'd give up everything to keep you safe ... until I was ready. I need Dad out of the way and soon. He's no use to me now that you're divorced. He's made a complete mess of things and is way over his head in debt to some particularly nasty men."

"His gambling debts, you mean."

"Yes, and how dumb is that? I like to gamble, too, seems to be the only thing we have in common these days, but I don't drink when I gamble and I don't gamble with sharks. All my debt is in his name. So poor Dad is in way too deep with men too smart for him to handle and those guys are going to keep on making trouble until he's out of the way for good. I thought they'd take care of that for me but now they've turned their attention to the ranch and the horses. Can't have that, now can I?"

She sounded indignant, Avery thought, feeling as if she were caught in some nightmare. Carlee was indignant that her father hadn't been murdered by thugs to keep her from having to do it. Avery felt sickened at the realization that she, a trained professional, had completely missed that Carlee lacked the ability to care about any human, even those closest to her.

"On top of all that, you and Leanne just keep pouring the ranch resources into rescue horses and then giving them away. That's not good business. Anyway, it just makes more sense to kill you now that I've got it all worked out."

"What? What have you got worked out?"

Carlee looked at her as if she were simple-minded. "Dad calls me for help almost every day. This time I told him to meet me here and I'd help him a little. Unfortunately, he's going to shoot your horse out from under you and you'll hit your head on some rock or break your neck or something. I'll figure that out before we get to the oak grove. I'll have to kill him trying to save you but, oh so sad, his death will be in vain as you'll be beyond saving. Your part's easy. All you have to do is keep riding."

Avery looked toward the oak trees growing ever nearer and tried her best to marshal her thoughts. She was alone and without a weapon, but she'd be damned if she'd die without a fight.

CHAPTER EIGHTEEN

Ahead of us are the oak trees that I believe to be Carlee's destination. The site is not ominous in the least, just a small grove with only one very old, very large oak among the several younger ones. However, I remain fearful of what it portends. Nonetheless, I am rather pleased with my human. We've managed to arrive ahead of the villainess and our Ms. Gorgeous. Mr. Military has proven himself a man of strength and stamina. Fortunately, we could take a more direct route than the horses though it involved Mr. Military scaling a few fences and fording a few rocky streams.

Now, Ms. Gorgeous must prove herself a woman of fortitude and ingenuity. I have no doubt that both traits will be needed in the moments ahead if all is not to end in disaster.

DIRKS SCRAMBLED UP the oddly shaped branches of the largest tree behind Trouble, praying that Avery and Carlee were too far distant to discern any real movements around the copse of oaks. His pulse thudded and he recognized the primal fear that gripped him. Avery, his woman, was in peril and every bit of strength and knowledge he could claim might not be enough to save her.

He watched the approach of the two horses. Avery rode at the front. Carlee followed close behind. The sun glinted on the pistol in Carlee's hand and Dirks' gut clenched. He had not been mistaken then. Unlikely as it had seemed, Carlee - not her father - was the threat to Avery's safety.

Dirks had a choice to make. Ease the rifle into position and risk a distance shot with Avery riding in front of Carlee or secure the rifle and ensure his pistol was at the ready. Either carried a peril. Any animal was subject to an unexpected movement and young horses particularly so. Once he pulled the trigger, if Avery's sorrel shifted the slightest in the wrong direction, she could be placed in the path of the bullet he released. Waiting until they were within pistol range would leave Avery at Carlee's mercy that much longer and he had no way to be sure this small thicket of trees was even their final direction although Trouble had led the way and certainly seemed confident that it was.

In the end, Dirks decided to trust whatever instinct or knowledge had steered the cat to this spot. The cat had been dead-on so far. Dirks held his breath and eased his pistol from its holster. Sweat that had nothing to do with the heat trickled down his forehead as he watched their slow approach. He sensed, rather than heard, Trouble shift position as the women neared their hiding place and prayed that neither woman would notice. If Avery felt their presence and glanced up, Carlee's gaze would follow hers and Dirks had no earthly idea how she might react at that point.

"I don't see your father."

Dirks tensed. Was Craig part of this after all? Dirks couldn't risk looking around for him. Not now when Avery and

Carlee were so close upon the tree where he and Trouble waited.

"Well, I don't really need him here right now." Carlee hesitated, seeming to weigh her options. "Besides, he's such a loser I can't even be sure he'll show up."

Dirks saw her grip shift, tighten on the pistol. Avery must have seen it as well. In a move that startled Carlee as much as it did him, Avery kicked her feet free of the stirrups, slapped her mount on the neck and leapt for Carlee's horse, all in one swift act of desperation.

Forced to hold his shot, Dirks dropped from the tree, landing hard on his feet just as a yowling black cat dropped from the limb beside him to land squarely on the hip of Carlee's horse.

As her panicked mount whirled at the weight of the cat and the feel of claws digging into tender hide, Carlee's shot went wild and she growled with rage. Before she could fire a second time, Dirks grabbed her arm, dragging her from the horse. She tumbled to the ground, and her pistol fell and discharged again. Dirks could only pray that shot, too, went far wide of any mark. With a rough twist of her shoulder, he pinned her, face down and planted a knee in her back. Only then, with heart still thudding, could he let his gaze find Avery.

She had landed on her rear a few feet away. For long moments, they simply stared at each other as both horses bolted away from the sound and smell of gunfire and one unleashed black cat.

That black cat sat guard between Carlee and her pistol and, at this point, Dirks couldn't be sure the cat wasn't capable of using it.

"Get Carlee's pistol, Avery." It was all Dirks could trust himself to say for a moment.

For answer, Avery scrambled to her feet, dusting the back of her jeans. She rubbed the fur between Trouble's ears before scooping up the gun.

Only when Dirks saw the pistol secure in her hand, did he ask, "Do you have your cell phone?"

Avery gestured in the direction the terrified horses had fled. "I'd say it's about halfway back to the barn."

"Then come get mine and call Tucker, then Farley."

As she walked toward him, Dirks let himself breathe a sigh of relief. Avery was safe. They'd sort the rest out, but – for now – that was all that was important, all that mattered.

THE DAYS CAME and went and turned into a week and then another. Avery worked and grieved and healed. Dirks had left her with a kiss and a promise that he'd be back but she wasn't sure how she felt about that. She wasn't sure how she felt about anything. He called her each night, sent her a text each morning and still she didn't know, wasn't sure. They'd actually known each other such a short while, a matter of days, really, before it had been time for him to leave. Was that enough?

"Avery?" At the sound of her name, she glanced over her shoulder. Leanne stood at the entrance of the barn, watching as she ran a brush lovingly over Jack's gleaming neck. "Ben – Sheriff Farley – drove out to see you. Do you want me to send him in here?"

"No, I'll come out. I'm done." She gave Jack a hug and led him back into the stall before slipping the halter from his head. It was the horses, Leanne and Tucker, the ranch itself, the work she believed in, that brought the healing she needed.

But she missed Dirks. Little as she liked it, as uncomfortable as it made her, she couldn't deny the fact.

The sheriff waited beside his truck. He'd placed his hat on the hood and the dry September breeze ruffled his silvering hair. "Avery." He studied her closely. "You look good. Rested."

He'd been present, witnessed as his men had loaded a hand-cuffed Carlee into the back of a patrol car. He'd watched as tears of shock and disbelief had slid down Avery's cheeks.

"I'm better," Avery said, smiling at him, "but I don't know about rested. It's been busy around here." And without Carlee they were short-handed but Avery wasn't ready to add anyone to their team just yet. Not yet, not this soon. She'd have to eventually, she knew, but bringing someone into their day-to-day lives was an important choice and they'd make it together, she and Tucker and Leanne.

"What brings you out this way?" Though she suspected she knew and dreaded to hear.

"I've got news of Carlee. Thought it best to tell you face-to-face."

Avery braced herself and waited.

Ben Farley sighed. "She waived all rights and refused a court-appointed attorney. Told the judge every detail of what she'd done and what she planned to do. And showed no remorse or shame or even a hint of emotion for any of it. It beat all I've ever seen, Avery."

"But they judged her as insane, right?"

The sheriff shook his head. "No, Avery, they didn't. She still might plead for that and might even get it, but for now, she's moving through the system. She'll have her day in court before it's finished, but ..." He sighed. "When it's all said and done, I expect she'll get one life sentence for murdering her twin and another for murdering her mother."

"I'll never understand," Avery whispered.

"No, ma'am, nor will I. She was a cool one, all along, could have been killed when she rolled that SUV."

Avery looked startled. "What do you mean?"

"There was a witness, a hired heavy on a bike trailing her and thinking it was you, planning who knows what kind of threat to get a payoff for his boss. Dirks put me on to him but it took a while for me to track him down. He was willing enough to talk when I did as long as it was off the record. Said Carlee was alone on the road ahead of him. No one forced her off."

"That's insane."

"Crazy business every bit of it," Ben agreed. "Speaking of which, have you heard anything from her dad?"

"Craig? No, I haven't and don't expect to."

"I heard he lit out after Carlee was arrested. Guess he's still running from his debt, but at least you won't be bothered over that again. Dirks Hanna and I made enough visits in uniform to be sure of that."

"Dirks?"

Ben looked at her quizzically. "You didn't know?"

"Seems like every time I turn around there's something I don't know."

"Well, looks like I stepped my shoe in it this time, but I'll leave the explanations to him." Ben gave her a hug before getting into his truck. "You call if you need me, Avery, any time day or night."

"I'll be fine."

Ben smiled as he closed his door. "I expect you will, at that."

She watched the sheriff pull out of the drive before turning back to her work, nearly stepping on the sleek black cat in the process. She scooped him up and rubbed her face against his soft fur. "You saved my life. I'll never forget that."

WELL, YES, I DID. Me and Mr. Military, who is long over-due for return. And that needs to be soon as I've been gone from my Tammy Lynn long enough. But though the danger has passed, Ms. Gorgeous is still in need of my attention. She doesn't wake us both crying out in her sleep now but her dreams are restless and her heart is in need of attention that only a human, and a human who loves her, can give. I'm a poor substitute for Mr. Military but I'm all she has for the moment.

I've tried to spend time with young Tucker as well. He fancied himself in love with Carlee and he has fared poorly these past few weeks. Ms. Gorgeous has tried to comfort him but needs as much as she gives there. Such a pity. I've heard the term heartless and perhaps even used it upon occasion, but truly, I don't think I'd ever before met a human who simply had no heart in the emotional sense of the word. I'd met those with an evil heart but none, like Carlee, where no heart existed at all. Neither heart, nor soul.

IT WAS time to convene a meeting of her team, Avery decided. A month had come and gone since Carlee had exited their lives in a way none could have foreseen. A month since she had seen Dirks. A month to pull herself together. Now it was time to be there, to be *present*, for her team.

At the end of the work day, they gathered in her garden. She with a glass of wine, Tucker with a beer, and Leanne with a tumbler of iced tea. Trouble shared the double-glider with her and she kept it moving gently because that was what he liked.

Avery took a breath and jumped right in. "I'm doubling our

part-time barn help. We'll have one morning, one afternoon student for each barn. I contacted the school and they're going to send us the applications and resumes of the students who are interested. I'll need you to look through those. It's also time to start building the clinic, Tucker. Dr. Snow is planning to retire next summer. He has someone to take on his small animal practice but would like to send his equine clients to you."

Tucker looked shell-shocked but only for a moment, before he grinned broadly. It was his first real smile since Carlee's arrest.

"Which," Leanne inserted, "means we'll need to start looking for someone to manage Barn Two."

"It does, yes, and I'll need both of you heavily invested in that selection process. We're a team and we're going to want to bring in someone with that same mindset. I'm also going to begin looking for someone to take over the accounts. I do it well enough, I suppose, but it isn't what I love and I can't manage it and my barn as well."

Her gaze went to Leanne as she spoke.

"You already know," Leanne said accusingly.

"Perhaps," Avery admitted, rubbing a hand along Trouble's back. "But you could tell us."

Leanne laughed. "Well, we don't know the sex but arrival will be mid-March."

Tucker hooted. "We're having a baby? Awesome! Uncle Tucker. Sounds good, right?"

"It does." Leanne leaned her head into his shoulder. "Uncle Tucker."

"And so ...?" Avery prompted.

"And so at some point I'll need to slow down, for a while at least, so I could take over the books then. But we'll for sure need someone to help you out now and be ready to take my place once the baby is here. I'm not a bookkeeper at heart either."

"It will take a bit of juggling but we'll work it out. I'll start talking with some of the colleges for prospects as well as place an ad or two in some of the journals we subscribe to."

They talked until nearly dark and it felt good to be finally looking forward instead of behind. Leanne drove away home and Tucker drifted back to his bungalow but Avery continued to swing and sip a second glass of wine.

It seemed almost as if she'd been expecting the headlights that turned into the long drive. Trouble seemed to be as well, purring against her hand but not bothering to come to attention as he eyed the sweep of light along the neat fences before the truck parked.

Avery stayed where she was, watching as Dirks walked toward her. He stopped, seeming to drink in the sight of her as much as she was of him. He held an envelope toward her.

"The acceptance of Summer Valley Ranch into the veterans' equine rehab program."

She took it without speaking, turning it in her hand. The program, her acceptance, was still important to her, but not, she thought, as important as this moment. Not nearly as important as this man standing in front of her.

Searching her eyes with his gaze, Dirks held out his hand to her and she took it. She allowed him to tug her to her feet, and – without hesitation – she stepped into his arms.

Ah, time now, at last, for me to make my way back to my lovely Tammy Lynn. I can leave here with a good conscience, knowing that I leave the security of Summer Valley Ranch in the very capable hands of my resourceful Avery Wilson and one Mr. Military.

ACKNOWLEDGMENTS

Heartfelt thanks to Janice Jones for the lovely stick horse in the cover art and Debbie Jones Kuykendall for an author's photograph which actually looks like me – only better!

ABOUT THE AUTHOR

Susan Y. Tanner continues to blend her passion for horses with her passion for writing. In *Trouble in Summer Valley*, she introduced readers to the rescue horses of Summer Valley Ranch where they prove their worth in therapeutic riding. In *Turning for Trouble*, her own rodeo experience brings that rough and tumble world to life. Her third romantic mystery, *Trouble in Action*, showcases the risky profession of stunt riding while giving a glimpse into historical reenactments. Published by KaliOka Press, these romantic mysteries are part of the Familiar Legacy series written in concert with some very talented authors.

Two of her historical romances, *Fire Across Texas* and *Winds Across Texas*, have been rereleased by Secret Staircase Books, an imprint of Columbine Publishing. Soon to follow will be *A Warm Southern Christmas*, *Highland Captive*, *Captive To A Dream*, and *Exiled Heart*. All were previously published by Leisure Books.

susanytanner.com

facebook.com/susan.tanner.376

amazon.com/author/susanytanner

SMALL TOWN TROUBLE

Trouble Cat Mysteries #5

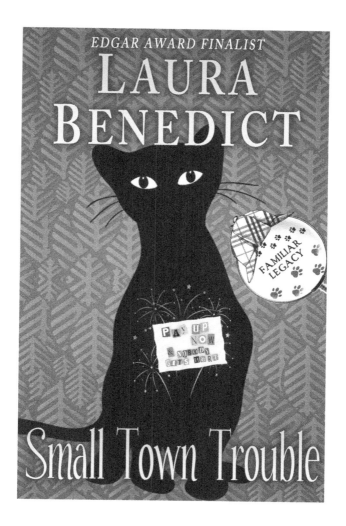

SMALL TOWN TROUBLE

Chapter 1

There's nothing like an overenthusiastic canine to ruin a stakeout. I have my eye on a blue sedan parked across the street from the Walsh Estate, where I'm visiting, but it's deuced difficult to concentrate with an obnoxious Jack Russell terrier barking up at me from the driveway. All of the other cars belonging to the partygoers—and it is a lavish affair--are parked in a nearby field, but the men who directed the parking are long gone. The dark-haired woman in the sedan is a latecomer, and she stares, unmoving, at the Walshes' posh house, her eyes hidden by sunglasses. With no small degree of nonchalance, I stretch across the top of the deliciously warm brick pedestal, and squint down at Jocko, the offending creature. Who has ever heard of such an idiotic moniker? Jocko, indeed.

I know for a fact that Sherlock Holmes never had to deal with such an annoying canine—not counting that Baskerville brute, of course. Sherlock, who is my role model and personal hero, made good use of an intelligent chap named Toby that was half-spaniel, but these Jack Russell types are thoroughly mad. They dash about the countryside, yapping constantly, chasing down rodents (an occupation much more suited to accomplished cats like me), and bothering horses.

I warn Jocko to calm down with a low growl. In return, he whines and pants and waggles that ridiculous curled tail. What a hopeless wretch he is.

At home in Wetumpka, Alabama, my human, Tammy Lynn, would never have such a beast hanging about. But during our visit with Erin Walsh, the daughter of the late Rita Walsh, Tammy's childhood babysitter, Tammy was called to Milan, Italy, to authenticate a priceless book that some monks found in their library. The Italian antiquities bureaucracy would only make it available for a few days, and she had to leave me behind. So my temporary residence is here, in western Kentucky, which is dreadfully far from Alabama.

It's true. I don't sound like I'm from Alabama. I spent much of the first of my nine lives studying that excellent Cumberbatch actor's Sherlock Holmes films, and acquired a bit of an English accent. Of course only other cats, like my brilliant detective father, Familiar, can hear it. But I have no problem motivating the humans around me when I engage in traditional feline vocalizations.

The woman in the car is staying put. I consider popping across the street or chasing the hapless Jocko her way to get some movement from her—angry-looking people who stare at houses usually mean danger— but the foolish dog would no doubt be run over by a passing tractor or pickup truck. One somehow feels responsible for the Jockos of the world.

Instead I leap onto the impeccably paved driveway, inches from Jocko's head, making him jump back a mile. Anyone who says cats can't smile has never seen me after I've played a clever trick.

The party has been in full swing since my third nap of the day, and most of the guests—employees and their families from Bruce Walsh's (Erin's father) car dealership—are swimming or fishing or careening about on noisy Jet Skis on the Cedar Grove Lake cove that meets the Walsh property. They've even set up a few picturesque changing cabanas near the property's strip of manmade beach. The less adventurous guests are in the swimming pool or eating. But I've done the rounds back there, and I want to avoid further contact with the youngsters and their sticky hands, so I enter through the carelessly open front door with Jocko panting behind me.

Hearing angry voices, I continue to the library door, which is open a few inches, and slip neatly inside. Hapless Jocko, who doesn't seem to understand that he could push the door open a bit further to enter as well, sits down in the hall and whimpers pathetically. But Jocko's not my concern right now.

Erin, a sweet co-ed who's home for the summer from the University of Kentucky, where she's preparing to study veterinary medicine, leans forward, her hands balled into fists at her side. Her face is pink beneath her freckles, a sign that she's angry and frustrated. I've seen that look on Tammy Lynn's face a time or two. But when I see the other woman, who wears a canny, unpleasant grin, I understand why Erin is frustrated. The other woman is her stepmother, Shelby Rae Walsh, who's only a dozen years older than Erin, and is Jocko's human mate. Shelby Rae thinks it's her job as a stepmother to meddle in Erin's business.

Neither of them glance at me as I stroll to one of the many tall windows overlooking the front garden, and settle on the back of an enormous couch with stripes like a cafe awning. From there, I can find out what's wrong between Erin and Shelby Rae, and observe the car out front. What does the woman in the car want? Is she dangerous? I intend to find out.

SMALL TOWN TROUBLE

Chapter 2

"What in the world were you thinking, child? Your daddy's going to be so upset. You know we think tattoos are trashy on women."

If she hadn't been so angry, Erin would've laughed out loud at her stepmother. Shelby Rae, with her bottom-grazing miniskirts and rompers, heavy makeup, and do-less family who had no visible means of support aside from the little helper checks (Shelby Rae's words) Erin knew Shelby Rae had been writing for years, had the market cornered on trashy. But it was her condescending child that made Erin want to wipe the Corral Me Coral lipstick off Shelby Rae's collagen-injected lips.

She didn't believe in the stereotype of an Irish temper, but she could swear she felt the anger in her bones.

"I'm not your child, Shelby Rae," she said. "I won't be talked to that way by you or anybody else. Daddy has asked you—and I've asked you a thousand times--to please stay out of my business."

Years ago she'd actually liked Shelby Rae, but that was back when she was in middle school, and her mother had died a few months earlier, and Shelby Rae—who worked as the receptionist at her father's car dealership—suggested to Erin's father that Erin might need a big sister kind of friend. She'd taken Erin to cosmic bowling, and down to Nashville to see a Selena Gomez concert, and to buy a bra that was a little more substantial than the training bra Rita had bought her the year before. It was Shelby Rae who drove her to the drugstore to pick out sanitary pads after Erin called her, whispering, "Shelby Rae, I started."

But two years later, her father asked her to come into the library—the very room in which they now stood—and, with a beaming Shelby Rae at his side, said, "We have wonderful news to tell you, honey."

If only her father had instead taken her out on a walk on the lake trail, or driven her in the boat to dinner at The Captain's Table on the other side of the lake, and told her, first, without Shelby Rae there. Or he could've asked her how she felt about Shelby Rae, and if she thought it was a good idea for him to marry her. She might have understood. She might even have been glad to have her suspicions confirmed. She wasn't blind or stupid. Her father sometimes stayed out late, and he and Shelby Rae shared significant looks when she came to pick up Erin. If only...

That's not what happened, though, and here they were,

fussing at each other in the house, instead of mingling out back with the guests attending the Walsh Motors annual employee summer barbecue.

"Oh, come on. Did you forget you have a tattoo on your backside?" Erin pointed at Shelby Rae's ample left hip. "You have a snake back there. What kind of person has a snake on their butt?"

Shelby Rae pursed her lips and stuck her recently altered nose in the air. "It's an asp. Like Cleopatra. And it's gold and blue. It's art."

Erin scowled. "I'm nineteen. It's perfectly legal if I want to tattoo my whole face." She pointed to her lightly freckled forehead. "I could get butterflies all across here. I could have a freaking butterfly parade, if I wanted to, instead of just an inch-wide one on my thigh."

In fact she'd completely forgotten about the new tattoo when she'd taken her shorts off by the pool ten minutes earlier. Seeing the tattoo, Shelby Rae had pulled Erin away from her best friend, Mackenzie Clay, and hurried her into the house, through the kitchen, and into the library. Erin only just now wondered why Shelby Rae had been watching her in the first place.

"You're being silly." Shelby Rae shook her head. "Only criminals have tattoos on their face."

"So I guess it would be okay if your Uncle Travis, who's out back drinking Daddy's beer and about to eat the biggest steak from the outdoor fridge, gets a tattoo on his face?"

Shelby Rae crossed her arms over her breasts. Erin knew she hadn't had to have those fixed like she'd had her nose done. She'd once overheard one of the salesmen at the dealership comment on Shelby Rae's enormous assets.

"Why are you so hateful, Erin? I have never done one

single thing except be nice to you! This is a very stressful time, with the lawsuit just ended. You haven't been here. You don't know what it's been like. That Owens woman has been hanging around, and I've hardly even seen your father for months." Her high voice stretched into a familiar whine.

The lawsuit. Erin's father wasn't a talker, and so had brushed it off whenever she called him from Lexington. But it had been in the papers. The brakes on Tionna Owens' car had failed in an intersection, just minutes after she left the dealership's service department. They'd checked out the car and told her it wasn't safe to drive, but she'd wanted a second estimate. The service manager even dutifully made a note that she refused service. She died less than two blocks from the dealership. The county didn't find grounds to prosecute, but the woman's wife, Bryn Owens, had brought a civil suit against the dealership, which had just been tossed out.

"He doesn't even listen when I try to tell him that woman is crazy," Shelby Rae continued. "Nobody listens to me!"

Erin sighed. "That's because you're a drama queen. Nobody needs your drama, and I'm sick and tired of it. I wish you'd just go away and stay out of my business." She knew she was being as dramatic as Shelby Rae, but she was beginning to wish she'd kept her apartment in Lexington and picked up a part-time job there for the summer. Bumming around New Belford and hanging around the house—even if she was often with Mackenzie—was turning out to be a bad idea.

Shelby Rae huffed out of the library, flinging open the door to reveal the startled faces of two women Erin didn't know. Shelby Rae glowered at them as they hustled away, obviously embarrassed to be caught listening, then picked up Jocko who was barking at her with frantic joy. They disappeared down the hall, Shelby Rae's heeled mules clacking on the polished wood floors.

Great, thought Erin. Now everyone would know they'd been arguing. How long would it be before her father was asking why Shelby Rae was so upset?

Erin walked over to the window. The library had always been one of her favorite rooms. She put a hand on the end of the high-backed sofa, and Trouble, the clever black cat that Tammy Lynn had asked her to look after, nudged her hand with his velvety nose.

"Sorry about that," she said, scratching the cat behind the ears. "I don't really hate her. She just gets to me sometimes."

The cat purred. Tammy Lynn had told her that Trouble was good at solving mysteries and had saved her more than once. But there were no mysteries to be solved in New Belford. The last disturbance was when two brothers—both drunk—got in a fight about which of them should inherit their mother's small cottage on the lake. The younger brother had shot the older brother, but when he was convicted, he cried, saying that his brother being dead was a worse punishment than prison. It turned out that there was a second mortgage on the house and neither one of them would've owned anything. No mystery there. Just Darwinism at work.

"We'll find something to do that gets us away from here." As she looked out the window, Erin stroked the soft fur on Trouble's back, and felt rather than heard the ebb and flow of his gentle breath.

There was a single blue car parked across the road. It was far enough away that its occupant was hard to make out. But she was certain it was Bryn Owens. It was hard not to feel bad for her. Bryn and Tionna had owned New Belford's only bakery together, and Erin and Mackenzie had liked to go there for coffee. But after Tionna died, Bryn put a closed sign in the window, and never opened the bakery again.

Erin knew what grief felt like. The pain in her gut had lessened considerably in the last seven years, since her mother had been killed, but it never really went away.

Trouble snapped to attention, slipping from beneath her hand to stand on his back legs and put his front paws against the window. The cat never missed a thing.

A rumbling motorcycle had pulled up behind the blue sedan, and shut off. Erin wondered if this was someone she was supposed to know.

A guy wearing blue jeans and a slim black tee shirt whose sleeves took on the taut, muscular shape of his upper arms and shoulders, put down the kickstand of his motorcycle and took off his helmet to push the sun-streaked hair from his face. Now she recognized his profile. His look was different—a little more relaxed and, frankly, sexier—than she remembered.

Noah Daly had been two years ahead of her all through school, and he'd been a loner. A bit geeky, but still a loner. A lot of girls thought he was cute, but their mothers made sure they didn't get too close because Noah's father, Jeb Daly, was bad news. Jeb had been in and out of jail since he dropped out of McClaren County High School, and everyone thought he'd turned over a new leaf when he married Annette, the teenage daughter of the minister at the First Church of Christ Disciples. He even held a job as a cook at a roadhouse near the county line for a few years. But when his only son, Noah, was about to enter high school, Jeb did the unthinkable: he used a gun to rob the New Belford branch of the Kentucky Patriot Bank.

It was the same bank that Bruce and Rita Walsh patronized. And the day of the robbery, Rita Walsh was in the building to drop off a dozen of her special mocha cranberry cupcakes to Amber Dawn Berry, a teller, and the sister-in-law of her best friend.

But it wasn't Jeb Daly who killed Rita. She'd been shot accidentally by the deputy, Zach Watkins, who responded to the silent alarm.

Five years later, her father had hired Noah Daly to work in the service department of the dealership. What had he been thinking? And what was Noah Daly doing talking to Bryn Owens?

SMALL TOWN TROUBLE

Chapter 3

"Here, Mom." Noah Daly handed his mother an insulated tumbler of sweet iced tea. She took the tea and smiled up at him from her chair at one of the umbrella tables by the pool. Only eighteen when he was born, she was younger than the mothers of most of the guys he knew. Her beauty had faded more quickly though: she'd long ago started dyeing her auburn hair to hide the gray, which showed up before she turned thirty, and she was on her feet a lot at her cashier's job, but didn't get much exercise, so she carried a little extra weight that she was self-conscious about. But the thing Noah noticed most about her was that her eyes didn't sparkle like they did when he was little. Still, unlike most of the guys he knew, he'd never once been ashamed to be seen with his own mother.

"Why aren't you out on the lake, honey? The jet skis look like so much fun. Didn't you bring swim trunks?"

Noah glanced around him. The women near the pool were in sundresses or shorts or bathing suits, and the kids were either in the pool or dripping water as they played close by. Most of the men he worked with—except for a handful who stood around the grill, drinking beer and talking to Junior, the catering chef doing the grilling—were in swim trunks down near the lake. All of their girlfriends were wearing bikinis.

"Not going in the water, Mom. Not in the mood. I just didn't want you to have to be at home today, with him there."

She leaned close to him, whispering. "You have nothing to be ashamed of, Noah."

"I don't want to talk about it, okay? We're here, and that's what's important."

A tall man wearing relaxed khaki shorts and a comfortably faded polo shirt ducked his head beneath the umbrella and laid one of his large hands on Noah's mother's shoulder. The hair at his temples was gray, but the rest was what Noah had heard his mother call strawberry blond. With his friendly green eyes, and booming voice, Bruce Walsh always seemed like he was about to share good news.

"So glad you could make it, Annette. I told Noah I hoped he'd bring you to the party this year." He nodded to Noah. "Even if young Noah here decides to bring along a sweetheart, you're always welcome to come, too."

Noah's mother tilted her face to him, and started to rise, smiling. "Mr. Walsh—"

Bruce Walsh didn't let her finish. "Please. Call me Bruce, and don't get up. We get to be the grownups here, right?"

"It's a wonderful party," she said, settling back down in her chair. "Look at all these cute decorations! Even these fancy tumblers are red, white, and blue. And all the children seem to be having a good time." As they watched, a small girl started down the pool slide, her arms above her head. She shrieked with delight before going in, and when she popped to the surface again, even Bruce laughed.

"Shelby Rae and I feel a deep sense of gratitude to the people who make Walsh motors successful. It's a family. I like to take care of that family." He held out a freshly opened bottle of Budweiser to Noah. "Something cold? Hot day to be out on that Yamaha of yours. You know, the invitation is still open for you and the boys in the department to fish off our docks any time."

"Thanks, Mr. Walsh." Noah took the beer with a nod. "I've come out here early a few mornings this spring. But I park over on the access road so I don't disturb you all. The yellow perch and bass are running big this year."

"Oh, that bass," his mother said. "That's something special."

Bruce agreed.

To Noah, the most impressive thing about Bruce Walsh was his sincerity. Sometimes he sounded like a politician, but Noah knew that Bruce always kept his word. When he hired Noah on, he said he didn't expect any more or any less from him than any other employee, but that it would be a great favor to him if Noah would keep his father, Jeb, from coming around after he got out of prison. Keeping the man who was ultimately responsible for Rita Walsh's death away from his place of business was a promise Noah had been happy to make.

Especially because he didn't want to have anything to do with his loser father, either. He was glad Bruce didn't know how that promise had already been tested.

Hearing raucous laughter over by the outdoor kitchen, Noah saw Bruce's wife, Shelby Rae, surrounded, as usual, by admiring men. She was too old to really appeal to Noah, and he wasn't into flashy women. The older guys in the service department referred to her as a gold digger because they knew her back when she was just the receptionist, and Rita Walsh was still alive. But after one of her infrequent visits to the dealership, the younger guys would talk about how hot she was. Now, a couple of those guys were checking out the plunge of her tight white top as though they wanted to fall in. She seemed to be enjoying the attention, but when an older man with thinning, dark hair rested his hand on her back, she whipped her head around so fast that her long, curled ponytail hit the man on her other side in the face.

"Quit it, Uncle Travis!" she said.

Noah smiled. The guy was creepy and obviously deserved it, but Noah watched as he merely chuckled and chomped down on his unlighted cigar, unfazed.

A couple of the other men dropped back, embarrassed. It could have been one of them instead of the intrepid Travis. He was her uncle? Talk about awkward.

Bruce and his mother were still talking. Noah wasn't sure what he'd missed, but the conversation had turned back to the expensive tumblers the party's drinks were being served in.

"Shelby Rae went a little crazy on making sure everything matched. I think she planned on about a thousand guests instead of a hundred and fifty. Everyone gets to take one home, but let me send a couple boxes of the extras home with you."

Annette laughed. "Oh, I couldn't let you do that. They're

so expensive. I'm sure your wife will want to return the rest." But Noah could tell from the way she was looking at the tumbler on the table that the idea excited her. They had so few nice things at home. She insisted that Noah put half his paycheck in the bank "for college, maybe, or a house of your own someday." He hated that she worked so hard but couldn't afford nicer things—even if they were just thick plastic drink glasses.

"You'd be doing me a favor." Bruce gave her a wide smile, and his eyes were kind.

Noah's mother blushed.

"Erin, honey?" Bruce called to his daughter, who was sitting beside Mackenzie Clay at the opposite side of the pool. "Can I get you to come here for a minute?"

Erin Walsh said something he couldn't hear to Mackenzie, who'd been in an economics class with him during his senior year of high school. Then she gave her father a small smile and lifted her long legs from the pool, and stood, taking her reflective gold aviators from her hair and putting them on so that her hair swung free. Unlike her stepmother, she was dressed down, wearing cream-colored shorts that rested softly on her narrow hips, and a heathered purple Allman Brothers Band t-shirt tied into a knot, briefly revealing a triangle of pale, flat stomach. The glimpse of her skin put a different kind of knot in Noah's stomach, and he glanced away.

He and Erin had never been friends, but they were always aware of each other. Neither of them had been allowed to come to his father's trial, because they were too young, but New Belford wasn't a very big town. He saw more of her when she started at the consolidated high school as a quiet freshman. People referred to her as "Erin Walsh, that girl whose mother got killed." But Noah thought of her as something more: the girl whose life his father had ruined. It didn't matter that Jeb Daly had been bluffing with an empty gun during the robbery, and it was Deputy Zachary Watkins who actually shot and killed Rita Walsh. His father was still responsible.

It wasn't until last Christmas that Noah started to think of Erin in a much different way.

She'd come into the dealership with Shelby Rae to be surprised with a spanking new Challenger that her father had ordered her for Christmas. It was a Hellcat, with a 700 horsepower HEMI engine that only had 42 miles on it—but Noah had put twelve miles on the engine himself after the service manager told him to take it out to make sure it ran perfectly before she arrived. The sleek black car was a beauty, with sports suspension, and paddle shifters on the wheel that meant the driver could switch to manual without even touching the stick.

Driving that car on the highway and a couple back roads he knew well had been among the sweetest fifteen minutes of Noah's life up to that point.

But the day only improved when, an hour later, Bruce Walsh called back to the department himself to ask that the car be brought around. Almost everyone was gone for the day, so Noah started the Challenger with the special red fob that engaged the full 700 horsepower (instead of the black fob that gave you only 500), and drove it around to the front of the dealership.

Erin stood on the sidewalk, her blond hair tucked into a knitted cashmere beret, her mittened hands covering her eyes like a little kid. Her father's arm was around her shoulders. When she uncovered her eyes, Noah saw pure delight and surprise come into them. She turned and hugged her father. When she finally pulled away, a lock of her blonde hair fell from her beret and brushed her lightly freckled cheek. It was in that moment Noah knew that, given half a chance, he could fall in love with her.

End of excerpt from *Small Town Trouble*
by Laura Benedict
Trouble Cat Mysteries #5

TROUBLE CAT MYSTERIES

Please join our Trouble Cat Mysteries page on Facebook:
fb.me/TroubleCatMysteries

www.troublecatmysteries.com

Familiar Trouble | Carolyn Haines
Trouble in Dixie | Rebecca Barrett
Trouble in Tallahassee | Claire Matturro
Trouble in Summer Valley | Susan Y. Tanner
Small Town Trouble | Laura Benedict
Trouble in Paradise | Rebecca Barrett
Turning for Trouble | Susan Y. Tanner
Trouble's Wedding Caper | Jen Talty

Bone-a-fied Trouble | Carolyn Haines
Trouble in Action | Susan Y. Tanner
Trouble Most Faire | Jaden Terrell
The Trouble with Cupid: 10 Short Mysteries Spiced with Romance | Multiple Authors
Trouble Under the Mistletoe | e-novella | Rebecca Barrett
A Trouble'd Christmas | e-novella | Susan Y. Tanner
Year-Round Trouble: 14 Original Cozy Holiday Mysteries | Multiple Authors

TROUBLE'S DOUBLE CONTEST WINNER
Buddie

"Shortly before my dog passed away from cancer, we noticed a little black cat that was little more than a kitten running around the neighborhood. One night, I happened to look out our front door to see a little black face with big green eyes looking in at us. I went to the door and, of course, she ran away. When my dog passed, I swore I would never have another dog because she was what I call my soul dog. A few weeks passed and I missed having an animal and noticed the black cat was back so I decided to feed it. She started coming every day and my sister and I decided to try and get her to come in the house using wet food. After a couple of weeks and leaving the back door open, (she was living under my neighbor's deck) she started coming in to eat the wet food and then beat a hasty retreat outside. Then one day, while eating lunch I hear a big bang at the back door and there she was wanting in! She would stand up at the back door and look in, sliding from side to side -- she looked like she was cupping her face with her paws looking into the house to see if she could see someone. From then on, she started staying in longer and longer, and now she only goes outside at night in the summer and sometimes stays in all night when it gets colder. She has made us laugh with her antics, sometimes looking like a gymnast jumping and rolling and running. She loves to have her neck scratched and insists on us petting her before we set her food down. While she can be sweet, she is full of sass and vinegar. She has the "stink eye" down pat when we say "no!" to her. She investigates everything: closets, under the bed, dressers and chest of drawers. She is very different from my beloved dog, but Buddie has quickly stolen our hearts."

— LORRAINE KRAFT

Made in the USA
Monee, IL
24 August 2022

12425047R00148